D1014475

BABYLON
SISTERS

*Also by Pearl Cleage
in Large Print:*

Some Things I Never Thought I'd Do
What Looks Like Crazy
    on an Ordinary Day . . .

This Large Print Book carries the
Seal of Approval of N.A.V.H.

BABYLON
SISTERS

Pearl Cleage

Thorndike Press • Waterville, Maine

Published in 2005 by arrangement with The Ballantine Publishing Group, a division of Random House, Inc.

Thorndike Press® Large Print Basic.

The tree indicium is a trademark of Thorndike Press.

The text of this Large Print edition is unabridged.
Other aspects of the book may vary from the original edition.

Set in 16 pt. Plantin.

Printed in the United States on permanent paper.

Library of Congress Cataloging-in-Publication Data

Cleage, Pearl.
    Babylon sisters / by Pearl Cleage.
      p. cm.
    "Thorndike Press large print basic" — T.p. verso.
    ISBN 0-7862-7199-X (lg. print : hc : alk. paper)
    1. Mothers and daughters — Fiction. 2. Women immigrants — Services for — Fiction. 3. Women refugees — Services for — Fiction. 4. Single mothers — Fiction. 5. Teenage girls — Fiction. 6. Birthfathers — Fiction. 7. Journalists — Fiction. 8. Secrecy — Fiction. 9. Large type books. I. Title.
PS3553.L389B33 2005b
  813′.54—dc22
                                      2005000747

For Zaron W. Burnett, Jr.,
who always brings the music;

For Deignan and Chloe Lomax,
who will continue the dance;

And for Michael Jondré Pryor Lomax,
whose smile is a song

As the Founder/CEO of NAVH, the only national health agency solely devoted to those who, although not totally blind, have an eye disease which could lead to serious visual impairment, I am pleased to recognize Thorndike Press★ as one of the leading publishers in the large print field.

Founded in 1954 in San Francisco to prepare large print textbooks for partially seeing children, NAVH became the pioneer and standard setting agency in the preparation of large type.

Today, those publishers who meet our standards carry the prestigious "Seal of Approval" indicating high quality large print. We are delighted that Thorndike Press is one of the publishers whose titles meet these standards. We are also pleased to recognize the significant contribution Thorndike Press is making in this important and growing field.

Lorraine H. Marchi, L.H.D.
Founder/CEO
NAVH

★ Thorndike Press encompasses the following imprints: Thorndike, Wheeler, Walker and Large Print Press.

By the rivers of Babylon,
there we sat down, yea, we wept,
when we remembered Zion.
How shall we sing the Lord's song
in a strange land?
— Psalm 137

Babylon sister, shake it!
— Steely Dan

ACKNOWLEDGMENTS

Special thanks to my family, especially my sister, Kristin Cleage Williams, who was the first one to stop and listen to my stories, and to my friends and neighbors for their love and support, especially Cecelia Corbin Hunter, Ingrid Saunders Jones, Shirley C. Franklin, Walt and Lynn Huntley, Ray and Marilyn Cox, A.B. and Karen Spellman, Lynette Lapeyrolerie, Zaron W. Burnett III, Johnsie Broadway Burnett, Doug and Pat Burnett, Marc and Elaine Lawson, Donald P. Stone, Don Bryan, Kenny Leon, Brother Kefing, Shunda and Jamill Leigh, Woodie King Jr., Michael L. Lomax, Dwight Andrews, Jimmy Lee Tarver, Granville Edward Freeman Dennis, Jill Nelson, Kay Leigh Hagan, Bebe Moore Campbell, Tina McElroy Ansa, Travis Hunter, E. Lynn Harris, Valerie Boyd, Valerie Jackson, TaRessa Stovall, Ayisha Jeffries, Helen and Gary Richter, Curtis and Barbara Jackson, Andrea Hairston, Maria Evans, and Maria Broom. Also thanks to the Shrine of the Black Madonna Bookstore and Cultural

Center and Brother Amir, Medu Bookstore and Nia Damali, Paschal's Restaurant, Stan Washington and *The Atlanta Voice*, *Booking Matters Magazine*, and ROOTS International. Thanks also to Gloria Wade Gayles for her revolutionary analysis of *Native Son* and to Tayari Jones for passing on the lesson, to Denise Stinson, Howard Rosenstone, and Nancy Miller for taking care of business, and to Bill Bagwell, and Ron Milner, out of sight but never out of mind.

1

My daughter is upstairs weeping. She's been up there in her room for three days, six hours, and thirty-two minutes, weeping. For three days, five hours, and forty-one minutes, I indulged her. A broken heart may not be as visible as chicken pox but the scars are just as bad. So I listened and I commiserated and I clucked sympathetically while she examined and reexamined every detail of her first love's betrayal. I took her meals upstairs on a tray, made tea to soothe her nerves and mine, and resisted every opportunity to say, "Phoebe, my darling, I told you he wasn't for you in the first place." The last thing you need in the throes of first heartbreak, when you're still not sure you'll survive it, is to hear the absolute, unvarnished truth spoken for the second time by your mother, who first uttered the words when you brought the young, betraying fool home and confessed, *Oh, Mama, I think he's the one!*

He was never *the one*. He was handsome and interesting and sexy and as serious as she was about saving the world by next

Tuesday at the very latest. He was also way too full of the blazing sexual energy of his emerging manhood to be anybody's *one* for very long. But at seventeen, how was she supposed to know? She handed him her heart, and everything else that wasn't tied down, and they were inseparable from October of her junior year until June, when they had to go their separate ways for the summer. She was determined not to let distance destroy their relationship, but once they were apart he seemed to be drifting away from her, and neither one knew what to do about it. After a summer of long-distance spats and tearful reconciliations, he confessed via a long e-mail that he had fallen in love with someone else and closed with a wish that they could always be friends.

That was three days ago, and I'm still sympathetic. I am her mother, after all, and I do love my child. But it was time for her to dry her eyes and blow her nose and get herself together. Nobody ever really dies of a broken heart except in the movies, and it is my opinion, motherhood aside, that more than three days in mourning for the demise of a relationship with any man is unseemly, not to mention a real strain on the women who have to help you through it. It was time for her to segue from self-pity to self-examination by asking the all-important question: *What is the lesson here for me?* Although it is deceptively simple, this question cuts to the heart of the matter because it turns that trembling, accusatory finger you're pointing at everybody else right back around to yourself. My darling daughter had spent enough time blaming her boyfriend. Now it was time for her to look at what she could have done differently to avoid this painful moment.

When she was younger, I would consider the lesson question with her so she'd begin to understand how it always leads to the heart of the matter. When she got older, I would just remind her to ask it, then leave her to think about the answer all by herself. That's what I intended to do tonight. She could review and evaluate her choices while she finished packing and I finished returning three days' worth of phone calls. I love having my office at home, and since Phoebe went off to boarding school two years ago, it's been not only convenient, but quiet, the last seventy-two drama-filled hours notwithstanding.

I'd better enjoy it while I can. Phoebe's going to college next year. She's got her heart set on Smith, and the Seven Sisters have never been a place for bohemian mothers living on a budget to send their darling daughters. It looks like after all these years of stretching my little inheritance and living by my wits, I'm actually going to have to break down and get a full-time job where somebody else signs the check and covers the health insurance. I'm going to try to keep some of my longtime clients. Most of them can't afford to hire anybody half as good as I am, and they've never needed me more.

What I do is coordinate and integrate services for programs assisting female refugees and immigrants. Atlanta is a magnet for people trying to make a new start in a new country, and even though the town's natives still think in terms of black and white, in reality we're looking more and more like the Rainbow Coalition. My job is to ease the transition on all sides by serving as a kind of conduit, clearinghouse, counselor, and all-around communications facilitator.

I tell people the language I speak is the future, and I love it. All you have to do is help a Cambodian family find safe housing or a Haitian mother register her children for school or reunite a Cuban father with a

14

son he thought he'd never see again or attend a Liberian wedding party to know that there isn't nearly as much difference between people as some of our governments and institutions want us to think there is. In my line of work, what I've learned is that most people are looking for pretty much the same things — health and peace and love and family and a community where you can wave at your neighbors and they wave back.

I love what I do, but it doesn't pay very well. My parents left me this house, all paid for, and enough money so that I could stay home with Phoebe and not have to worry about the basics. When my volunteer work at the Red Cross turned into a lot of freelance consulting, I was able to make enough to finance our annual trips to somewhere we'd never been before and to send Phoebe to a private boarding school up north when she decided she wanted to go.

But the last of my inheritance paid for her senior-year tuition, and there's not enough coming in to keep us afloat and to finance four years of college. She keeps offering to get a job, but our deal has always been, *You get the grades and I'll get the money.* Besides, it's only four years. I can stand almost any job that long if it pays well enough. After that, Phoebe's on her own, and I can feather my empty nest any way I want. Until then, I've got to toughen this girl up and get her back to school.

I brewed a fresh pot of coffee and poured us each a cup to signal that the tea-sipping phase of her healing was officially over, then went upstairs to tap on her half-open door.

"You awake?"

From inside the silent, darkened room my daughter's voice was a pain-filled quaver. "Come in, Mom."

I pushed open the door with my foot. Once inside, I could see that there was one small candle burning on the bedside table. The air was faintly perfumed with the roses Amelia brought over yesterday when she came to check on the progress of the patient. Amelia Douglass has known Phoebe since she was eight years old and is more like a favorite aunt than a next-door neighbor. Phoebe herself was curled up in the center of the bed under a wool blanket her grandmother brought back from South America years ago and which is so smotheringly heavy that we use it only on those rare occasions when the furnace goes out in one of those freak Atlanta ice storms and we want to stay cozy until Georgia Power gets around to reconnecting our block.

But there was no ice storm. It was, in fact, the end of August, and the temperature outside at nine thirty at night was still eighty-five degrees. I suppressed a smile. Baby Doll was playing this scene to the hilt. The candle flickering over her sweet little face was the perfect theatrical touch. Right out of *Camille*. My child intends to major in performance studies. Looking at the scene she's constructed here, I know she'll make the dean's list.

"I brought you some coffee," I said casually, like she's always in bed with the lights out at nine thirty on a Friday night.

She sat up slowly and reached out to clutch the cup I was offering. Consistent with her cold-weather motif, she wrapped both hands around it and breathed deeply, as if we were huddled in a tent at the foot of Mount Everest.

"Thanks, Mom."

That quaver in her voice sounded so genuinely sad, I was tempted to sit down on the edge of the bed and spend another hour or two cooing and comforting. I know that's what she wanted, but part of being a good mother is knowing when to exercise some tough love, even in a raw moment like this one.

"Can I turn the light on?" I said. "I can't hardly see you."

"I look a mess," she said, running her hand over her hair, cut short and curly. The flickering candle threw her shadow on the wall dramatically. *The award for best lighting design goes to . . .*

"You can't look a mess to your mother," I said, turning on the lamp. "It's against the law."

She managed a shaky smile, but she was right. She looked a mess. Not a terminal mess. Just an *I haven't had a shower or brushed my hair or changed my clothes in three days because I've been too busy crying* mess. Her suitcases were open at the foot of the bed, but her clothes were strewn around like she'd closed her eyes and thrown them in the air to see where they would land.

"I see you've started packing," I said, taking a seat at the foot of the bed. She was propped up now against a nest of pillows, the two-ton blanket still draped over her knees. She gazed around at the colorful piles of her back-to-school clothes like she was seeing them for the first time.

"I was trying to get it organized," she

18

said. "But . . ." Her voice trailed off like no further explanation was necessary since I was clearly familiar with her situation.

"So you want some help?" I said. "You know you're not going to want to tackle all this tomorrow."

She took another sip of her coffee, put it down slowly on the table near the candle, and sighed deeply.

"Mom?"

"Yes?"

"There's something I have to tell you, and you're not going to like it."

This is not a sentence the mother of a seventeen-year-old girl in the middle of a marathon crying jag wants to hear. *Trust me.* The possibilities are endless, and endlessly depressing. I willed myself to remain calm and not jump to conclusions.

"What is it, sweetie?"

She just looked at me while a big fat tear rolled down her cheek. She dabbed at it with a soggy tissue that had seen better days. *Please tell me this girl isn't —*

I interrupted that thought before my brain could finish it. "What's wrong, Phoebe?"

"I haven't finished packing because I'm not going back to school," she said, her voice a mixture of misery and defiance.

"Not going back to school?" I said, not sure whether I was more surprised or relieved. This was a fantasy, not a problem. "Why?"

It was a rhetorical question. There was no possible answer that would result in my agreeing to such a move. Phoebe was a straight-A student at Fairfield Academy. This was her senior year, and she was practically guaranteed admission to any school where she applied. This was no time to take a break.

"It's just too painful," she said with a delicate shudder. "I'll have to see *him* practically every day. Everybody will know he broke up with me for . . . *her.*"

Phoebe's voice cracked on the word, and she tried to collect herself. I didn't rush the moment. I wanted her to get it all out before I inquired as to whether she had lost her whole mind. In a nice way, of course.

"I just don't think I could stand it," she said. "You understand, don't you, Mom?"

I chose my words carefully. I was a modern mother and I wanted to be compassionate, but absolutely clear in what I was saying.

I patted her knee through the rough wool. "I understand that at this moment, it may seem like the whole world has fallen in on you," I said calmly. "But hiding at home is not the way to get through this. Sooner or later you'll have to go back to school, and the longer you wait, the harder it will be."

"Why do I have to go back at all? You homeschooled me when I was little. Why can't we do it again?"

"Because I can't teach you calculus," I teased her gently.

She was not amused. "I've already had calculus."

"Listen, sweetie," I said. "I know you loved him, and I know it's hard to face your friends, but dropping out of school your senior year isn't an option. It doesn't make sense."

Two more tears rolled down her cheeks. For maximum guilt-producing effect, she didn't even bother to wipe them away. I patted her knee again, and noticed her perfectly pedicured toenails, sticking out from underneath the blanket, were painted a summery shade of pink.

"Is that all you wanted to tell me?"

She didn't answer immediately, and I held my breath one more time.

"Yes," she whispered faintly.

"Then let me tell you something," I said.

"You are a smart, resourceful, kind, generous, talented young woman. You have a mother who loves you, a godfather who adores you, and a sister circle that thinks you're pretty special. You fell in love with a boy who couldn't see it, didn't appreciate it, or was so totally intimidated by it that he left you for somebody else."

The tears came in an ever-increasing flow, but she continued to ignore them, so I did, too.

"It happens sometimes, and it's always hard because you can never really know why people do the things they do."

"He said he loved me!" she wailed, as if she still couldn't get her mind around the lie.

"I know he did," I interrupted her quickly before we headed back down that path. "But that's not really the question, is it?"

She didn't answer, but I was determined to press on. "Is it?"

"I know what you're going to say," she said, sounding annoyed. "You're going to say, 'What is the lesson here.' Right?"

"Right."

She stared at me, and an expression flickered across her face that I couldn't identify. She lifted her delicate little chin

22

and looked me in the eye. "Is that all you wanted to tell me?"

Her words took me by surprise. Or *my* words did, thrown back at me like so much bad business. Was she getting smart with me? There was no denying the sass in her tone, or the deliberate defiance of her question, and I opened my mouth to assert the unmistakable fact that she was the child and I was the mother and what she'd better do was get her narrow little behind out of that bed and clean up this room and herself, not necessarily in that order, and claim temporary insanity had made her even *think* she could talk to me like that.

But then I stopped myself. She wasn't mad at me. She was mad at herself, and she had that coming. Being angry was all part of answering the question she didn't want me to remind her to ask. My work here was done. So I stood up and smiled down at her instead of taking the bait.

"Yes," I said, picking up my coffee cup and heading for the door. "I guess that was it."

She didn't call me back to apologize, but she didn't get up and slam the door behind me either, which would have meant the insanity was more than temporary and would require immediate intervention. I'm a modern mother, but I ain't no fool.

2

By the time I got downstairs to my office, the phone was ringing off the hook. It was almost ten o'clock, but I'm used to people calling me at all hours. A lot of the people I work with don't conduct their business from nine to five. I snatched up the phone before the voice mail clicked on, since some folks are reluctant to leave a message. Their accents make them too self-conscious.

"Babylon Sisters," I said quickly. "Catherine Sanderson speaking. Can I help you?"

I named my business after that Bible verse the Melodians overlaid with a reggae beat a couple of years ago, which made it an unlikely international hit: "By the rivers of Babylon / There we sat down / And there we wept / When we remembered Zion." Most of my clients still felt like "strangers in a strange land," so I added "Sisters" to let them know I was family.

But the voice on the other end didn't have an accent. It was offering an apology.

"Ms. Sanderson? Sam Hall here, and let

me start right off with a sincere apology for calling you so late into the evening. I just couldn't let another day go by without trying to at least touch base."

Sam Hall? The name didn't ring a bell, but he had a great voice. Deep and rich and too sexy for a business call, even one that came this late.

"No problem, Mr. Hall. What can I do for you?"

"The question is, Ms. Sanderson, what I'd like to do for you."

Too bad that voice was wasted on somebody with such a lame opening line. The voice was pure Teddy Pendergrass, but the rap sounded like a used-car salesman. "Do I know you?"

"We met briefly at the Child Prostitution Task Force luncheon last week, but I wouldn't expect you to remember me. You were surrounded by people who had been deeply moved by your remarks. I was one of many."

He had seen me doing my most recent dog-and-pony show. I do a lot of public speaking, mostly about issues affecting women and girls in the international community. These days I consider each speech almost an audition, since I'm job hunting in sort of a semi-official way. The day of that luncheon speech, there was a terrible story in the paper about the death of a four-year-old whose immigrant parents were living on the street. I was righteously indignant, and even though I was definitely preaching to the choir, when I sat down they gave me a standing ovation. Afterward, so many people pressed their cards into my hands, I hadn't had time to sort them out yet.

"That was an extraordinary day," I said, sliding in behind my desk. "The spirit ran high."

"You made it extraordinary," he said. "That's why I'm very anxious to talk to you, and my boss is, too."

"Who's your boss?"

"I am proud to say that I am vice president of operations and development for Miss Ezola Mandeville. You may be familiar with her work."

Of course I was familiar with her work, although I had never met her. Ezola Mandeville was an Atlanta legend, a former domestic worker who got sick and tired of being sick and tired and started organizing other maids and cleaning women to demand better wages and more humane treatment. She worked for an old white woman who depended on her completely, and actually had a lot of respect and even some affection for her, but who did not appreciate her increasing visibility in what was becoming a full-fledged movement. When the old woman's friends began to complain that Ezola was stirring up their maids, several of whom had suddenly demanded advance notice and extra money for overtime, it was the last straw.

Her mistress reluctantly fired her the next morning, confident of finding a suitable replacement without much trouble and certain that, deprived of their leader, the other maids would return to their former state of docility and life would go on as it always had. She knew she would miss Ezola, but the world she knew didn't have a place for friendship between white women and black women, so she ignored her feelings and put an ad in the paper for a new maid.

The only problem was that Ezola was not prepared to go quietly. She was a fiercely independent woman, alone in the world by choice. Her job made it possible for her to pay her own way, and she did not intend, as she said to herself, to spend the next five years learning the ways of a whole new set of white folks just because these women didn't want to pay cab fare when their maids left those mansions at midnight to catch the last crosstown bus home.

So on Monday morning, instead of looking for another job, Ezola showed up at her employer's house, where she stationed herself at the foot of the long, winding driveway to inform any of the other colored women who answered her mistress's ad that the job was already taken and that their best bet was to move right along.

It took only one day for the word to get around that Ezola fully intended to keep her old job, and three more days for her mistress to realize she couldn't make it without her. The legend has it that the white woman finally took that long walk down to the street, and after several minutes of intense negotiations, they arrived at a compromise that guaranteed Ezola overtime pay for evenings, cab fare home after parties, and weekends off unless she wanted to work. None of the other maids got as complete a package as Ezola, but all of them got something, including a new sense of their own power and their mistresses' vulnerability.

When the old lady died a few years later, she surprised everybody by leaving Ezola a hundred thousand dollars, which her former maid used to open a training and job-placement agency for women involved in janitorial services. In ten years, it had grown into a multimillion-dollar enterprise with contracts from some of the biggest hotels and office complexes in Atlanta as well as select private homes in the same Buckhead community where she used to work. She was the regular recipient of awards for her innovative approach to preparing the women for work before sending them out to any job site. Employers praised her unique ability to motivate workers and pointed to the low drop-off rate in a field with notoriously high turnover. For her part, Ezola guaranteed any woman who wasn't afraid of hard work a job whenever she wanted one.

"I'm flattered that Ms. Mandeville knows my work," I said. "Was she at the luncheon, too?"

"*Miss* Mandeville," he corrected me smoothly. "She doesn't like to be called *Ms.,* but no, she wasn't there. She depends on me to be her eyes and ears, and I'll tell you, Ms. Sanderson," he caressed that *Ms.* like he wanted me to know *he* had no objection to it. "I gave her a *big* earful of you after I heard that speech. You're the answer to our prayers."

He was laying it on pretty thick, but that voice made it sound like the gospel truth.

"I don't know quite what to say, Mr. Hall. Can you be a little more specific?"

His laugh was even better than his voice. "My apologies again. I fully expected to leave another voice-mail message, and when you actually picked up, it sort of threw me."

I hadn't even gotten the first one. How long had I been sitting upstairs commiserating with Phoebe, anyway? Three days or three weeks?

"What was the message?"

"The message was an invitation to you to come and break bread with me and Miss Mandeville at your earliest convenience in order to explore the possibility of your coming to work with us on a project that is right up your alley. Are you interested?"

His timing was perfect. It's never too late to call if you've got good news.

"I'm very interested," I said, reaching for my calendar. "Monday looks good for me."

"Then Monday it is," he said. "Miss Mandeville likes to use her personal chef. Can you join us at noon at our headquarters?"

"Of course." I knew exactly where their

building was. It was hard to miss it. Mandeville Maid Services was housed in a newly renovated five-story building in the historic, but perennially depressed Auburn Avenue area. Ezola was reputed to have paid cash for her property, and her decision had single-handedly revitalized an entire block and endeared her to city hall.

Every black mayor since Maynard Jackson had tried in vain to come up with a plan to bring back the glory of what had been preintegration black Atlanta's main commercial strip, but the lure of huge, upscale malls like Lenox Square and Phipps Plaza had made the small storefronts of Auburn Avenue seem quaint reminders of a time that was as gone with the wind as Scarlett O'Hara's plantation. Ezola bought the building for next to nothing and put the money she saved back into her business. When her staff had expressed concern about location, she said people who were looking for maids still expected to come to the black community to find them, and Auburn Avenue was about as black as you could get.

"Well, you've made me a very happy man, Ms. Sanderson. I'll look forward to seeing you on Monday."

"I'll be there," I said. "Please give my

best to *Miss* Mandeville."

"I'll do that," he said, pleased that I had remembered about that *Ms.* "Good night."

"Good night."

I hung up the phone and immediately grabbed a handful of cards to see if I could find one that would give me a little more information about Sam Hall and his boss. I wondered what kind of project they were talking about and how many of the stories I'd heard about the reclusive Miss Mandeville were true. She had a reputation for being strong and ruthless, which could probably be said of most successful businesspeople, but in a woman it still seemed extraordinary, and to some people, slightly inappropriate. That's fine with me. I've never been a stickler for *appropriate*. What I need to know is, what's the going rate for being an answer to somebody's prayers?

I was so engrossed in my search and my speculation that I didn't know Phoebe was standing in my office doorway until I looked up and saw her watching me intently. She still had the big blanket sort of gathered around her shoulders, and just looking at it made me feel sweaty.

"Hey, sweetie," I said, pleased to see her up and about. "Feeling better?"

"Mom," she said. "We have to talk."

3

It was too late for more coffee, so I poured myself a glass of merlot and went to join my daughter in the living room. She had politely declined my offer of juice or another cup of Sleepytime tea. I settled into my favorite rocking chair, loving the gentle sway of it that was as familiar as my own heartbeat. I bought it the day I decided to keep Phoebe, because good mothers are supposed to nurse their babies in rocking chairs. Even then, before I had a clue about how hard it is to actually raise a sane and loving child in a brutally insane, often unlovely world, I knew that was my goal. I wanted to be a good hands-on mother. A rocker was the first step, and I sat in twelve chairs before I found the right one. It had a tall back, a cane bottom, and carved arms that encircled me like a hug. It was perfect. I couldn't wait for Rich's department store to deliver it, so I made them tie it to the top of my car and drove home with the radio up loud and my chair up top, and it was a moment of perfect certainty that I was doing the right thing.

When I look back at it, I am always amused that I thought everything would be as easy as finding the perfect rocker. What planet could I have been from to think being a good mother has anything to do with certainty? After seventeen years with Phoebe, I now understand that a strong hunch is usually the best you can hope for. That, and a poker face. An unintentionally bemused smile can derail an honest mother-daughter exchange faster than the ring of a cell phone. Just because you know she'll laugh about it all someday doesn't mean *this* is the day.

Phoebe curled up on the side of the couch where she always sits when we watch TV and tucked that damn blanket around her bare feet. Over our heads, the ceiling fan whirred softly. I took a sip of my wine and smiled at my miserable-looking child.

"What's going on?"

Relieved of my earlier fears that I might be a grandmother before I turned forty, and having stated my position on the not-going-back-to-school question, I felt confident that I could handle whatever was knitting my baby's brow in such consternation.

Phoebe took a deep breath. "Don't take this the wrong way, Mom, but I think this whole thing is your fault."

"What whole thing is that?"

"This whole thing with Bradley."

She had told me she would never speak her faithless boyfriend's name again and that she would appreciate it if I didn't either. It was, she said, *just too painful.* I was tempted to point out that she must be feeling better, since his name rolled off her tongue with ease, but my curiosity got the better of me.

"My fault? How can it be my fault? I always liked Brad. I just didn't like him for you."

"That's the whole point. You could tell he was wrong right away, and I never suspected a thing." The thought made her so indignant that she shrugged off the blanket and leaned toward me. "Why do you think that is?"

I wondered if I should go alphabetically or chronologically. "I'm thirty-eight and you're seventeen. I've had more experience with men than you have. I —"

She shook her head vigorously. "No, no, no! That's not it at all."

I took another sip of wine. "I don't know what you're talking about, sweetie. Start at the beginning, okay?"

"*Okay.*" She paused dramatically, closed

her eyes, took a deep breath, and then opened them with a look of renewed determination.

"There is a theory," she said, slowly, "that women's romantic relationships with men are totally shaped by their fathers. If it's a bad relationship, those women will seek out men who are like the father over and over in order to see if they can resolve issues that began in early childhood."

"I've heard that theory," I said.

"Do you believe it?"

My own father flickered across my mind. Smart, funny, passionate, dangerous, free. I adored my father, but I don't know how good our relationship was. He was not a man who had much interest in anything other than his work and his wife, including his only daughter. He was always kind to me in a distant, distracted sort of way, but I never felt like he'd miss me if I weren't around. Or even notice.

"I'm not sure," I said. "There's probably some truth to it."

"Do you think your relationship with Granddaddy is what drew you to my father?"

For the last couple of years, Phoebe has been badgering me for information about her father. When she was little, I told her he had died in an accident before she was born. She accepted that for a while, but when she got older, she wanted more details. Didn't I have a picture? Didn't he have a family? Weren't they her family, too? Didn't they want to meet her?

Her questions were outrunning my ability to lie. One day I found myself looking through a magazine for a photograph of some unknown young brother whom I could pass off as Phoebe's father, and I realized I couldn't sustain this level of subterfuge. I didn't even want to. I hated lying to my own child. The problem was, I wasn't prepared to tell her who her father was. How could I? He didn't even know she existed. That had been my decision when I had her alone, and I wasn't about to risk her showing up at his door one day, searching for her roots and exposing my decision for his scrutiny after all these years. He had made his choices and I had made mine, starting when I got pregnant during my senior year at Spelman. I loved him, but even then I knew a child wasn't in his plans.

Already an award-winning student journalist, he had just snared the job of a lifetime as West African bureau chief for a respected black newsmagazine, and that was all he talked about. It was his dream come true, and he was ecstatic. I was on my way to graduate school at Howard in international affairs, hoping for a diplomatic career, and we were already making plans for me to come over and visit once he got settled and as soon as I saved enough money for a round-trip ticket. I was also keeping busy by pretending to be fine with our impending separation because I knew I had no choice. That was always part of our deal. We considered ourselves citizens of the world, and we had fallen in love first because of a shared passion for understanding world events and wanting to, as he said, "play a role in the major stories of our time." We spent almost a year engaging in those long, lovely, late-night conversations that start with politics and end with an escalating series of intimate exchanges and self-revelations that resonate so deeply you feel like you must fall into each other's arms or die.

It was wonderful and overwhelming. For a shy nineteen-year-old virgin, it was a lovely introduction to sexual pleasure without guilt, and we discovered each other together as if we were brand-new beings in a world all our own. Sex with him was an explosion of new feelings, physical and emotional, and I couldn't get enough of either one. I told him that I loved him and he said he loved me, too, but he never made any secret of his plans to leave for Africa the week after graduation. He never made promises he didn't intend to keep about marriage or family or a conventional existence with a fixed address and a predictable future. I pretended that was fine with me because I knew his freedom was as important to him as his work, and the idea that he would sacrifice or even modify either one because we happened to fall in love never entered his mind. For almost two years, everything was about as close to perfect as I could stand it. Then I got pregnant with Phoebe.

When I got the test results, I thought for a long time about whether or not to tell him. Of course I was going to have an abortion, so what was the point of interjecting all the drama? But that *of course* wasn't as firmly entrenched as I hoped it would be. In fact, there was another argument being made by some other part of my brain that ran more toward fantasizing how lovely it would be if he threw his arms around me and told me not to even consider an abortion because he was going to marry me immediately. We would start our family in West Africa so he could still do his work, I could go back to school in a year or two, and our child would be nurtured within the circle of love that had created that life in the first place.

But I always knew that was a fantasy. He was a great boyfriend, but that didn't mean he was prepared to be a great father. So I pushed that hopeful thought as far back in my mind — and my heart — as I could and I called the Feminist Women's Health Center to schedule the procedure as soon as they could take me.

I waited until the week before he was leaving to tell my lover I was carrying our child, and his face told me my fantasy was just that. He didn't look happy. He just looked scared, disappointed, maybe a little pissed. So I hurried to tell him that he didn't need to worry because I was going to get rid of it. I cringe now when I think of using those actual words. *Don't worry. I'm going to get rid of it.* Like she was a cockroach or something.

To his credit, he winced when I said it and reached out to pull me close. "Are you sure?" His voice was gentle, non-judgmental. We were playing the parts we had learned. It was a woman's right to choose and the progressive man's role to be supportive.

There are probably more terrible questions, but at that moment I couldn't think of one. Of course I wasn't sure! I loved him and I wanted him, and something in me really wanted to have this baby, but I didn't know how to tell him that. I couldn't even admit it to myself yet. My generation is still struggling to find the balance between love and freedom, sex and romance, family and career. Sometimes we get it right, but more often, we don't. That struggle is the legacy of the women's movement and our mothers' efforts to incorporate the theories of middle-class, white feminism into their highly *untheoretical* black female lives.

As my mother told me once when I was quoting Gloria Steinem as the ultimate authority on all things feminist, "What you have to understand is that colored women weren't *involved* in the women's movement. We were the women who moved!" She was right, of course, but moved *where?*

"I'm sure. I've already made the appointment for next week."

"Oh, baby," he said. "I'm so sorry." And he sat down with me on his lap and rocked me back and forth until I had worked up enough nerve to ask the question.

"Will you go with me?" I whispered.

"Of course I will," he said, and tightened his arms around me. *"Of course I will."*

After that, we didn't talk about it anymore. We made love one more time, but everything was so different, we might as well have been total strangers. The next day I went back to my apartment, and he kissed me at the door like it was the last time. And it was.

I called him that night, and when he answered the phone he was so drunk he wasn't making any sense. He just kept telling me how sorry he was until I told him I'd talk to him tomorrow and hung up. But I didn't talk to him in the morning, or that afternoon, or late that night, or ever again. When I finally went by his place, frantic, and let myself in, all his clothes were gone and there was an envelope for me on the coffee table with three hundred-dollar bills and a note that said, *I'm so sorry, baby. I can't do this with you. Be strong. B.J.*

I think it was the *be strong* that pushed me over the edge. I sat down on that bed we'd rolled around on together so many times and I cried as hard as I ever cried for anything or anybody. I felt a part of me that loving him had opened up closing like a steel door as the hip, undemanding, unconventional woman I was pretending to be dissolved in those tears. Because he had done the worst thing a lover can do. He had committed the unpardonable, unforgivable sin. He had left before I had a chance to stop loving him.

Phoebe was watching me, and I realized she was still waiting for me to answer her question. "I think my relationship with my father made me a more independent woman."

"But did it lead you to my father?"

She was pressing me, so I tried another sidestep. "It probably influenced all the men I was close to in different ways."

"But did it influence you when you picked my father?"

"Your father was one of the men I was close to, so I guess it did."

Phoebe stood up then, dragging her blanket with her so she looked a little like one of the old Hollywood depictions of Native Americans gathered outside their tepees with winter rolling in. She walked over to the window and pulled the drape aside to look out into the dark street, then turned back to me.

"If you don't tell me who my father is, I'll never be able to figure out men. You're dooming me to a lifetime of heartache and you don't even seem to care!"

I let that slide and tried to remain calm. "We talked about this before. It wasn't a period of my life I'm particularly proud of, but I can't sanitize it now just to make you happy. Your father could be one of several men I was sleeping with at the time. They were nice guys, but nobody I wanted to invite into the rest of our lives. So after graduation, we went our separate ways. They have their lives and I have you."

This lie evolved out of my desire to be absolutely sure she'd never be able to narrow down the possibilities and stumble upon her real father because he was standing around in my past all alone. I even went so far as to construct fake diaries to cover my college years, which listed four or five boyfriends, as young girls' diaries often do, but never once mentioned her father. I left the diaries around where she could find them to bolster my story, so I figured she had believed what I had told her. I was wrong.

"I don't believe you. You're not that kind of woman."

Her tone irked me. A broken heart gives you a little leeway, but it doesn't give you license. "What kind of woman is that? Nonmonogamous?"

"Indiscriminate!" She spit the word in my direction defiantly.

Uh-oh. I thought. *She's pushing it.* Then she walked back over to the couch, sat back down, and crossed the line.

"How many are we talking about anyway, Mom? Can you narrow it down a little? Two or three? Five or six? *Ten?*"

This is what I get for sending her to private school with a bunch of rich white girls. From what Phoebe says, they talk to their mothers any kind of way, and their mamas let them, but this conversation was over. I stood up.

"Let me tell you something, and I'm not going to say it again. The way you were conceived is none of your business. The number of lovers I've had, or never had, is none of your business either." She tried to say something, but I held up my hand and she was silent, proving that she's not completely crazy. "You are a blessed child because you have a mother who loves you more than life itself. A mother who has given you the tools you need to be an independent woman who won't have to take shit from a living soul. A mother who is going to pay your way through college."

I was getting angry, and the good mother is never supposed to get angry. What kind

45

of example does that set for your child? I took a deep breath. "I'm sorry, Phoebe, but if that's not good enough, then I can't help you."

Tears were running down her face again, but I was too mad to offer her sympathy or a tissue.

"I'm going to the newsstand to pick up tomorrow's papers," I said. "There's plenty of food in the kitchen if you're hungry. I won't be long."

She wiped her face with a corner of the blanket and issued a shaky last word. "I just . . . don't know how . . . you can say . . . you love me . . . and still not tell me . . . who my own father is."

"I've told you what I know, sweetie," I said, grabbing my keys and heading for the door. "That's the best I can do."

Which was, of course, not true. A lie is never the best you can do, even when you tell yourself it is. It's just a way of buying some breathing room until you can work up enough courage to tell the truth. And that can take a lifetime.

4

The air outside was warm and moist and smelled like rain. I took a deep breath and started walking. There was no reason for me to go to the newsstand now. That was just an excuse to let me and Phoebe have a little cooling-off period while I collected my thoughts. Phoebe's father is the only operatic moment in my otherwise pretty routine life. I don't mean boring. I love my work. I love my friends. I adore my daughter. But it's all contained within the twenty-four hours of an ordinary day. The stories begin, run their course, and then come to an end. But not B.J.

Burghardt Johnson is the one moment in my life that made me feel everything bigger and wider and deeper than I ever had before. I loved him from the moment I laid eyes on him, and I probably always will, but that doesn't mean I can explain why to anybody. Even his daughter. Maybe *especially* his daughter.

As I walked down Peeples Street and turned down Abernathy Boulevard, a man passed me with a tip of his Braves cap and a pleasant "Good evening." I returned the greeting with no thought that he might do me harm and realized again how lucky I was to live here. Pick any spot on earth these days, and nine times out of ten it isn't safe for a woman to be out alone there after dark. In some places, she isn't much better off in daylight. Here, women could walk around without fearing for their lives. I could take my problems outside for an airing and not have to worry that I wouldn't make it home in one piece. That's one of the reasons I live in this neighborhood. It's why I raised Phoebe here. I wanted her to be fearless.

On the surface, West End is just another African-American urban community on Atlanta's southwest side. The main commercial strip, named for Rev. Ralph David Abernathy, a giant of the civil rights movement, has the classic inner-city mix of fast-food joints, soul- and health-food restaurants, beauty supply stores, barbershops, wig palaces, mom-and-pop grocery stores, and a liquor store or two. Of course, there are churches, from the Shrine of the Black Madonna to St. Anthony's of Padua and all manner of Baptists, Methodists, Muslims, and mystics in between.

The Mall West End, crowded with shoppers any day of the week, has an array of nail shops, dollar stores, discount books, clothes on a budget, and a dizzying range of athletic-shoe outlets. Across from the mall, the new Krispy Kreme doughnut shop has relocated to a spiffy new facility with the added temptation of a truly dangerous-to-the-waistline drive-through. New condos are going up across from the mass transit station, and the omnipresent, ever-charming street vendors now do a booming business with nearly as many residents as train riders. A few blocks away, the Atlanta University Center adds five thousand college students to the mixture in a way that guarantees a pizza joint will stay open, a sandwich shop will thrive, and a smattering of Jamaican and Chinese take-out places will always have a line on Saturday night.

The streets are free of litter and loiterers. Buildings and landscaping are neat and well kept. Streetlights shine unbroken and potholes are nonexistent. Walking by the twenty-four-hour beauty salon on my way to the West End News, I could see two stylists working with clients in side-by-side chairs. All four women were laughing and talking as easily as if they'd been in somebody's kitchen on Saturday afternoon, heating their hot combs in the stove, telling the stories that women tell when they're safe and happy and there're no men around.

Next door, the florist who closes at midnight was putting the finishing touches on the bouquet that would be featured in tomorrow's front window. It was a wild profusion of tropical blooms, heavy on the shop's signature birds-of-paradise and sure to be snapped up by a romantic with a sense of adventure. There is only one word to describe West End's nighttime streets: peaceful. That's what makes this neighborhood different. But it wasn't always this way.

A few years ago it went through a period of economic transition that left it fragmented and newly vulnerable to the same crimes that plague poor communities from Los Angeles to Washington, D.C. Rape, robbery, street crime, domestic violence, and child abuse were rampant, and then crack came and the situation became almost intolerable.

My father had died by then, and my mother wasn't sure it was safe for us to stay in our house without him. For a long time, things just slid from bad to worse.

Then suddenly, inexplicably, the bodies of black women began showing up in neighborhood Dumpsters, behind vacant homes, in the trunks of abandoned cars. A little girl was murdered by two crackheads who stole her lunch money. Finally, a young mother was raped and killed on her way home from the grocery store and her body left on the railroad tracks. Her funeral was crowded with mourners, and when her brother collapsed in despair over his baby sister's casket, he was led away by one Mr. Blue Hamilton, who was heard reassuring his friend that this crime would not go unpunished.

And it didn't. A series of tips led to the identification of the man responsible for the murders, and he was arrested. When the court released him on a technicality, despite overwhelming evidence that he was guilty and without remorse, the neighborhood prepared for the worst, but two days after he returned home, the man disappeared and was never seen again.

That was how Blue Hamilton became a neighborhood legend and the unofficial patron saint of southwest Atlanta. He had transformed our ordinary African-American urban community into a peaceful, crime-free zone where women could walk unmolested any hour of the day, and the crack houses had been replaced by carefully tended gardens and community playgrounds. It was the safest eight or ten square miles in Atlanta. On the streets Blue controlled, going out after dark was as safe as going out at high noon. Some people argued with his methods and called him a gangster, but I remember what it was like before he took charge of the men around here and I'm proud to call him a friend. He's the reason I can be out here, walking in the moonlight, *thinking*.

Phoebe is going to have to get over herself. My solution may not have been the best one, but she's always had one hundred percent of me, and she has a great godfather in my best friend Louis.

Louis is the only other person who knows Phoebe's real father, but he had been sworn to secrecy by me right after I told him I was pregnant. I knew I could trust him. We'd been keeping each other's secrets for years. We first met as infants when our mothers, who were best friends and lived around the corner from each other by design, delivered us within a few months of each other. Louis arrived in the fall and I made my appearance on what is now Martin Luther King Jr. Day, but back then was only January fifteenth.

We were thrown together immediately, and there is ample photographic evidence of us grinning in the bathtub, naked as jaybirds, or napping in the same crib, piled up together like puppies. Our mothers found these photographs endearing. As teenagers, we found them mortifying. As adults, they provided us with hours of teasing as well as evidence of our lifelong bond. We tried to go steady once when we were thirteen, but it was a disaster. We called it off after one excruciatingly awkward kiss, renewed our pledge to be friends for life, and never looked back.

Louis was the only person I considered asking to go with me to the clinic. He was standing right beside me when they did the preabortion sonogram and showed me the little peanut-shaped *thing* that was, or was not, going to grow up to be a real live baby, depending on what I decided in the next few hours. He held my hand when we sat there, surrounded by every kind and color and class of woman, some with partners, some with friends, some grimly alone, all just waiting. He heard them finally call my name and felt my hesitation just like I did. And when I turned to him in tears and told him I didn't want to do it, he just hugged me real hard and took me home so I could tell my mother.

Her reaction didn't worry me. My mother had been wealthy and unconventional all her life. She was only eighteen when she fell in love with my father, a professional gambler twice her age. Horrified, her parents disowned her and moved to Florida. She married my father immediately, and when she got pregnant with me two years later, he bought her this house. She spent most of my childhood traveling with my father while I stayed with a series of nannies until I was thirteen and convinced them I could stay by myself.

Once she determined having a baby was really what I wanted, the idea of a grandchild delighted her. She encouraged me to give up my ratty little student apartment and move in with her. She had plenty of space and she was lonely in that big old house. For my part, I was talking a lot bolder than I felt. I knew raising a child alone was a huge responsibility, and I had sense enough to welcome her assistance. As for the identity of the father, she didn't press me. My mother and I settled on a version of *don't ask, don't tell* that suited us both.

Too bad she wasn't around tonight, I

thought, opening the door of the West End News and stepping inside. Maybe she could help me make her granddaughter stop asking the one question I was not prepared to answer. In the meantime, I'd grab the *New York Times* and a few fashion magazines for Phoebe as a peace offering. Maybe spending a few hours with the rich, famous, and disturbingly thin would take her mind off her troubles and my past. Otherwise, it was going to be a very long night.

5

When I got home, my daughter had left a short note: *I'm at Louis's house. I'll be late.* She didn't even sign it. To tell the truth, I was relieved. Louis had limitless patience for Phoebe's dramas, major and minor. I probably wouldn't have survived her adolescence without him, and tonight he was just the port in a storm she needed.

I put the newspaper in my office, took the magazines upstairs, and laid them on her bed. The candle had been extinguished, but the smell of roses was overpowering in the hot stillness. I turned on the ceiling fan and opened the window to get some air moving. That's when I spotted Amelia doing laps in her pool. When she works late, she often swims at night. She was moving through the water with barely a ripple, strong and graceful as a creature who was born for the sea. One of the reasons she bought that house ten years ago was because of the pool. It was full-size, completely tiled in shades of blue, green, and gray, and on the bottom it boasted a life-size mermaid mosaic that had fascinated me all my life. The mermaid was inexplicably and beautifully brown, and her long black hair flowed out from her head in curling tendrils that wound around the entire floor of the pool. She wore the mysterious smile that seems to be every self-respecting mermaid's expression of choice, and she was holding a pale pink conch shell up to her ear as if to listen for the ocean's roar or a midnight confession.

The story was that many years ago when West End was the far frontier of what was Atlanta, and beyond which there was only woods, the wealthy white men who built these houses had engaged in a friendly competition. Each one wanted his mansion to feature something that would suitably impress his neighbors with the owner's wealth and status in the world. Of course, it probably never occurred to them that black people would ever live in these homes. If it had, perhaps the original owner of Amelia's house never would have built that pool. It is doubtful that our house's original owner would have one-upped that pool by building a four-room playhouse in his yard, now my yard, for his daughter, then my daughter, to dress and undress their dolls and invite their friends for tea.

Amelia and I hadn't had a chance to talk since she came over yesterday to check on Phoebe, so I headed outside to bring her up to date. Our backyards were separated by a low stone wall and a wooden gate that was always open. By the time I walked through it, she had finished her workout and was drying herself with a fluffy white towel. At forty-two, Amelia looked ten years younger, and she intended to keep it that way. Tall and slender in a sleek black Speedo, she wore her hair in a short natural that didn't interfere with her swimming or her sense of style. She had one son, Jason, who was a freshman at Yale Law School and fully intended to go into practice with his mother once he passed the bar.

Her ex-husband, Jason's father, also a lawyer, was an arrogant, overbearing man, with whom she shared cordial relations for the sake of her son. She was always urging me to use the pool, but I was usually too busy to take her up on it. Tonight, the water looked so clear and inviting I almost jumped in with my clothes on.

"Hey, you!" I said, coming through the gate. "Finished already?"

She looked up and laughed. "Hey, yourself! That was fifty laps, for your information. How's Phoebe?"

"She's certifiably insane, but I think she'll live," I said, kicking off my flip-flops and dangling my feet in the cool water.

She wrapped the towel around her waist like a sarong and flopped down on one of the striped canvas deck chairs. The mermaid's hair seemed to be rippling gently.

"Still in mourning?"

"Sort of. She's decided it's all my fault because she hasn't had a chance to observe her father, in order to better understand herself, and therefore make better romantic choices."

Amelia rolled her eyes. "Tell her not to worry. I saw my father every day of my life and men are still a mystery to me."

"I tried to explain that to her, but she's really pissed."

"Don't worry about it," Amelia said, sounding sympathetic. "I remember when Jason first got his little heart broken. Some girl he was crazy about told him she just wanted to be friends because he was too nice. He told me I had ruined his life by not raising him to be a typical male asshole — my description, of course, not his!"

"Did you apologize for being such a bad

mother?" I said, laughing.

She raised her eyebrows. "Did you?"

"Not in this life!"

"So you *know* I didn't! I told him I had raised him to be a peaceful presence on this earth and that any girl who couldn't see that was a waste of his time. He didn't speak to me for two weeks, and then he met a girl who thought he was the cat's pajamas and all was forgiven."

The old-fashioned expression made me smile. I remember my mother bestowing that one as a high compliment, too, although why feline night wear should be considered something wonderful was still beyond me.

"So there's hope for me and Phoebe?"

"Of course there is. Look at Jason. Butter wouldn't melt in his mouth now, but I swear he's responsible for every gray hair I've got."

"You haven't got any gray hair!"

"I owe it all to my stylist," she said. "The reality is a much grimmer picture."

"Your secret is safe with me."

"Speaking of secrets," she said, "can I ask you something?"

"Sure." The sky was clear and there was the barest sliver of a new moon. Phoebe used to have a book that showed the stars at different times of the year. When she was little, we spent hours on the back porch trying to identify the constellations. "Ask away."

"Why don't you just tell her about her father and let her figure out how to deal with it the best she can?"

Amelia didn't know his identity, but I had shared the rest of the story with her. I was surprised by her question. "How long do you think it would take for her to track him down?"

"So? What if she does? Kids do it all the time."

"So what if he's less than thrilled to discover that he has a seventeen-year-old daughter?"

"What if he's not?"

"Not what?"

"Not 'less than thrilled.' What if he's delighted to find her after all these years?"

Sometimes Amelia annoyed me by playing the devil's advocate. Maybe that was what she was doing now. It was probably an occupational hazard for lawyers, but I always found it counterproductive. Not to mention the fact that the devil has plenty of advocates already on the job. One more is just overkill.

"You make it sound like he's been

searching for her or something," I said. "Trust me. This isn't that story. The last thing he wants is to take on the responsibility of a teenage daughter. When I told him I was going to have an abortion, he couldn't get on that plane to Ghana fast enough."

"Sometimes men change when they see forty staring them in the face," she said. "It's a mortality thing."

Amelia seemed to be suddenly on the side of complete disclosure, although she had never before expressed an opinion on the matter, other than to show mild surprise when I explained that my solution had been to falsely claim multiple partners as a way of throwing Phoebe off the track. She suggested that simply refusing to reveal the name might have been a better way to go, but she respected the creativity and thoroughness of my approach.

As we sat there, a thought occurred to me. "Has Phoebe been lobbying you about this?"

Amelia grinned at me. "I wouldn't describe it as lobbying, but she definitely mentioned it when I saw her yesterday."

"Well, you can tell her for me it won't work." I sat up and wrapped my arms around my knees. "The potential for her to really get her feelings hurt is too great. Why risk it?"

"Her feelings or yours?"

I raised my eyebrows and looked at her.

Amelia looked back at me. "You realize I know this is none of my business, right?"

"I'm the one who brought it up," I said. "Go ahead."

"Phoebe is a very strong young woman. You can't always see it because you're her mother, and to you she's always going to be your baby girl."

"Only until she graduates," I said, knowing she was right. "Then I'm cutting her little ass loose."

"Too late," Amelia smiled. "They already did that. In the delivery room, remember?"

A wispy little cloud moved across the moon and disappeared behind the giant pines at the edge of Amelia's yard. She was a good friend trying to pull my coat, and I appreciated it, as always.

"How could I forget?"

"Then stop worrying! She can handle it. If you tell her or you don't tell her, she's going to be fine." Amelia sat up and looked at me. "You're the one I'm worried about."

"*Me?*"

She hesitated. "You know I know this is —"

"— none of your business," I said with her. "So why are you worried about me?"

"Because you're such a terrible liar."

"What do you mean?" I couldn't decide if that was a compliment or a criticism.

"Good liars keep it simple. The fewer details the better. You, on the other hand, have concocted a big, complicated mess of a story that never sounded very convincing and gets weaker every time you tell it."

"Do you think she knows I'm lying?"

"I think she's confused. She doesn't know what to think."

"She's not the only one," I said, kicking my feet in the water to watch the mermaid's tail ripple.

"Don't beat yourself up too bad," Amelia said. "It made perfect sense at the time, right?"

I nodded. "Most of it still does."

"Then all you have to do is work on that little part that doesn't."

We had been friends for a decade because Amelia was honest without being judgmental. She always told me exactly what she thought, as only a lawyer can, but she never required me to agree or make a move based on her point of view. She had no timetable. Once she had her say, she left you to your own devices and moved on to other things. Which was what she did now.

"So, did you talk to Sam Hall yet?"

I was glad for the change of subject. "He called me tonight."

"Thank God! He was driving me crazy."

"Where do you know him from?"

"I represented a client in a case that involved Ezola Mandeville. She sent him to talk to me. How about that voice?"

"Makes it hard to keep your mind on business, doesn't it?"

"You got that right, but how about her aversion to the word *Ms.?* What's that about?"

"I'll ask her. We're having lunch next week."

"Really?"

"They're probably planning a project he says is right up my alley."

"You think you could work for her?"

"I've got to go to work for somebody, and you won't hire me."

"I can't afford you!"

"He said I was the answer to their prayers. How about that?"

"Better not get too cocky until you know what they were praying for!"

From Amelia's yard, I could see the light come on in my kitchen window, signaling Phoebe's return from her godfather's house around the corner. She was probably rummaging around in the fridge looking for something to eat. Three days of herb tea and saltines had probably taken their toll. Baby Doll needed dinner.

"Well, I know what I'm praying for," I said, standing up and hoping my daughter's visit to Louis had improved her disposition.

"What's that?"

I leaned down and gave Amelia a quick kiss on the cheek before heading home. "Wisdom, patience, and tuition money, not necessarily in that order."

"Just be yourself!" Amelia called after me, and I knew she was right. Flawed or fabulous, I'm the only mom she's got. All I have to do is love her and *be myself*. Everything else is extra.

6

When I opened the back door, at first I thought I had gone to the wrong house. The kitchen table was set with two places and a vase full of sunflowers I recognized from Louis's front yard. Phoebe was at the counter cracking eggs in a bowl, and while Sade's *Lovers Rock* is not exactly upbeat, it was music, and the vibe in the room was definitely not hostile.

"What's all this for?"

"For you." She shrugged her shoulders and managed a crooked smile. "For us."

"It's beautiful," I said, and walked over to hug her and kiss her newly nontearstained cheeks. "I was coming in to cook something for you."

"I'm making an omelet. Is that enough?"

"If you throw some cheese in there it is," I said, opening the refrigerator and reaching for the block of sharp cheddar I knew was in the cheese drawer.

I got the grater and stood next to her at the counter, enjoying the familiarity of the routine. We had been cooking together since she was old enough to handle a whisk, and we knew each other's kitchen rhythms the way longtime partners in a ballroom dance competition know when to glide and when to dip. At five-eight, Phoebe has a good three inches on me, although she'd like to be taller so she could slam-dunk a basketball. She doesn't want to actually play the game. She just wants to be able to leap into the air and slam the ball through the net, alone and unopposed.

When she told me that was one of her recurring dreams, I couldn't have been more surprised. I never had any kind of sports dream. The idea that Phoebe produced her own fantasies, apart from any we might share, was a revelation to me. It seemed such a completely separate act, kind of like the first time your kid tells you no, and means it. It's a moment of such unequivocal *otherness* that it sends a shiver down the spine of an overprotective mother such as I know myself to be. *You mean this is not attached to me like my arm?* you think, amazed. *This is not just an extension of me?*

"Mom?" Phoebe said, keeping her eyes on the eggs starting to foam under her expert strokes.

"Yeah?"

"I'm sorry."

"For what?" I said, still grating. "Wearing that blanket around for three days?"

She poked me in the side with her elbow. "Don't make fun of me!"

I put down the cheese. "I'm not making fun of you. I'm just glad we're going to have a nice meal together."

"That's just what Louis said." She smiled a little. Not one hundred percent, but a smile.

"He did?"

She nodded and condensed their conversation into Louis's gentle suggestions as to how we could make peace.

"He said you would probably appreciate having dinner with me tonight. Especially if I cooked it."

I laughed and hugged her again, being careful not to tip the bowl. "Your godfather is a living saint."

"Yes, I know," she said, turning back to the eggs, adding a pinch of salt and a dash of pepper. "He said that, too."

She poured the eggs into the pan with a buttery little sizzle. I had grated more than enough cheese, so I popped in two pieces of whole wheat bread for toast and watched her tend her omelet with the practiced eye of a cook who's comfortable in the kitchen. Either the storm had passed or we were dancing around in the eye of it. At this point I didn't really care. I was just happy to have her back. When people say *tough love*, they're usually talking about the kid, but I think it's harder on the mother. It's infinitely easier to *defy* authority than to *be* authority.

When we sat down, Sade was still crooning about how somebody had already broken her heart, but across the table from me, Phoebe was serving up a perfect omelet as her peace offering in the same way I had offered up those fashion magazines. We still knew each other better than anybody else did, and maybe the things we didn't know just weren't worth knowing.

"To us," I said, raising my orange juice in a toast.

"To us," Phoebe said, and we clinked our glasses and agreed to disagree on who owed who what explanation of things that cannot always be explained. At least for the moment, a peaceful meal was all we required.

7

Sunday passed too fast. Phoebe packed up, cleaned up, and chose a pair of low-slung jeans, a tiny little top, and a brand-new bright pink jacket to return to campus looking rested, gorgeous, and unconcerned, no matter what story was making the rounds. I spent the day poking my head in to offer suggestions and answering e-mail to get a jump on Monday morning. There was no way to prepare for the meeting with Sam Hall and *Miss* Mandeville. They had sent for me. All I had to do was show up and let them make me an offer.

Phoebe and I shared a dinner of lemon roast chicken, a tossed salad, and fresh strawberries with Louis; then we all went over to Amelia's for a good-bye toast of sparkling apple juice and headed for the airport. It was sunset. The sky over the freeway was as beautiful as a beach postcard, and suddenly I started feeling sentimental. The summer had spoiled me. I wasn't going to see my baby again until Thanksgiving, and that was three months from now. Who knew what adventures Baby Doll would have between now and then, or how much time she'd have to share them?

"Mom?"

"Yeah?"

"I'm going to miss you."

"I'm going to miss you, too," I said. "You're going to have a great year. I can feel it."

"You know I'd never do anything to hurt you, don't you, Mom?"

"Of course I do," I said, watching a big Delta jumbo jet coming in for a landing above our heads as we neared the airport. "What made you say that?"

"Nothing," she said. "I don't know. Nothing."

Interesting answer, but the passenger drop-off lanes at Atlanta's Hartsfield-Jackson airport are no place to pursue such complicated questions, so I didn't try. A big SUV swung out and I swooped in behind it and pulled up next to the curb. Phoebe was gathering her things.

"You okay?"

She leaned over and kissed me good-bye, waving at the skycap nearby for assistance. "I'm fine! I'll call you when I get there!"

"You'd better! I love you!"

"Love you, too!"

And she was gone. Checking her bags, stamping her ticket, boarding the airplane, ready to confront her demons, romantic and otherwise, and handling her business the way a third-generation free woman is supposed to do. My baby was growing up. Now all I had to do was figure out how to pay for the next four years and she was on her own. If I do my job right, she'll be ready, and so will I.

8

When I pulled up in front of Mandeville Maid Services per Sam's instructions, at just before noon, a young woman in dark blue pants and a white shirt with *Valet* stitched above the left breast pocket took my keys, handed me a ticket, and directed me inside. I was wearing my corporate clothes: gray suit, white blouse, black pumps. If there was a job to be had, I intended to leave here with it. When I identified myself to the female security guard, she told me politely that Miss Mandeville's office was on the fifth floor and pointed me to the elevator on the far side of a bright, plant-filled atrium that ran from the hardwood floor of the lobby to the stained-glass windows in the ceiling. A small sign pointed to a clinic on the building's lower level, and another arrow directed visitors to the office of the social services coordinator with a question and an answer: *Got a problem? We've got an answer!*

Ezola's inclusion of a well-woman clinic on-site had garnered a flurry of news coverage, all well deserved. The jobs she was filling rarely included health benefits, although healthy employees are always better for business. So Ezola hired two women doctors, and gave any woman she placed access to the clinic as long as she was employed. She hadn't been generous enough to spring for hospitalization or maternity benefits, but she was definitely on the right track. The lobby floors were spotless, and the plants were so green I couldn't believe they were real until I got closer and saw a young woman watering and pruning nearby. It was an impressive setup, and it seemed to be humming right along just fine. What could they possibly want with me?

Before I had a chance to speculate further, the elevator's mirrored doors opened and a short, bald man in a beautiful pinstriped suit was standing there smiling like he was so happy to see me, he could barely contain the joy.

"Ms. Sanderson," he said, coming forward and holding out his hand in greeting. "It is a pleasure. I'm Sam Hall."

The voice was the one I had heard on the phone, all right, but none of my mental speculation had led me to picture Sam as a short, slightly round, clean-shaven guy with a very expensive suit and a very firm handshake.

"Welcome to Mandeville Maid Services," he said. "You just passed your first test."

"And what test was that?"

"You arrived on time," he said. "You'd be amazed at how many people are careless about it. Five minutes here. Ten minutes there. It adds up, and that's not how we do business."

This woman must be a real terror.

"The renovation is lovely," I said.

"Thank you. Now will you follow me? Miss Mandeville is really looking forward to talking with you."

He led me down a short, heavily carpeted hallway that ended at two oversize oak doors. He knocked softly, and a buzzer deactivated the lock with a click. Her level of security surprised me, but I guess it shouldn't have. These are dangerous times. Sam pushed open one of the big doors and moved aside to let me pass.

I stepped into a large, very formal-looking room that had an imposing cherrywood desk at one end, and at the other a dining table elaborately set for two that could easily seat six. In between was an area made for more casual conversation, with two love seats facing each other, a couple of wing-back chairs, and an oversize throne-looking thing that was sprayed antique gold and upholstered with tufted red velvet. It looked like a child's idea of a chair fit for a queen, and Ezola Mandeville was sitting in it as I stepped into her office.

She stood up and smiled pleasantly, although she didn't come forward to greet us. Sam closed the door and walked with me over to where she was standing. She looked as intimidating as her photographs. Maybe more so. *Fierce* might be a better word to describe her. She probably wasn't much taller than I was, but it wasn't about height. There was a real presence, an almost palpable strength, rolling off her in waves. I couldn't imagine trying to tell her no.

As she stood there majestically, in front of her unapologetic throne, I was aware of her strong arms and hands that ended in short, thick fingers and nails shaped square for efficiency, not fashion. She was rangy, but not thin. Her broad, dark brown face was clean of makeup and dominated by her small but expressive eyes and high, sharp cheekbones. Her mouth was full-lipped and firm, and her hair was twisted into a bun, pinned tightly at the back of her head. A plain dark blue linen dress with a single strand of pearls and a pair of low-heeled pumps completed her outfit by doing nothing to draw attention to themselves. When you saw Ezola Mandeville, you remembered her, not her clothes.

"Miss Mandeville," Sam said. "I would like to present Ms. Catherine Sanderson."

"Thank you for coming," Ezola said, shaking my hand with a grip as firm as Sam's, although her voice was surprisingly light, almost girlish. Neither one of them looked at all the way they sounded. It was like meeting a popular radio deejay and realizing that he was a lot closer in appearance to Biz Markie than Wesley Snipes.

"It's an honor to meet you," I said. "I'm a great admirer of your work."

"I'm so happy to hear it. That'll make my job that much easier. Please sit down." She indicated the chair closest to the throne and I took it. It wasn't until I sat down that I realized how much lower my chair was than Ezola's. She was giving Sam instructions in the crisp way of someone who is used to saying things one time and one time only. Sam was watching her and nodding attentively. I decided he wasn't really unattractive. It was just that, based strictly on his voice, I had been expecting someone else. In my mind, Sam Hall was a cross between Denzel Washington and

Sam Jackson. When he turned out not to be anything like either one of them, I felt like he had cheated.

He assured Ezola that he would communicate her wishes to the kitchen and then turned back to me.

"So good to have you here, Ms. Sanderson," he said, extending his hand. "I look forward to seeing you again."

I had assumed he would be staying for the meeting, but he was gone before I had a chance to say good-bye, pulling the big door closed behind him.

Ezola Mandeville turned to me in my little sawed-off chair with a question.

"You eat meat, don't you?"

"Yes," I said, wondering if that was another test.

"Good, good." She lowered herself onto her throne as she nodded her approval. I guess I passed again. "I've had some people up here recently who acted like I was putting their lives in danger by serving up a nice porterhouse steak. Asked me hadn't I heard about mad cow disease!"

She rolled her eyes in disgust. "What kind of question is that? Of course I know about mad cow disease. I remember when Oprah got tried for even talking about mad cow disease. But what does that have to do with a nice lunch of steak and potatoes? Nothing!"

I had to agree with her on that one. Mad cow disease was so far down on my worry list that I rarely considered it at all. When I want to freak myself out about an illness, I just look at the AIDS statistics and that's enough for me. But this woman didn't invite me up here to talk about cows. We were here to talk turkey.

"Here's the way I like to do business," she said. "We talk first, and eat after. That way we can both enjoy the meal without trying to figure out what the other one's thinking. I'm a busy woman and I know you are, too. We could waste a lot of time trying to be mind readers."

"That sounds good to me," I said. "Sam didn't really tell me very much when we talked on the phone."

She smiled and nodded, as though that were as it should be. "He's very high on you. I need to be able to tap into the community of women you know like the back of your hand, and Sam says you can make that happen."

"I'm flattered," I said.

"Don't be," she said. "I want to help women stand on their own two feet, Miss Sanderson, but I'm not in the missionary business. I intend to make a profit and I intend to make this business grow, but there's one thing standing in my way. Do you know what that something is?"

I shook my head.

"Sorry black bitches," she said as easily as she might have said, *Would you care for a cup of tea?*

"Excuse me?"

"Let me tell you what I mean. I'm in the maid business. If *you* don't want to clean it up, I can send you a woman who will. It's hard work, but it's steady, there's no shame in it, and it pays enough to keep a roof over your head and clothes on your back, but I got more jobs than I can fill. Why? Because no black woman wants to be a maid anymore. Nobody wants to clean up after everybody's gone home or change a hundred beds a day or scrub the toilets out. These girls will do it for a week, a month, maybe three months, if they really need the money, and then they disappear. They don't quit. They don't call in. They just don't show up one day, so the job gets half-done or not done at all. Then the white man who hired me to get it done right calls to say he's not paying for the mess he got and what am I going to do about it?"

I understood exactly what she was talking about, but her characterization of these women as *sorry black bitches,* however shaky their work habits might be, didn't sit well with me, and I couldn't let it stand.

"I don't think calling them bitches helps the situation."

"It doesn't," she said. "Nothing does. I've tried everything. They think they're too good for this work. That's why I call them sorry. They don't see the value of an honest living."

"Why do you call them bitches?"

She let the question sit there for a minute. "To see if you're paying attention," she said finally. "And to see whether or not you'd agree with me."

"I always pay attention," I said, "and I never call women bitches. I don't care how sorry they are."

She just looked at me and I looked right back. I wasn't working for her yet so I had nothing to lose.

"Good," she said. "I don't either. I hate that word."

She got up slowly and walked over to the floor-to-ceiling window that let her gaze out at her employees going about their assignments. She turned back to me. "Can I tell you a story?"

"Certainly," I said, wondering how many more tests I'd have to pass before she fed me.

"Most people," Ezola said slowly, "have heard the story of how I once got fired for organizing maids."

I nodded.

"What they haven't heard is *why* I started doing it."

All the stories focused on shorter hours, higher pay, more humane treatment. Classic labor-movement goals. Seemed pretty clear to me.

"I don't mean the obvious reasons." In spite of her earlier statement about not having time to read my mind, Ezola was doing a pretty good job of it. "I mean why would I, a poor, colored woman working as a Buckhead maid, suddenly think about doing something like that? What made me do it?"

The history of black female activism is littered with tired feet, sore backs, one too many demands from the mistress or master of the house, one too many off days canceled at the last minute, one too many boxes of old clothes instead of a raise in pay.

"It was a book," she said, and her tone was almost reverent. "One book that changed everything for me. And do you know what book that was?"

I shook my head. I couldn't imagine.

"It was *Native Son* by Richard Wright."

My surprise was total. Wright's tragic novel from 1940 chronicles the fate of Bigger Thomas, a hapless black kid born into the most wretched poverty who accidentally smothers the drunken daughter of his wealthy white employers and then, in a panic, burns her body in the furnace. His arrest and conviction become a cause célèbre, galvanizing or polarizing the book's white characters, depending on their political persuasions.

"I don't understand," I said, honestly confused by what she had found in the grim pages of the novel that sparked her own activism.

"You've read the book?"

I nodded. "In college."

"You remember it?"

"Pretty well."

"Well enough to answer a question for me?"

Ezola needed to change her name to SAT.

"I'll do my best," I said. "It's been a while."

"It's an easy question," she said. "Why did Bigger kill that woman?"

If you remember the book at all, you remember that. "He was afraid of being discovered in a white girl's bedroom," I said, trying to remember the character's name.

"Mary," said Ezola, still effortlessly reading my mind.

"Yes, Mary. She was drunk and he had carried her upstairs. . . ."

The scene came back to me, piece by piece. Mary's drunken staggering. Bigger's rising panic.

"He was afraid of being discovered."

"But why did you assume I was talking about Mary?"

Slowly, another scene swirled out of my memory, but dimly. Not nearly as clear as Mary's death scene. There was a woman in this one, too, but who was she? What was her name?

"There was another woman," I said, wishing I could call up more details, but try as I might, she remained a mystery.

"Bessie," Ezola said softly. "That other woman's name was Bessie, and she was a colored woman, just like us, who helped Bigger out of the goodness of her heart and got bashed in the head for her trouble."

Now I remembered. After he killed Bessie for no reason except misdirected rage, the hero added insult to injury by stuffing her body down an air shaft, rendering her *invisible*. Ezola's point was beginning to dawn on me.

"That white woman I worked for had that book in her library for some reason. Maybe one of her kids brought it home from college. I don't know. She didn't have any other black books I ever saw, but she had that one, and one day it was out on the table, and before I dusted it off and put it back up where it belonged, I opened it up and read a little of the first page. I had never read a book written by a Negro before. I knew there were some, but I quit school after the tenth grade, so I never actually saw one. But that *Native Son* book just grabbed hold of me and wouldn't let go. I sat right there all afternoon and read almost that whole book. When it was time to go, I put it in my purse and I read it all the way home on the bus, ate my dinner, and kept reading until I was done.

"That next morning, I couldn't get Bigger and Bessie out of my head. I understood about Mary, him being so scared and all, but why had he killed Bessie? I took the book back, and after I gave her breakfast, I asked Mrs. Wyndom, that was her name, if she'd read it. She said she had, and I said then maybe she could help me understand why Bigger killed that woman. She always liked to think she was helping me improve my mind, so she gave me this long explanation about how dangerous it would be for a black man to be in Mary's bedroom like I didn't know that, and on and on until I realized she wasn't thinking about Bessie at all. That poor colored woman never crossed Mrs. Wyndom's mind."

I was fascinated with Ezola's line of reasoning and sorry that my first reaction had been the same as the clueless Buckhead matron's. It reminded me of traveling with my parents to one small Caribbean island or another when I was just a kid, newly alive with a passion to right the world's wrongs and full of a reformer's zeal. I was amazed and ashamed at how they could ignore the poor people who were always around the fringes of the tourist zones we frequented, looking for a chance to sell you something, or begging a few coins. Even the people who were working at the hotels were invisible to my mother and father as they dressed in their beautiful clothes, kissed me good night after telling the babysitter what time to put me to bed, and swept out to the gangster-owned casinos for a night of high-stakes gambling that would probably have financed the babysitter's family for a year or two.

It made me feel guilty that we had so much while other people had so little, and one night, as my father was putting on his white dinner jacket, I asked him if it didn't make him feel bad to ignore them.

"They're not my responsibility," he said, shrugging them off like a cheap suit, "and they're certainly not yours. Why don't you go down to the pool and leave the people's revolution to the people?"

After that, I stayed home in Atlanta when they traveled outside the country. Neither one of them pressed me for the real reason why. I think they were relieved not to have to drag me along, trailing my privileged American guilt behind me like a whiff of Jungle Gardenia.

"That white woman didn't see me or Bessie," Ezola was saying, "and it made me mad, and the more I thought about it, the madder I got. No wonder these women worked their maids so hard. They never even saw us. By the time I got off work that day and walked that long, uphill stretch from Mrs. Wyndom's house to the bus stop, I had decided one thing. I wasn't going to be invisible anymore. I was a full-grown woman and I figured it was time to start acting like one. I owed it to myself, and I owed it to Bessie."

She came back and sat down across from me again. I'm sure she told that story a lot, but it moved me. I forgave her for the *black bitches* test question and waited for her to wrap it up.

"And that," she said, "is what all this is about. Bearing witness for Bessie by looking out for all the hardworking colored women people never even see. That's why I do what I do, and if you decide to come and work for me, that's what you'll be doing, too."

It was easily the most intense job interview I'd ever had, if that's what this was, and it was impossible to resist. My work was already about saving women. Of course I wanted to bear witness for Bessie. I was already doing it for Maria and Ashima and Migdalia and Shanequa. It was the same testimony, and I had already been sworn.

"But that's what you're already doing, isn't it?" she said, watching me closely. She was good at this and she knew it. Now she was ready to close the deal.

"Yes, I guess it is," I said. "What can I do to help you?"

As if on cue, there was a soft tap at the

door. Ezola pushed the buzzer to admit a white-jacketed waiter bringing our food in covered silver dishes like room service.

"Now *that*," she said, standing up and waving him in to set things up, "we can talk about over lunch."

Which was exactly what we did.

9

By the time I left Ezola Mandeville's office, we had hammered out the broad outlines of a relationship that seemed mutually beneficial, and my job search was over before it got started good. She was interested in targeting immigrant and refugee women to offer her services, and she needed my help to reach them effectively. It was a great idea. Many of these women needed immediate temporary work to help support their families, and they were motivated to work hard by the dreams that had brought them to America in the first place. I was happy to make the hookup. If they were going to be doing service work, Ezola's operation would be more protection than they were going to find anywhere else, decent wages, and even a few benefits. It seemed like a winning combination all the way around.

Plus, the money she was offering me was enough to cover all of Phoebe's college costs and let me put a little aside for myself. The only problem was, I had a company. So I made a counteroffer that allowed me to start working for her free-lance while I finished my current projects. She reluctantly agreed and I promised I'd be on board full-time in three months. How I was going to get it all done was something I'd have to figure out later. But for now we shook hands to seal the deal and enjoyed our coffee with a slice of sweet-potato pie.

Outside, I gave my ticket to the young woman at the valet stand who stamped it *paid* and called for my car to be brought around front. As I stood there waiting, I could hear the radio she had playing quietly beside her. She was listening to black talk radio, something I almost never do, since I can be ignorant all by myself. An indignant woman was urging the show's listeners to support the first black *American Idol* winner because she thought he wasn't getting as much airplay and publicity as the white runner-up had gotten, including being featured solo on the cover of *Rolling Stone*, a magazine this woman had probably never read in her life.

"Buy his CD on day one," she was urging all those within the sound of her voice. "These white folks need to be taught a lesson once and for all."

I closed my eyes and took a deep breath.

Sometimes these Atlanta Negroes drive me crazy. All they ever talk about is race! Not race in the sense of the human family. Not race in the sense of the complexities of living in the global village, with its awe-inspiring displays of cultural diversity. Those discussions would be interesting, certainly challenging, and might even result in some concrete changes in lifestyle or public policy.

But no! In Atlanta, racial discussions continue along the lines established all those years ago when former governor Lester Maddox was at his segregated restaurant handing out pick handles to keep the Pickwick the bastion of white supremacy and bad food it had always been. Black folks on one side, trying to get in. White folks on the other side, trying to keep us out. It's such a simplistic, counterproductive way of looking at things, especially when all the people in charge around here are black. We're still bitching like the last twenty years never happened at all. It's exhausting.

Sometimes Louis accuses me of being an elitist, but I'm not. I just wish we had a bigger worldview, that's all. The fact that *Brother Ruben*, as she kept calling him, garnered a big record contract, earned the love of legions of fans, appeared on countless magazine covers and TV shows, and received a Grammy nomination meant nothing to the woman who was calling. In her mind, he was black, and therefore a victim in need of the protection that only racial solidarity can afford.

"What do you think about what she said?" I asked the young woman in the booth.

She glanced up at me quickly to see if she could be candid and then shrugged her shoulders. "If you askin' me, it seems like she's makin' it into a sympathy thing. You know, buy the brother's CD to help him out. But he don't need that. He can really sing. You know what I mean?"

"I know exactly what you mean."

The host apparently did, too. "Y'all ain't gotta do Brother Ruben no favors, though," he said. "Check him out."

The voice belonging to the brother in question was one of those full, rich, chocolate voices that only come out of the mouths of black men. Jerry Butler has one. Isaac Hayes has one. The Temptations had five between them, and Barry White had at least two all by himself. Ruben Studdard wasn't in their league yet, but he was working on it, and the boy definitely had promise.

Sort of like Atlanta, I thought as my car pulled up to the curb and the young valet hopped out, accepted my tip, and closed the door behind me. Big and corny and full of passionate potential that it never quite fulfills. But just when you think you know everything there is to know about the place, it turns the note you expected to hear in a direction you had never considered and you find yourself heading home with all the windows rolled down, singing your ass off, and being eternally grateful for even the possibility of perfection.

10

The problem when your two best friends become a couple is that they're never around when you're up for a spontaneous celebration. They're always at lunch or on their way to the movies or strolling in the park or simply not answering their phones because they've got better things to do. Although I was dying to share my good news, Amelia and Louis were nowhere to be found. When I got home and called her office Amelia's secretary said she'd left early, and the answering machine was on at the newspaper even though it wasn't even four o'clock.

This was serious. Louis always wrote his weekly columns on Monday, since the paper was in production on Tuesday to hit the stands on Wednesday. But today he had not only left early, but closed the office. Amelia and Louis had been friends since I introduced them, but four months ago she took him to a Sweet Honey in the Rock concert at Spelman, and ever since then they'd been thick as thieves. They were still being cool around me, but I could feel a new energy between them.

I used to try to tease Louis that he had printer's ink for blood, but he took it as a compliment. The *Sentinel* was his life. He was the owner, editor, and publisher. It was the only job he ever had, starting as a delivery boy when he was just a kid. His father, Louis Adams Sr., had founded the *Sentinel* in 1964 and raised his son to believe their mission, "to tell the truth to the people," was worth the sacrifices they had to make as a family to get it into the hands of its readers. In the early days, the paper was often under attack by the Ku Klux Klan for encouraging black voter registration. The office was firebombed twice, and Louis told me he had answered the phone at their house many times as a child to hear a snarling male voice threaten his father's life or his mother's safety.

But those were the glory days. The staff had dwindled to Louis, his longtime receptionist, Miss Iona Williams, a couple of interns from the A.U. Center, and two freelance reporters who covered everything from church news to city hall, and none of it very well. The only reason to pick up the paper at all was to read Louis's blistering editorials. He was as passionate about politics as his father had been, and as well informed. He had contacts all over the place who fed him information so his columns, which he ran in large type on the front page in a move right out of *Citizen Kane*, were full of unexpected tidbits that made them required reading for anybody who wanted to traverse the labyrinth that is our local political scene. The *Sentinel* was a losing proposition economically, but for Louis it was both a legacy and a labor of love. Imagining Louis without the *Sentinel* was like imagining Louis without his lopsided grin. Impossible.

So a group celebration was out, but I was still full of nervous energy from my meeting with Ezola, and I didn't feel like getting right back to work. Outside, the sky was an unbroken expanse of blue, and the breeze was blowing cool air from the north Georgia mountains. I opened the back door and stepped outside. As if to banish any lingering doubts that this was a perfect day, an impossibly red-breasted robin was singing itself silly in the middle of my sunflowers.

That's when I decided to take Amelia up on her standing invitation of a swim. I'd have the pool to myself. Just me and that mermaid and all that sunshine. Maybe it was time for a little reward after surviving my recent trials by fire. We're always quick to fuss at ourselves when we do it wrong. I want to reward myself when I do it right. My daughter isn't mad at me anymore, and my best friends are falling in love before my very eyes. Maybe it was standing my ground with Phoebe. Or maybe it was being in the room with Ezola's strange energy and Bessie's ghost, or maybe even something in Sam Hall's shiny bald head, but I felt like I could go Amelia's fifty laps, and fifty more, without even breathing hard.

Which is, of course, the real test. Not just can you do it, but can you make it look so easy everybody thinks they can do it, too, until they try it and come up winded, gasping for air, and hoping nobody's watching. That's not me. I've worked hard to get here and I'm ready for my close-up. *Been* ready. Why do you think I bought a new bathing suit, just in case?

11

The next week flew by in a blur of closing out old files, creating new ones, and reading through the mountain of material Sam had sent over to familiarize me with their Mandeville Maids. He was in Miami on business all week, which was fine with me. By the time he got back, I'd have some ideas ready for him to review.

Louis and Amelia had congratulated me on my new client, and on surviving Phoebe's last visit. I had teased them about their whereabouts when I tried to share my good news. They looked properly sheepish, and their answers were evasive enough to confirm my suspicions. I wondered if Phoebe had noticed it, too? I'd have to remember to ask her next time we talked.

The house had returned to its pre-Phoebe state of calm, and I was getting loads of work done, but the truth was, at the end of the day I really missed her. Our closeness was partly a result of my raising her alone, but more because we enjoyed each other's company like good friends do.

When she first went to Fairfield two years ago, I was a wreck. She wanted to go. It was her idea, so I wasn't worried about her making the adjustment. What threw me was how quiet the house was. I was so used to her music, her voice, her friends, her radio, her computer, her television shows, her favorite DVDs, her guitar, that when she left, the silence was almost overwhelming.

For some reason, I started listening to a lot of opera, Puccini especially, since he's the one my mother liked and these were her records I was playing, especially *Madame Butterfly* and *La Bohème*. All those doomed sopranos and impossibly passionate tenors helped me fill up the house with other voices that didn't remind me that my baby was now off on her own in the world, growing up and having adventures while I was just rattling around in a big, empty house. For the first time in a long time, I was lonely. Sure, I had my friends and my work, but there I was, still relatively young, still reasonably attractive, all dressed up with no place to go. I had had only two lovers, if you can even call them that, since Phoebe's father left for Africa. They were nice enough guys, and I wasn't looking for mad love as much as a friend I could sometimes sleep with. I thought it would be easy, but once you get out of school, it's much harder to meet single men.

The ones I did meet never seemed to have it all together in one place. The ones I liked to talk to were already married or didn't appeal to me sexually. The ones who appealed to me sexually usually had no interest in the things I cared about. Only twice did I think I had found somebody interesting, but neither one worked out. In both cases, the sex was terrible. One guy was so inept that teaching him would have required more effort than I was prepared to put in, and the other one had seen one too many porno movies and firmly believed that the best position in which to have sex was doggie style, no matter how many times I assured him this was a male fantasy, not a female preference.

After those disasters, I tried a couple of vibrators, but they made me feel pathetic, *Sex and the City* notwithstanding, and I didn't want to explain what they were to Phoebe, since I knew she would find them sooner or later. She's gone through my drawers and closets since she was a kid, just like I used to search through my mother's things looking for clues to who she really was. Trying to crack that mysterious code. So I got rid of the machinery and made sure to masturbate au naturel at least a couple of times a month to keep everything in working order, but that was pretty much it.

That was still pretty much it. I don't think about sex much when Phoebe's home. I think my maternal instinct keeps my libido at bay, but lately when she leaves, I can't help it. Amelia says thirty-five to forty-five is a period of intense sexual energy for women because we are facing the end of our childbearing years, and the urge to express all we are and know sexually is *overwhelming* — her word, not mine.

Well, I'm thirty-eight, and it wasn't that bad yet, but the devil does find work for idle hands, so I put on my mom's scratchy old album of Leontyne Price singing *Madame Butterfly* and went to get the mail. I was delighted to find a letter from Phoebe sitting on top of the stack. E-mail had encroached on our letter writing, but we still managed to sneak in a real letter, on real stationery, with real stamps, every now and then, and it was always a treat.

I dropped the rest of the mail on the coffee table and carried Phoebe's letter over to the couch so I could curl up and savor it. I tucked up my bare feet, unfolded the pages that smelled vaguely of my daughter's scent, and read these words.

Dear Mom,

I know you won't like what I have to say, but you know I would never do something like this if it weren't really important to me. I have a right to know my father.

She underlined *my father* in red like I might miss it.

You have made a decision not to tell me what I want to know, and I respect that, but now I'm asking you to respect the decision I have made.

I closed my eyes and took a deep breath. What was this girl talking about?

I have taken your college diaries back to school with me. I've only taken the ones that would fit the time period when I might have been conceived. I've made a list of the possible candidates — your lovers —

She underlined that, too, just to make sure I was paying attention.

And I've sent them all a letter outlining my

situation and requesting that they have a DNA test and forward the results to me, with a copy to you.

She's got to be kidding! She has to be!

I know you're probably mad at me now, but I had to do what was best for me and not let you talk me out of it. Please don't try to contact me. I've moved off campus with two girlfriends and I've changed my cell number. I just don't think I can talk to you again until you can tell me the truth about my father. It's just too painful. Please don't hate me, Mom. This is my life we're talking about. Not yours. If you need to reach me in an emergency, Louis will be able to find me, but only in an emergency.

A final red streak under that for emphasis and then the usual sign-off.

Love you, Mom.
Phoebe

12

There are only two kinds of offices that house black newspapers. One is at the top of a long, rickety set of wooden stairs that would drive the fire marshal crazy if he ever inspected anything in these neighborhoods, which he doesn't. The second is the ground-floor storefront in some bustling black commercial strip with the name of the paper printed in big white letters across the plate-glass window in the front. The *Sentinel* took the second option and occupied a row of four connected storefronts on Martin Luther King Jr. Drive.

At the *Sentinel*, just like at every other black newspaper office I've ever visited, the first person you encounter when you come through the front door is a middle-aged-to-ancient black woman who answers the phone, routes calls, greets visitors, and keeps up with who's in and who's out and when they'll be back. In the midst of these duties, she also clips newspapers — her own home publication and as many others as the editor deems appropriate. Her desk is always piled high with well-stuffed folders that need to be filed under headings like, *Black Mayors, 1974–1976,* or *Police Brutality* or *Denzel Washington.* They are also the ones who rewrite the church news column so it's ready for the world, open the mail, and remind the editor to go home and get some sleep every once in a while.

It was a full-time job back in the days when the *Sentinel* had six full-time reporters, four in town and two traveling the South to bring back coverage that placed Atlanta in the wider context of *region.* The *Sentinel* was the only black newspaper in town to send a reporter to the Pettus Bridge. They even had a reporter jailed in Albany and held without bail until Louis Sr. drove down with a lawyer from the Gate City Bar Association and brought him home. In those days, it wasn't unusual for the crusading editor to sleep on the big, well-worn leather sofa in his office. After his mother died, Louis Jr. was accustomed to waking up alone at home and calling his father at the *Sentinel* to say he was making breakfast and did Louis Sr. want him to cook enough eggs for two, as if this were the normal exchange between father and son.

But the *Sentinel*'s glory days were behind

it now, and the full-time staff had dwindled to Louis and Miss Iona Williams, who was still holding down the position of honor just inside the front door. Miss Iona, as everyone called her, had been the voice on the *Sentinel*'s answering machine for as long as anyone could remember, urging callers to leave a message and "don't forget to do something for freedom today." She had also been Louis Sr.'s longtime companion after he was widowed young, but had never married him out of loyalty to his wife, who was one of her best friends from girlhood.

At sixty-plus, Miss Iona was still a beauty. Her skin was smooth under the flawless makeup she was never seen without, and her salt-and-pepper hair was cut in a short pixie that had been her trademark style as long as I'd known her. One of those rare people who truly understands the difference between style and fashion, Miss Iona was wearing a dark green dress from the fifties that looked as modern as today. She was my role model. Sixty-five and sexy was a goal worth striving for, but today I doubted I'd make forty before my insane child gave me a heart attack.

When I walked in looking for Louis,

Miss Iona greeted me warmly. "Hey, girl! Where have you been hiding?"

"Just trying to stay out of trouble," I said, hoping I didn't look or sound as agitated as I felt.

She cocked her head to the side and raised her eyebrows. "Is it working?"

That made me laugh. "It's not working worth a damn!"

She laughed, too. "I didn't think so. How's my Baby Doll doing?"

My mother's friends always called her "Dolly," which is why we first started calling Phoebe "Baby Doll." When she was an infant, she looked just like my mother. It was almost as if they had used me as their conduit. To Dolly's buddies, Phoebe would always be Baby Doll.

"She's her grandmother's child. That's all I've got to say."

"Nobody up there at that school is bothering her, are they?"

Old black people always assume overt hostility runs rampant in environments like Fairfield, but it's almost never like that anymore. There are so many people from so many places that national boundaries are more likely to cause friction than squabbling between citizens of the same country. "No. She's fine. She's driving me crazy all by herself."

Her desk sat just outside of the glassed-in cubicle that was Louis's office and had once been his father's private sanctum. I could see him in his office talking animatedly with a young woman who was frantically taking notes. "I need some advice from her godfather. What's he up to?"

"One of the freelancers brought in something about migrant workers in south Georgia, but she doesn't know how to follow it up. He's trying to help her find the thread."

Louis was always talking to reporters about finding the thread that ran through a story and held it all together.

"Otherwise," he'd explain patiently, "all you've got is a bunch of facts. What's holding it all together?"

For Louis, what was holding it all together was a deep and abiding love for and faith in black people. He believed we could do better, and he lived his life as if we already were.

When he looked up and saw me, he smiled and held up one finger to say he was wrapping things up. The young reporter had one more question, which Louis answered as he walked her to the door. "How soon can I get that rewrite?"

Louis said, sounding like the editor in the *Superman* movies.

"Before five," the woman said over her shoulder, already headed back to her desk.

Miss Iona turned away to answer another call with her trademark greeting. "This is the *Sentinel*, black Atlanta's beacon of truth; how can I help you?"

Louis leaned over and kissed my cheek as he walked me into his office and closed the door. "I've been expecting you all morning. Did your mail come late?"

I was carrying Phoebe's letter in my purse to read it to Louis, but it seemed he had already seen it.

"You knew?"

He nodded. "She copied me."

"And you didn't call me?"

"I've been trying to call her."

"Did she really change her number?"

"She did, and her roommate says she's living off campus but she's not at liberty to tell me where. I left word for her to call me. I think she will."

"This is a nightmare." I sat down on the big brown leather couch that took up half the space in the room. "What am I going to do?"

Louis sat down at the other end of the couch and took my hand. On the other side of the glass, Miss Iona was charming a FedEx man half her age.

"Do you think she really did it?"

He wanted to say, *Of course she didn't do it,* but he couldn't lie, especially not to me. He clutched at the only available straw. "Did she really take the diaries?"

Louis, of course, knew all about what had once seemed like a great plan and now seemed like the gateway to hell.

"Yes."

"Did you list first and last names?"

"Of course."

"Don't say, 'of course,'" Louis said calmly. "I can't be expected to know the correct form for young girls' diaries. It could as easily be first name, last initial, or something like that."

"Sorry. Yes, I listed first and last to make it more convincing."

"That makes them pretty easy to find. All she has to do is Google these guys."

I groaned. "This is beyond awful. I can't even imagine what the letter she's sending them says. She didn't send you a copy of that, too, did she?"

"No. Just her letter to you and a little note asking me not to be mad and to contact her old roommate in case of emergency."

"This is an emergency!"

"Calm down," Louis said in that soothing way men have when they just don't get it. "If anybody contacts you, tell them your daughter made a mistake. What can they do?"

I groaned again. "Show up? Be indignant? Ruin my reputation for having at least the sense I was born with? Ask me what the hell I'm talking about, since I never had sex with a single one of them?"

"Am I in there?" Louis said with a grin to show he wouldn't mind if I'd thrown his name in the pot for good measure.

"Of course not!"

"Always the friend, never the fantasy," he said, and shook his head in mock despair.

"If you can get serious for a minute," I snapped, "I could use some advice."

"Okay, okay," he said soothingly. "Don't worry. She'll get it out of her system. Your secret remains intact, and, truth be told, these guys will probably be flattered you ever thought of them that way. Don't forget, you were a *babe* back then!"

The almost-flattery didn't distract me from the can of worms my daughter had opened and put down before me like an episode of *Fear Factor*. "I'm still a babe, but I can't even remember whose names I listed!"

"Well, that means I still have a chance," Louis said, grinning, determined to tease. "Maybe you put me on there and just forgot."

He still wasn't taking this as seriously as I wanted him to. "That's not funny."

"Yes, it is," he said, standing up and grabbing his jacket off the back of his chair.

"I'll bet their wives won't think it's so funny."

"Are they all married?"

"That's the point, Louis." I stood up, too. "I don't know! I haven't seen these guys in seventeen years!"

"Come have lunch with me and Amelia." He pronounced it like it was all one word. *MeandAmelia.* "I'll buy you a couple of apple martinis and you'll begin to see the humor in all this."

"No, I won't. What if these guys start showing up at my door?"

"Tell them to come see me," he said. "I'll explain everything."

"Phoebe is the one who's got some explaining to do."

"Soon as we find her," he said, ushering me out the door like a man with a lunch date he didn't want to miss. "I promise."

"Don't tell Amelia," I said as we left the

office in Miss Iona's capable hands and headed over to Paschal's. Louis Sr. had been a regular at the old Paschal's in the days when the original owner fed civil rights workers his world-famous chicken on the house as his contribution to the movement. Louis Jr. carried on his father's tradition from a booth in the corner of their expanded new place over on Northside Drive.

"Why not?"

"I don't want her to say I told you so."

He laughed. "Amelia never says I told you so."

"This is so stupid, she'll make an exception."

"All right," he said, taking my arm as we crossed the street. "Then so will I. Just for you, my lips are sealed."

13

"Am I glad to see you," Amelia said, standing up to hug me as soon as we walked in. "Phoebe copied me on that insane letter!"

"So much for secrets," I said, taking a seat next to my friend.

"I got one, too," Louis said, sliding in on the other side of Amelia and giving her a quick peck on the cheek. "A letter, not a secret."

She beamed at him for a second before turning back to me. "Secrets are a waste of time. We need to put our heads together and come up with a way to handle this girl's madness. Are you okay?"

Madness was what it felt like to me, too.

"It never dawned on me she'd ever do something like this."

"Me, either," Amelia said. "She never even mentioned the diaries to me."

"She asked me about them once or twice," Louis said. "Right after you left them out for her to find a couple of years ago."

"And you're just now telling me? What did she say?"

He shrugged, looking uncomfortable. *How did I ever think I could pull this off?*

"She asked me if I thought they were true."

"What did you tell her?"

"I told her somebody would have to be pretty crazy to lie in something they wrote just for themselves."

Amelia was beaming again like she could just eat him up. I wanted to smack both of them for being so happy when my life was suddenly such a mess.

"Thanks a lot," I said, signaling the waiter.

"What was I supposed to say?" Louis asked me after ordering a round of drinks. Alcohol for me. Sweet tea for them.

"Fake diaries don't do much good if nobody vouches for them," he said gently, and he was right.

"Why don't you just call these guys?" Amelia said. "Maybe you can head them off at the pass."

"I can't call them. I don't even have a list of their names, much less current phone numbers."

"Don't you remember who you wrote down?" Amelia said, sounding surprised as the waiter returned and put our drinks down, hovering discreetly for a moment, then gliding away when ordering didn't seem to be on anybody's immediate agenda. Paschal's waiters never rushed their customers. If you wanted to linger, they were prepared to let you. The candied yams weren't going anywhere, and neither were the collard greens.

"I didn't want to remember them," I said, trying once more to explain my convoluted reasoning. "They were just guys I had classes with. Friends of friends. Lab partners. Imaginary lovers, not the real thing."

Amelia was nodding like she was in the process of taking a deposition. "Nobody who maintained contact with you?"

"Not a one. They barely knew me."

"Then you know what?" Amelia looked at Louis, then back to me. I could tell she was rolling the facts over in her mind to clarify her thinking before she gave me an opinion.

"What?" All I needed was for Ezola Mandeville to hear some sleazy stuff like this on the wire. Atlanta's black community is a small universe, and gossip travels fast, especially when you're riding high and the fun is seeing you fall.

"I wouldn't do anything at all," Amelia said. "If they don't contact you, let sleeping dogs lie."

That sounded too easy, and even if it worked, there was still the question of the appropriate punishment for my daughter. She was too old to spank.

"What about Phoebe?"

Amelia shrugged. "Honor her request and don't contact her at all. She'll come to her senses."

"Sometimes I wonder."

"I'll make sure I find out who she's staying with and where," Louis said. "Just give her some space."

"*Space?* I'd like to give her a piece of my mind!"

Sometimes this modern-mother stuff requires a little too much understanding for me.

"Didn't you drive your mother crazy?" Amelia said, reaching for the menu now that she had given me a survival strategy that made sense, at least temporarily.

"It skips a generation," I said. "Like twins."

"That's not how I remember it," Louis said, grinning at me like he was fully prepared to give me a few choice examples.

"Change the subject," I said. "Please!"

Amelia immediately obliged by launching into a funny story about a case she had just tried where the defendant spoke French, her client spoke Cambodian, and the translator was certified only in Spanish. Louis followed up until the food arrived by telling us about his upcoming appointment to talk to some young black entrepreneurs from Detroit who had contacted him about investing in the *Sentinel*. By the time we were finishing our meal, I had decided that my friends were right. The best thing I could do right now was just be still, be patient, and wait for the storm to pass.

14

It was almost two o'clock in the morning, but my mind and my heart were still racing. Sleep was out of the question. If anyone had told me there would ever be a time when I wouldn't be able to pick up the phone and call my daughter, I would have laughed at the absurdity of such an idea. I wasn't laughing now. Louis called at midnight to say she was fine and, as he put it, "filled with the righteous fire of adolescent indignation."

Sure she was. Indignation was one of her favorite emotions. She got that from me. We don't just get mad; we get righteous. We cannot *believe* that you will not bend to our considerable will, and our outrage comes in equal measure with our incredulity. I was sure her telling of the story of why she had to take such drastic measures was a real tour de force, with me as the evil mother with the promiscuous past and her as the dutiful daughter who must finally take matters into her own hands. I couldn't argue with her casting me in that role, but I had hoped it would never come to this. I had hoped — I had *believed* — that I could be everything she needed when it came to family, and that my ability to make a life without her father in it would be her choice, too. But it wasn't.

Her father. I never even thought of his name anymore, only his status. It was always easier that way. Everything was clear when he was defined by his biological relationship to my child, not his emotional relationship to me. He was my first love and my first lover, a dangerous combination for a die-hard romantic like me. He was still the only man I ever wanted to wake up next to every morning and go to sleep next to every night, but what's that old Rolling Stones song? "You Can't Always Get What You Want"? They got that right.

He was also the only man I ever knew who listened as well as he talked, gave as good as he got, and made me feel like he saw me the way I wished I was: strong and sexy and free as a bird. I saw my life unfolding with him right there beside me, making jokes, making love, having adventures, having children when we had enjoyed each other enough to share ourselves with kids and all they bring.

He saw his life unfolding as a successful foreign correspondent, traveling the world unencumbered. It was proof of my naïveté that I thought our two fantasies could not only coexist, but complement and complete each other. My life for those few months when that dream was in full effect and love was in bloom was like something out of a romance novel. I knew the kind of woman he wanted and I played her part so well I forgot she wasn't really me.

Then one night when we were making love, I didn't get up and put in my diaphragm. One night I just didn't want to untangle myself from the honey-colored jumble of his arms and legs and hips and thighs and fumble around with spermicides and stubborn rubber discs that are the slipperiest thing known to woman other than the place you're trying to put it. The magic was so thick between us that night, the feeling was so strong, the moment so right, I felt that if I broke the spell we might not be able to get it back, and I couldn't risk it. That's the way your mind works when you're twenty and your hormones always cast the deciding vote.

So I did a quick calculation of the odds, threw caution to the winds, and had the best unprotected sex of my life. Later, curled up in his arms, I remember thinking, *If that makes a baby, so be it.* Of course, I never thought it really would. It was only one time! *Did I do it on purpose?* I don't think so, but that's the other problem with hindsight, especially seventeen-years-down-the-road hindsight. Who knows?

All I know for sure is that I couldn't risk his having the wrong reaction, so I took away that chance by not letting him have any reaction at all. I pretended to be the independent woman who took responsibility for her mistake — it was, after all, my diaphragm, not his — and handled her business without a lot of drama. I wanted to say, *I love you! I need you! Let's try to make it work! Let's think outside the damn box and all that bullshit! Let's be free and happy and stay together forever!*

But I didn't say any of that. I told him not to worry and he took me at my word. And that was that. Except it wasn't.

15

Three days had gone by without the arrival of any DNA samples or disgruntled pseudo-suitors. Phoebe was still AWOL, but she had spoken to Louis twice and expressed concern that I might never forgive her. I told him to tell her to hold that thought, but I was starting to relax a little bit. Amelia's advice had been both wise and efficient: *Do nothing.*

That did not apply to my new project, however. The more I learned about Ezola's operation, the more I admired it. It was going to be a pleasure to be the bridge between Mandeville Maids and the immigrant women who needed her services. I already had a legal pad full of notes and ideas, and Sam Hall wasn't even due back in town until Friday. I expected to hear from him the first of next week, so I was surprised when he called from Miami late Wednesday afternoon as I was closing down my office for the evening.

"Ms. Sanderson? Sam Hall," he said. "Did I catch you at a bad time?"

"Not at all," I said, turning down the music so I'd be able to hear his voice. Even though I'd corrected my visual, the voice alone was still good for a shiver or two. "Are you still in Miami?"

"Yes. I understand you and Miss Mandeville had a productive session."

"We did," I said. "I guess that means we're going to be working together."

"We are indeed. Actually, I'm going to FedEx you some material about an event we've got coming up next week. I know you're just getting your feet wet, but if you could pull together some remarks for me, I'd appreciate it."

"Of course," I said, even though serving as speechwriter was not part of my contract. "When do you need them?"

"Yesterday," he said cheerfully. "But right now I've got to run, Catherine. May I call you Catherine? Now that we're officially coworkers."

"Of course," I said. "Catherine is fine."

"Then I'm Sam." And he was gone.

I wondered what event he was talking about, but for now I was through working. I had cooking to do. Our brand-new book club was meeting this evening at Amelia's, and I was making pasta.

It was Miss Iona's idea. She was devoted

to Oprah Winfrey, and ever since Oprah started a book club, Miss Iona had been hot to start one, too. First she tried the women at the senior center near her house, but they weren't interested or couldn't see well enough to take pleasure in reading anymore. Then she tried her church, but they wanted to limit their selections to Christian fiction and inspirational books, and Miss Iona wanted more variety. So she finally invited me and Amelia, Flora Lumumba, who's in charge of the community gardens, Aretha Hargrove, a painter and photographer who is carrying her first child, and Blue Hamilton's new wife, Regina, who does PR, to come to her house to explore the possibility of forming a book club that would meet for dinner every other month or so and talk.

Miss Iona suggested that we keep it small, just the six of us, and that we start with Jill Nelson's novel *Sexual Healing*, because nobody could be neutral about the questions she was raising. We agreed the meal would always be communal and that nobody had to feel guilty about bringing takeout as long as it wasn't pizza.

"Are we going to name ourselves?" Aretha said, folding her hands over her belly in a protective gesture that seems to come to mothers in their sleep the moment that egg starts becoming the magic of somebody's ears or somebody's eyes or somebody's little flat feet. Last year she had married Kwame Hargrove, the son of a popular politician, sister Senator Precious Hargrove, and the celebration had ended with a community-wide party that went on peacefully until dawn. Standing in for her parents, who had died in a car accident when she was a kid, Blue Hamilton not only walked her down the aisle, but at the bride's request, sang the most amazing a cappella version of "Ave Maria" I've ever heard in my life.

"I guess we should have a name," Miss Iona agreed, "but I'm not good at that stuff. Anything you all choose is fine with me."

"I like Babylon Sisters," Amelia said. "But it's already taken."

They all looked at me. I was flattered that they liked the name I'd already chosen, especially since my business was going on hiatus as soon as I was full-time with Ezola. I liked the idea of keeping the name alive. There was absolutely no reason not to share it. This could be that start of a whole movement of Babylon Sisters stuff. Babylon Sisters dry cleaners,

Babylon Sisters day-care centers, Babylon Sisters nail shops. The more the merrier.

"If that's the name you want," I said, "I'd be honored."

"Babylon Sisters Book Club," Regina Hamilton said, nodding her approval. "I like that a lot."

The story in the neighborhood is that Blue and Regina knew each other in another life, lost each other for a few hundred years, and then found each other again right here in West End. Neither one of them ever confirmed it, and nobody has nerve enough to ask either one of them about their personal histories. I don't believe in reincarnation myself, but it's a beautiful story, and they are so clearly in love that if it's not true, it ought to be. She was probably a real Babylon sister a lifetime or two ago, and the name just stirred up the memory.

"Me, too," said Flora. "Shall we vote?"

Flora rides herd on the group of independent old folks who are the heart and soul of West End's award-winning community gardens program. She's big on participatory democracy, but she's used to calling for the question.

"All in favor," said Miss Iona, raising her hand and wiggling her crimson-tipped fingers.

It was unanimous. The Babylon Sisters Book Club was now officially launched, and I was looking forward to our discussion tonight at Amelia's. The women in *Sexual Healing* had taken matters into their own hands and opened an upscale, full-service brothel catering to sisters in need of some serious TLC. The idea was intriguing, but I couldn't imagine any of us throwing down a credit card and disappearing into a private room for an afternoon of technically proficient but soulless sex. The problem is, the part that makes it sweet is the part money can't buy and time can't seem to erase. I'm curious to see what my sisters think, but right now, all I've got to do is concoct a pan of my best spinach lasagna. Sexual healing is a sometimes thing, but a good meal with your girlfriends is a guarantee.

16

The lasagna had another half hour to bake, which gave me more than enough time to dash up to Mr. Jackson's package store and pick up a bottle of Chianti to complement my culinary skills. I had invited his wife, Barbara, to join our book club, but she was always busy at the store, so I didn't really expect her to be able to come. I had my keys in my hand and a light jacket across my shoulders, since summer was now officially over and fall was in the air, when the doorbell rang. I opened it to find a tall, thin, very uncomfortable-looking man standing there. He looked vaguely familiar, with his close haircut and his large, square glasses, but mostly what struck me was how uncomfortable he was.

"Yes?"

"Catherine?" he said, achieving the impossible by sounding even more uncomfortable than he looked.

"I'm Catherine. Can I help you?"

A look of shocked surprise crept across his face. "You don't even remember me, do you?"

"I'm sorry," I said. "You look familiar, but . . ."

"Bobby Hicks," he said. "We had Chemistry together senior year. Dr. McBay's class?"

"Oh, my God! Bobby! Of course! Sure! How are you?"

I stuck out my hand, wondering what would have brought my old lab partner to my doorstep after all these — *Oh, shit! How clueless can I be? He got one of Phoebe's letters!*

He shook my hand without much conviction. Bobby Hicks had been a very smart, very boring boy who was a perfect lab partner because he understood everything and loved to explain it, repeatedly. The problem was, he loved to explain everything. *Repeatedly.* There could be only one reason for his visit, but what was the damn protocol? Was he supposed to bring it up or was I?

"I guess you're wondering why I'm here," he said.

"I think I have an idea."

"You do?"

"It's okay," I said. "I know you're not her father."

"Well, there was never any question about that," he said, sounding relieved and annoyed in equal measure. "But what

132

made her think . . . I mean, how did your daughter get the idea I might be . . ."

He couldn't seem to finish a sentence.

"Listen," I said, "would you like to come in? I can explain."

He stiffened up and took a small step back, like I might lure him inside and then take advantage of him. "I'd prefer we talk out here."

"Fine," I said, wishing I could get my hands around Phoebe's neck. *Modern mother, my ass!* "Would you like to sit down?"

"Thank you," he said, taking one of the porch chairs.

I sat down, too. I felt sorry for Bobby. It wasn't his fault. If I had gotten a letter like that, I'd probably be pissed off, too. I tried to be clear but not waste time on too many details.

"My daughter is on a quest to find her biological father. She went through my diaries and sent letters to any man whose name she found there."

"My name was in your diaries?"

"Yes."

"As your lab partner?"

"Yes." That wasn't a lie, but the part about me and him being more than friends was. "The point is, she was wrong to send you a letter like that, and I can promise you she won't contact you again."

He looked at me. "My wife opened it. It came special delivery and she thought it might be important, so she opened it."

"I'm so sorry, Bobby. Please tell her how sorry I am to have upset her."

"I'd appreciate it if you'd call her yourself."

"What?" He had to be kidding.

Without further explanation, he reached into his pocket and pulled out a cell phone, punched in a speed-dial number, and extended it to me.

"Her name is Monica."

"I don't think that's appropriate," I said, but I could already hear her voice on the other end of the line. There was a baby or two wailing in the background.

"Bobby? Are you there? Bobby? Who is this?"

Bobby was looking at me like we were back in Chemistry class and I had forgotten my homework. I took the phone from his hand because I couldn't think of a way not to. "Monica? This is Catherine Sanderson."

Silence. I was going to kill Phoebe for sure. I never had this kind of foolishness in my life. Now, here I sat in the middle of a scene straight out of *One Life to Live*.

"I want to apologize for my daughter. She's working out some issues and this was her way of forcing my hand. Bobby and I were never more than friends. He's not her father."

I looked at Bobby, sitting there glowering at me. "In fact, we weren't even friends. We were just lab partners."

"I know," Monica said. "I was in that class, too. You probably don't remember me. You were too busy talking to my husband."

I resisted the temptation to remind her that they weren't married then and apologized one last time.

"Well, I'm sorry about everything," I said. "Bobby's completely innocent. He won't hear from my daughter again."

She was saying something else shrill as I handed him back the phone.

"Monica, it's me!" he interrupted her tirade. "Now do you believe me? I told you we never even . . . *did it!*"

Just the thought made me feel a little queasy. I stood up.

"Take your time and finish your call," I whispered with a small wave. I still had time to get my Chianti without overcooking my lasagna and, as far as I was concerned, this conversation was truly over.

"Monica?" he said, standing up, too. "I'll call you right back."

He snapped the phone closed and looked at me, suddenly uncomfortable again. That was an improvement over the glowering, but not by much. I wondered if there was a more direct way to say good-bye and get him off my porch.

"I'm a teacher now," he said, apropos of nothing. "Tenth-grade Chemistry and Biology."

"Still doing that science, huh?" I said, heading for the front steps and pleased that he took the hint and walked with me.

"Yeah. Same old, same old."

His tone had changed completely. He sounded almost wistful. What was going on?

"Well, I'm sure your students are lucky to have you," I said, although I wasn't sure of anything of the kind. His little gray Honda Civic was parked right behind the big old green Buick I inherited from Louis a couple of years ago and that I'm still driving. His car looked old and sad, just like he did.

"You think so?" he said, fishing in one pocket after the other for his keys. He hadn't changed a bit. Still awkward. Still confused.

"Don't you?"

"I don't know what they think," he said. "They probably hate me."

He was suddenly awash in self-pity, his voice almost a whine. I could tell he wanted to tell me his troubles, but that was not going to happen. I'd had enough.

"Well, good seeing you, Bobby," I said, opening the car door. "Sorry about the circumstances. You take care, now."

"You, too." He watched me climb in, but before I could pull away, he tapped on my window. I reluctantly lowered it and he leaned down to look me in the eye. "You should have told me, you know?"

"Told you what?"

A slow, goofy smile spread across his face. "That you felt that way about me. Maybe we could have worked something out."

Was boring Bobby Hicks hitting on me? How much worse could this get?

"Maybe we still could," he said.

I put the car in drive. If it was going to be worse than this, I wasn't going to stick around to see. "Go home to your wife," I said. "Before I call her back and tell her being lab partners was just the tip of the iceberg."

He must have believed me, or his fear of Monica's wrath far outweighed his desire to rekindle our imaginary romance, because by the time I got to the corner and looked in the rearview mirror, he had pulled off the other way and disappeared.

17

Bobby's unexpected drop-by had really rattled me, but I still managed to get the wine, and the lasagna was perfect. We were only six, but we could have easily fed a dozen. Flora had grilled a variety of fresh vegetables from her prizewinning garden, with just a touch of olive oil and herbs. Aretha had roasted a free-range chicken with tarragon. Miss Iona had brought a pan of her legendary macaroni and cheese, and Regina had made a salad with fresh tomatoes and basil and mozzarella cheese that melted in your mouth. For dessert, Amelia had constructed six colorful parfaits.

The wine flowed freely and so did the conversation. The book was a jumping-off point for a wide-ranging discussion that touched on sex, love, AIDS, desire, birth control, romance, religion, and whether or not any of us could imagine paying for sex, no matter how good it was supposed to be or how long the drought had lasted. We ranged in age from Aretha, at a blossoming twenty-five, to Miss Iona, who admitted to sixty-plus, with a few stops in between for the rest of us, but everybody said no way to the brothels. Paying for sex was beyond where their imaginations could take them. More important, as I picked up in the easy ebb and flow of our confessions and critique, my sisters had no reason to consider such an option because all of them were currently having sex. Every single one, including Miss Iona, who was keeping company with Mr. Charles, one of the senior gardeners, who was seventy-five if he was a day, and Aretha, who was due to deliver in less than a month. I was a minority of one.

Even Amelia had chimed in with an anecdote and answered my raised eyebrows with a giggle and a conspiratorial wink. Maybe I should have taken Bobby Hicks up on his offer just to see if I still remember the basic moves. I'd hate to have an opportunity present itself and be too rusty to take advantage of the situation.

As the evening started winding down, we found ourselves examining what it takes, other than sex, to make a relationship last.

"The thing is, you gotta have truth or the whole thing falls apart," Aretha was saying. "I tell Kwame everything."

"Some women think that telling a man the truth will ruin a relationship faster than infidelity, but I think they're wrong," Amelia said. "I have found that truth is a great aphrodisiac for men. If you tell them the truth, they know you don't need their approval. It changes the balance of things in a way that is always sexier than pretending. Don't forget, it's a short step from feigning an interest in football to faking orgasms, and an equally mind-deadening waste of time."

"I never told any man everything," said Miss Iona, rolling her eyes. "There's some things men don't need to know."

"Like what?" Amelia smiled.

"Like whatever I decide not to tell 'em," Miss Iona said. "Telling a man the truth about everything all the time takes the mystery out of it. I'd rather keep them guessing."

"Not me," said Flora, whose husband was a well-known defense lawyer flirting with a career in politics. "I like to lay my cards on the table."

"Me, too," Regina said. "I believe that old Mark Twain thing about if you always tell the truth, you never have to remember anything."

"I'm not saying you have to lie," Miss Iona said, clarifying her position. "I'm just saying you aren't required to tell everything you know."

"What's the difference?" I said. The distinction was starting to elude me.

"A lie is a deliberate distortion of the truth," Amelia said. "I think Miss Iona's talking more about letting people draw their own conclusions."

"Exactly." Miss Iona nodded, pleased. "Too much truth will drive a man crazy."

Aretha just laughed. "Does Kwame look crazy to you?"

"As a bedbug," Miss Iona teased her, knowing Kwame was as solid as a rock. "I've been meaning to speak to his mama about that very thing."

Our evening floated to a close on the music of our laughter, and I thought how lucky Kwame was to have found a woman who would gift him with her secrets, because she trusted him to handle them as gently as he was going to hold their baby. Thinking truth could do that was crazy, all right. Crazy like a fox.

18

Amelia's office was a bustling beehive of activity tucked away on a quiet midtown street whose only other commercial entity was a quiet little French bistro on the corner that Amelia used to woo her upscale clients and reward her associates after a successful trial. We had gone there for lunch to celebrate Jason's acceptance to Yale and when Phoebe made the honor roll at Fairfield her first semester, but today both of us were too busy to linger over cappuccino in the middle of the afternoon.

I had spent the morning lobbying members of the city council in support of increased funding for homeless shelters and wondering if Bobby Hicks was an aberration or the first of many uncomfortable encounters. Last night after everybody else had divided up the leftovers, hugged one another good night one more time, and headed home, I stayed around to tell Amelia about my visitor. She was appalled that he made me speak to his wife, but not surprised that he hit on me, pointing out that Louis had said some of them would probably be flattered at the thought, however far from reality it might be. She voted on the side of his being an aberration, not a trend, and told me to come by her office around two so she could introduce me to her new intern.

Miriam St. Jacques had been working for Amelia for a couple of months as a general office assistant, and she was looking for a younger sister she had lost track of. That was all I knew, but Amelia supervised a bilingual staff of lawyers who did a lot of work with clients of mine. It was not unusual for them to have interns or part-time employees who needed assistance.

When I walked in, Amelia was standing in the lobby shaking hands with a distinguished-looking Japanese gentleman who was bowing and smiling happily at whatever deal they had just closed. Amelia was smiling, too. He nodded politely as he passed me on his way out, and Amelia watched him head for his car, which was waiting with his driver at the curb.

"Good afternoon, Counselor," I said. "Doing good or doing business?"

"The idea that those two things are mutually exclusive is such a twentieth-century idea," she said, grinning. "Mr. Tanaka wants to do business in Atlanta. He needs a translator."

"You don't speak Japanese."

"No, but I'm fluent in African-American with a specialty in Atlanta Negro dialects."

"You're crazy." I laughed, waving at the receptionist and following Amelia to her office. Every cubicle, every desk, was occupied with people who were moving through their tasks efficiently and without visible stress in spite of the obvious need for more space. Amelia was going to need to expand pretty soon or they'd be taking statements on the front porch.

Sitting at the desk outside of Amelia's office, frowning intently at a computer screen, was a striking girl who looked about eighteen. Her skin was very dark and so smooth it seemed to have no pores at all. She had huge, dark eyes and a strong nose over a perfectly round, full-lipped mouth. An unexpected dimple in the middle of her chin was a lovely surprise. The only thing that marred her appearance was a painfully cheap wig perched on top of her beautiful head like a hat from hell. The long bangs and feathery layering of the clearly synthetic hair partially obscured her face and made you want to brush it aside so you could admire what God had made in this girl.

She stood up immediately when she saw

us coming her way. She was tall and skinny, with the awkward grace of hopeful young womanhood, and I knew who this was at once.

"Miriam St. Jacques," said Amelia, "this is Catherine Sanderson. Catherine, this is Miriam."

She smiled shyly from under that godawful wig, and I shook her hand and smiled back. Amelia ushered us into her private office and closed the door.

"Sit down, sit down," she said as we crowded in and took our seats around a small round conference table. Miriam looked very nervous, but Amelia got right down to business, turning to the girl as if she didn't even notice the wig hat working its show.

"I've told Catherine a little bit about you and your sister, but why don't you tell her what's happened up to this point?"

That didn't seem to reassure Miriam.

"All of it?" she said so softly I could barely hear her. She spoke English with a French accent, but it was easy to understand her.

Amelia shrugged. "All that you think it's important for her to know."

That was still too open-ended. This girl's country had been a poor, angry, violent place for most, if not all, of her life. How could she begin to tell me where she'd been and what she'd seen? She looked at me helplessly.

"Why don't you tell me how you came to Atlanta?" I said, knowing she was here now on a temporary visa, due in no small part to Amelia's sponsorship. "Did your sister come with you?"

She nodded, relieved at a question she could answer directly. "We came together, Etienne and me. From Florida."

I smiled, trying to get her to relax. "Etienne is an unusual name for a girl."

She smiled a tiny smile back. "My father wanted a son so badly, to be named Etienne, as he had been named for my grandfather. When my sister was born, and Mama said there would be no more children, he insisted on calling her Etienne anyway."

"How did you get to Florida?"

She looked at Amelia, who nodded. "It's okay. She's a friend."

"My parents paid a man to bring us, my sister and me, on a boat. There were fifteen of us. All women. My sister was fourteen." Her eyes filled with tears, but she blinked them back. "She's fifteen now.

"Some people met us with a van, two

vans, when we landed. It was a beach, but it was very dark and there were no lights or signs, so I don't know where exactly we were. I'm sorry."

"That's okay," I said, imagining the terror of such a landing. "Did you know the people who met you?"

She shook her head. "No. They were men, four men. They loaded us in the vans, seven in one, eight in the other. We had to sit on the floor. No seats and no stopping. No food. They gave us water, twice, and told us to be quiet unless we wanted to go to jail or back to our country."

She couldn't even say its name.

"Some of the girls were crying, but my mother had said these men were going to help us get jobs, so we could become citizens, so I told my sister not to be afraid. I told her everything was all right, but it wasn't all right."

Her eyes filled up again and she shook her head miserably. "When we finally stopped driving, we still didn't know where we were. Most of us spoke French, maybe a little English, but the men who drove us were speaking Spanish, so it was hard to know what was going on. They put us in a house with so many women, one bathroom, sleeping on the floor."

She wrinkled her nose at the memory.

"They told us that was where we had to live, and that if we came outside, our neighbors would call the police and they would come take us away."

What she was describing was not news to me. People who come here illegally are terrified of being discovered and sent home to face whatever made them flee in the first place. Nobody risks life and limb to head out across miles of ocean on a rickety old boat if they've got any better options at all. Whatever made Miriam's mother spirit her away from Haiti into the arms of shadowy strangers must have been every mother's worst nightmare. Could I have kissed my Phoebe and put her on that boat? I hope I never have to find out.

"Tell her about the jobs," Amelia prompted gently.

"Yes, yes, the jobs. They got us jobs cleaning."

"Cleaning what?"

"Office buildings. The big glass ones. After everyone has gone home for the night. They would pick us up in darkness, drive us there, wait for us to finish, and take us home in darkness."

"Did they pay you?"

"They paid us nothing. Barely enough to feed ourselves. The rest of the money they kept for themselves."

Somebody was amassing a sizable fortune trading on frightened people's misery. Maybe Ezola's programs were working so well, she was pricing her maids out of the market. These guys could charge less because they didn't pay anything. It was all profit.

"I told my sister it was wrong what they were doing and I was going to make them pay us so we could get our own place and live like human beings, but they sent my sister away. I tried to stop them, but I couldn't."

She stopped and took a deep breath, fingering a gold locket around her neck.

"They told me she ran away, but Etienne would never run away without me. Mama told us to stay together. She didn't run. They took her." Her voice cracked a little, and she pursed her lips as if to keep herself from saying any more.

"Took her where?"

"They wanted her," Miriam said softly. "I know they wanted her even though she was a child. They wanted her and I think they took her. If I had stayed there, I think they would have taken me, too. So the next time they dropped us at work, I slipped out through the basement and ran as far as I could away from there until I was in a place with houses and trees. I hid until morning. When it got light outside, I saw a woman, a white woman, but she had a little girl, so I ran up to her and told her some people were after me and they had kidnapped my sister. She took me to the police."

When Phoebe was a kid and we traveled internationally to places where she didn't know the language, I told her that if she ever got separated from me to find a woman with a child and ask her for help. Miriam's experience had proven the wisdom of that advice.

"Did the police help you?"

"They asked me so many questions," she said, getting agitated. "How did I come to the United States? Who were the men in the vans? How long had I been in Atlanta? Did my parents have enemies? Where was the house where we were taken? So many questions and I couldn't answer any of them."

Amelia broke in before Miriam got too worked up. "They blindfolded them coming and going to the job site, but we've got some clues based on things Miriam remembers that might at least narrow it down to a certain neighborhood."

"Good," I said. "These places move around a lot just to stay one step ahead of the law and anybody else who's looking for them, but they tend to stick to one general area."

These would be places where people were too poor or too high or too scared to care who lived in the house with the boarded-up windows and the two rottweilers chained up in the front yard.

"The thing is," Amelia said, "it looks like these guys are using more and more of these women as prostitutes in the same way they use them as janitors. What Miriam is saying bears out what we've been hearing."

"Do you have any proof?" I'd been hearing the rumors, too.

Miriam shook her head, the wig trembling slightly. "Just things some of the women said. Two other girls ran away before they took my sister. Both of them were very young, like my sister, and very beautiful."

"Show her the picture," Amelia said.

Miriam opened the locket she'd been fingering and showed me a small photograph of a smiling young girl, her open face so alive you would swear you could hear her laughter.

"I have to find her," she said softly. "Whatever they have done to her, she is still my baby sister and I'm supposed to take care of her."

She closed the locket slowly and dropped it back inside her blouse. "I promised my mama."

Something about the simplicity of the way she said it really touched me. Like there was no question of whether she would do this, only a question of how.

"I'll see if I can find out anything," I said. "Give me a couple of days to poke around."

Gratitude washed over Miriam's face, and she grabbed my hand and squeezed it. "Thank you," she said over and over again. "Oh, thank you."

"It may take some time," I cautioned her. "These guys sound like pros."

The smile faded from her face, and I immediately felt bad for robbing her of a moment of optimism in what was a terrible situation.

"Don't worry," I said, to reassure her. "I'm a pro, too."

As I walked to my car through the crisp fall day, I thought about how many women were going through what Miriam had just described. I had heard so many stories of sexual abuse, but so far no organized ring had emerged in this area. I hoped this wasn't the start of something bigger. Forced prostitution was my great fear for these women, and many of the people who work with me share it, but we don't know what to do to stop it from happening. The sexual marketplace, voluntary and involuntary, is such a brutal, dehumanizing, scary place that nobody on the outside can stand to look at it long enough to clean it up. Probably because at some level, we all know that what the elders say is true: *When you look long into the abyss, the abyss also looks long into you.*

19

Saturday I spent the morning looking for information on Miriam's sister, but the trail, if there ever was one, was months old, and nobody had any leads at all. The afternoon was devoted to putting words into Sam Hall's mouth, figuratively speaking, of course. He needed a speech for a ceremony honoring a group of Mandeville Maids who had earned their GEDs while working full-time. They were the flesh and blood at the heart of Ezola's promise of a better life, and this ceremony meant something to her, Sam said, even if she wasn't going to actually attend.

I had never written a speech for anyone else, but I think I was able to strike what I hoped was the right balance between informative and inspirational. I tried not to be corny. These were not kids finishing high school. These were grown women reaping the rewards of their own discipline and hard work, and they deserved a little *rah, rah* for hanging in there.

By the time I wrapped up everything it was sunset, and I hadn't even been outside to get the mail. That's the problem with working for yourself: there's nobody to make you stop and smell the roses — literally. I couldn't remember the last time I had enjoyed the pleasures of my own front yard. I grabbed the mail and took a deep breath of twilight. The woman across the street was watering her lawn while her husband played a game of catch with their son in the driveway. It looked like a scene out of some mythical small-town America, and that's exactly what it felt like. I waved at my neighbor and she waved back. I had sent Phoebe away so she could understand the big picture, but something in me hoped she'd always appreciate the beauty of a snapshot as tiny as this one peaceful block.

Thinking about Phoebe must have conjured her up. An envelope that bore her name was on the top of the stack, and the return address said, *Smith College, Office of Admissions, Northampton, Massachusetts.* She was waiting for this letter. She had completed all the requirements for early admission, and her interview had been, according to her, a mutual admiration society. They had encouraged her to apply and spoken with her several times during the process to be sure she was still interested. It was her first and only choice. Without thinking, I went back inside and reached for the phone. She would want me to open it and give her the news immediately. She would want to share this moment with me. . . .

But I couldn't call her. I didn't have her number. I couldn't forward it to her because I didn't have her address, either. She was out there in the world, and the only way I could reach her was to call Louis. It hurt my feelings and it made me mad, but mostly it wore me out. It wasn't my choice, but I had to live with it, and today it was just too much. I tossed the letter on the table and gave myself permission to think about it later. Amelia had invited me for a swim and I intended to take her up on it.

I shifted through the rest of the mail, mostly bills and pleas for money from one desperate group of do-gooders or another, and I say that with love. I'm a do-gooder myself, although I think I'm more pragmatic than most. Telling an employer on-site day care is the right thing to do is usually less effective than showing how much money can be saved with fewer late or absentee mothers.

There was one envelope that wasn't a bill and didn't seem to be a solicitation. The return address was a post office box in

San Francisco. A lot of the young people who come through the Red Cross here go on to work on the West Coast, and I was famous for my glowing recommendations when they were job hunting. Probably somebody who needed a reference, I thought, tearing it open to see who needed me to put in a good word. No such luck.

Dear Ms. Catherine Sanderson,
I received a letter from someone claiming to be your only daughter. She wants me to take a DNA test to see if I'm her biological father.

Here we go again. I sat down on the couch and read on.

She gave me this address as to where I should send a copy of the results, which is why I'm writing to you at my partner's suggestion.

His partner?

I do remember you from choir, but I don't think we ever had sex. I don't even remember us being close friends. On the other hand, I was trying so hard to play straight back then, I probably groped more girls than Arnold Schwarzenegger. And with all the cheap wine and bad dope that was floating around, who knows?

I know, I thought. *I know.*

All that's over now. I'm gay and married.

You gotta love San Francisco!

But if you think I might be the daddy and you want me to take the test, I will. My partner and I have a small design firm, and we're not rich, but if she's mine and you need some help, I'll do the right thing.

Yours sincerely,
Jerome L. Pettigrew

20

"Of course I know him," I said after I found Amelia and Louis in her yard and read them the letter aloud. "He was in the choir with me. He could really sing, so he was always trying to hog the solos."

"Well, his partner was a lot more understanding than that other guy's wife," Amelia said. She had paused in the middle of her daily fifty laps to hear my late-breaking news, and she was treading water effortlessly over the mermaid's tail. Louis wasn't swimming. He was watching.

"I didn't even know he was gay!"

"Don't feel bad," Louis said. "Back then, he didn't either."

"But everything turned out for the best," Amelia said, gliding away from us.

"How do you figure that?"

"He moved to a gay-friendly part of the country and fell in love. That's not too shabby," she said, resuming her laps.

"So he's doing fine and I'm trapped in some kind of past-lives limbo," I said, flopping down on a chair beside Louis and realizing he was dressed in his Sunday-go-to-meetin' black suit, a little formal for an evening by the pool. "Where are you coming from all dressed up?"

He sighed deeply. "I've been meeting with two possible investors."

"How'd it go?"

"They want to run a ten- to twenty-page supplement in every issue with ads for strip clubs, escort services, and porno products of all kinds."

"You're kidding, right?"

"Welcome to Atlanta. The Amsterdam of the South."

"I know Miss Iona ain't havin' that, so what are your other options?"

"I can close it down and go teach in a journalism school somewhere, or I can find a story we can cover the way we used to and make people remember what the *Sentinel* is all about."

"I vote for option two."

"You and me both. Now all I need is a real reporter and a great story."

"I'll keep my eyes open."

"I'd appreciate it." Louis's eyes were following Amelia up and down the pool as if he were afraid that one of these times she'd get to the other end and just keep swimming.

"Phoebe's letter came from Smith

today," I said, trying to sound casual. Louis knew how much Phoebe's heart was set on Smith. He turned away from Amelia and looked at me.

"Is she in?"

"I didn't open it."

He looked surprised. "Aren't you going to?"

I shook my head. "Not the way things are. I think it would just piss her off."

"Do you want me to tell her?"

I nodded. "I'll bring it by tomorrow. You can read it to her or send it on. Let me know when you know, okay?"

"I will."

We both sat there for a minute, watching our friend cutting her graceful path through the water and thinking about my daughter, stamping her little feet in frustration somewhere out in the world. I had underestimated her reaction to an obvious lie from the person she depended on most to tell her the truth — *me*. It was time to figure out how to face up to my own lesson in all this and admit to my child that I knew a lot more than I was telling, but not yet. I just wasn't ready to let Burghardt Johnson back into my life if I didn't absolutely have to. The last time I let him get close to me, I almost lost myself. But this time I stand to lose my daughter, and nothing is worth that.

"I just miss her," I said.

Louis nodded. "I know."

"What if I was wrong?"

He reached over and took my hand and patted it like a kindly uncle. "Wrong about what, my guilt-ridden friend?"

"Wrong about not telling her."

"What about not telling *him?*"

"In spite of what seems to be the current consensus, I'm pretty sure I wasn't wrong about that."

Louis shrugged. "Sometimes a miss is as good as a mile, Cat."

"Meaning what?"

"Meaning that if I had a daughter as special as Phoebe is, I think I'd like to know."

"You're not B.J."

"Not even close," Louis said, trying to tease me out of my funk. "He's a lot taller, but I'm much better-looking."

"Yes, you are," I said. "On his best day."

"You might mention that to Amelia if you can work it into the conversation."

"She doesn't even know B.J."

"I mean about how good-lookin' I am."

I laughed. "No problem."

Amelia executed a perfect turn and headed back in our direction as Louis reached into his wallet and handed me a card with several phone numbers on it.

"What's this?"

"I think you should call her."

"Amelia?"

"Phoebe."

"I want to," I said. "I've never wanted to do anything more, but I can't risk it. If she hangs up on me, I'll have to catch a plane up there tonight and act like an old-fashioned black mother."

"I'm going to give you the number anyway, in case you change your mind."

"It's her mind that needs changing, remember?"

"I think she's sorry she ever sent those letters."

That was music to my ears, but Louis had said *I think*. "Did she *say* that?"

"She said she missed you. Is that close enough?" He was still holding out that card like he was prepared to dangle it there all night. Louis was the eternal peacemaker.

"She gets her stubbornness from me," I said, slipping the card in my pocket so we could move on.

"Third generation," Louis said, glad he had made me smile, "but that's okay. I like stubborn women. The meaner the better."

I followed his eyes back to the pool. "Then what are you doing with Amelia?"

He turned back to me with that lovely lopsided grin. "You really want to know?"

I grinned back. "Absolutely."

"I'm falling in love with her."

21

After Amelia got out of the pool, Louis volunteered to serve the drinks, and we let him. I lay back in the chair next to my friend, who was wrapped in a fluffy white robe that made her cocoa-colored skin look like rich milk chocolate. She looked peaceful, and I couldn't resist suggesting a reason why.

"So," I said, "how long have you and my favorite editor been keeping company?"

She opened her eyes and had the nerve to blush. "Since the Sweet Honey concert."

That was exactly when I had noticed the change. I congratulated myself on being so observant. They went out friends and came back soul mates. "What happened?"

She laughed a little and shook her head. "The hell if I know. I've always liked Louis, you know that, but we've got three divorces between us, and I'm not looking for complications in my life right now."

We spend half our lives longing for love and the other half running from it. "Go on."

"Well, you remember you said you couldn't go, so I had an extra ticket. When Louis said he had never seen them and would love to go, it seemed like the perfect solution, except I wasn't sure I wanted him to go."

"Why? You two have been going to the movies for years."

They like the big-budget Hollywood stuff like *Spider-Man* that I wouldn't see on a bet.

"Yeah, but movies, or dinner, or even another concert is one thing. Sweet Honey is different. It's special. It's completely and unapologetically and magically black and female. You know what it's like! It's a ceremony or a ritual or something with real power, and I wasn't sure he could handle it."

She was right about that. The annual visit of the famous a cappella quintet to Spelman College's Sisters Chapel was a gathering of the tribe like no other. Amelia and I used to take Phoebe, and the three of us would dress up in our most celebratory colors and our most special silver bangles and earrings that hung to our shoulders so we could feel them swaying against our necks when we started dancing in the aisles. Then we'd head out into the night like the beautiful black birds we knew ourselves to be.

Sweet Honey will bring that out in you, and by the end of the concert, the sisterhood is so thick you can cut it with a knife. That much unadulterated *womanness* makes some men uncomfortable. They feel overwhelmed, intimidated, ill at ease. To compensate, they talk too loud or demand the attention of a sister who is still savoring a private moment or in some way impose their will when they should just relax. Amelia didn't want to put Louis in a situation that would bring out the alpha male in him. Once you see a man act like that kind of an asshole, it's hard to forget. You keep wondering when he might do it again.

"So he was all right?"

She grinned at me. "He got it, Cat. He totally *got it*. It was the same kind of energy *we* have at the Sweet Honey shows. In fact, it was as good as having you there, except afterward, we got to take it all home to bed."

I laughed. "Well, I can't compete with that. Guess I'll have to find a new best friend. Two, actually."

"Don't even try it," she said, smiling. "You're going to have to be my maid of honor."

I sat up and looked at her, gazing serenely at the pink blush of the evening sky. "You're getting married?"

"Of course," she said. "How many men can totally *get* Sweet Honey, make me laugh, and make me come all in one night?"

"When were you going to tell me?"

"As soon as he asks me."

I was confused. "He doesn't know yet?"

"Miss Iona said I don't have to tell everything I know." Amelia turned toward me with a grin. "Neither do you, by the way. I think it's more romantic if he comes to it on his own."

"He's halfway there already," I said. "Maybe a little closer than that."

"He's still playing catch-up then," she said, as Louis stepped out of her back door with a bottle of champagne and three glasses. "I'm almost home."

22

I made it until midnight without calling her. It took me that long to figure out what I was going to say. Baby Doll had imposed only one condition to end our estrangement. She wanted me to admit that I had lied about the fantasy gaggle of possible baby daddies and tell her the truth. Although I thought her use of the fake diaries to send letters to those guys without my permission was really a terrible thing to do, she was doing it in self-defense because of the big lie I kept trying to get her to swallow, or at least pretend she did.

Turns out, she learned the things I taught her about how important truth was so well that she was now applying the same standard to me. She wasn't prepared to pretend. Even if her method was wrong, her question was legitimate, and I was prepared to answer it. Part of it, anyway. I was prepared to tell her the diaries were fakes and admit that I did know who her father was. But his identity was still going to have to be my secret for a while longer. I was going to ask her to respect that, woman to woman, and I hoped that she would.

Then I was going to tell her she got a letter from Smith.

I made myself a cup of tea and sat down with the number Louis had given me in my hand. Phoebe is everywhere in this house, in this room. There are baby pictures, and christening pictures, since my mother insisted. Pictures of us with the family we stayed with in Martinique the summer she learned to speak French and play blackjack. There are pictures of her with Amelia and Jason at his graduation from high school, and one of her and Louis on horseback the time they took lessons together on a dare from me and loved it so much they went once a week for years.

In every picture, my daughter is fully engaged in the world around her. Her eyes reflect curiosity, happiness, confidence, and peace. She is an unself-conscious beauty whose intelligence and good health shine through at every age. Maybe Louis was right. Maybe her father *would* want to know. The thing that's hard for me to explain about B.J. is that I don't hold it against him for leaving. Loving somebody doesn't mean you have the right to change who they are, even when you wish they could be somebody else, just for an hour or two. Which, of course, they can't. I know that now, but I also know that whatever else we did, or didn't do, our baby girl turned out perfect.

Except for being stubborn as a mule, which, no matter what Louis says, is a trait she gets from her father's side, not mine. Mothers can't be stubborn. We have to see all, know all, understand all, and forgive all. Or get as close as we can, anyway. It was time for me to show her how it's done. I smoothed out the card, picked up the phone, and punched in the first of the three numbers I had to use to get through Phoebe's protective sisterhood shield, when I realized there was somebody already on the other end of the line. I hadn't even heard it ring.

"Hello?"

"Catherine?" said a voice I thought I'd never hear again. "Burghardt Johnson. It's been too long."

There was no way to prepare. No way to figure out what to say to make it through such a moment without sounding like an idiot. His voice sounded exactly the same as it had on all those late-night phone calls when he had spun his dreams for me like the finest silk on a golden loom. His voice was all it took for all those memories to come flooding back. All those memories I am careful to keep locked away for examining when I'm finally old enough to understand and probably too old to care. There they were, reminding me that I had been in love once, too. And how long ago was that, anyway? Two years? Ten? Almost twenty?

"It has been a long time," I said. "It's good to hear your voice."

That was nice. Truthful. Just the right note of friendly surprise. Warm without being too fuzzy.

"You sound exactly the same," he said. "How long has it been?"

Nineteen years, fifteen months, and sixteen days, but who's counting? I hadn't realized *I* was counting until the number popped up like the lottery when you win and the identical digits suddenly leap off that ticket like they're six feet tall.

"Long enough," I said. "Are you in Atlanta?"

Our airport is one of the busiest in the world, and sooner or later, everybody you know passes through it. "Not yet, but I'll be there next week. I'm working on a story about Haitian refugees, and several of my contacts out there told me that if I was serious, I needed to get in touch with a sister named Catherine Sanderson."

After eighteen years, he was calling me professionally? I didn't know if I was relieved or disappointed. Confusion seems to be the zone I immediately gravitate to when I'm around B.J. When I had told him what I intended to do about Phoebe and he didn't try to talk me out of it, I had the same problem. Did that mean I hadn't made any progress at all?

"I do work with a lot of refugee programs," I said, marveling at how quickly I clicked into that tone. Two could play this game, whatever the hell it was we were playing. "Was there something specific you needed to know?"

He didn't say anything for a minute; then I heard him release his breath in a long whoosh, or maybe he was still smoking.

"There's something very specific I need to know," he said. "Do we have to do it like this?"

"Like what?"

"Like I pretend it's not a little strange for me to be calling, and you pretend I'm just another reporter trying to research a story."

"Is that what we were pretending?"

"Can we start again?"

"Sure," I said. "The phone didn't ring so the call doesn't really count anyway."

"Shall I hang up?"

"You don't have to do that," I said, surprising myself with how quickly I assumed control. Maybe I had made some progress after all. I guess that's what learning to be strong will do for you. "Let's just have a moment of silence and then I'll answer."

"All right," he said. "How long a moment?"

"As long as it takes," I said.

"As long as it takes for what?"

"For me to figure out what to say!" And that was really the truth, even though we were falling into the kind of easy back-and-forth we'd always had. *That was then and this is now.*

"Don't think about it," he said. "Just go with the flow."

"Nobody says 'go with the flow' anymore," I said.

"Where I've been, everybody says 'go with the flow.'"

"Then go with it," I said. "Starting now."

I sat there, holding the phone while he exhaled again. This time it sounded more like a sigh than a smoke, but I still had no idea how to play this scene. I guess I had no choice but to take his advice and *go with the flow.*

"Babylon Sisters," I said. "This is Catherine. Can I help you?"

" 'How can we sing the Lord's song in a strange land?' " he quoted another part of the verse from which I'd taken the name. "I like that."

"Good. Are we still pretending?"

"I'm not. This feels much better. How about you?"

"Much better. So are you really coming down here?"

"Yeah, and people really did keep telling me to contact you. They didn't know I knew you, of course."

"Are these the same people who were telling you to go with the flow?"

He laughed. "I take it you're not a big fan of New Age clichés?"

"I'm not a big fan of clichés. A great journalist I used to know told me once that clichés were the last refuge of an undisciplined mind."

"*Used* to know?"

"I haven't seen him in a very long time."

"Do you miss him?"

"Are we pretending again?"

"Maybe just a little."

"I miss him like crazy," I said. "How's that?"

"Best news I've had in ages," he said,

sounding like he really meant it. "I'll call you next week. We've got some catching up to do."

Suddenly the thought of sitting down with him over a glass of wine, trying to fill in the last two decades, did not appeal to me. Amelia had said to let sleeping dogs lie, and that was what I was going to do.

"B.J.?"

"Yeah?"

"Let's don't."

"You don't want to see me?" He sounded disappointed.

"I'd love to see you. I just don't want to . . ." *To what? Take a stroll down Memory Lane? Have to ask you why you didn't even bother to say good-bye?* "I'd like to start from where we are now, you know what I mean? I don't want to spend a lot of time talking about the past. Okay?"

"No problem," he said quickly, like I was about to hang up on him. "We can pretend we just met."

"No pretending," I said. "Let's just be who we grew up to be and let it go at that."

"No pretending at all?"

"None."

"You drive a hard bargain, Cat."

"That's part of my charm, remember?"

"How could I forget?"

23

Miss Iona had gone to visit her sister, so Louis was in the office alone when I walked in and dropped the Smith letter on his desk.

"And good morning to you," he said. "What's that?"

"Phoebe's letter. I think you'd better handle it."

He turned it over in his hands gently. "I really figured you were going to break down and call her."

"I did. The call didn't go through. There was already someone on the line."

"On Phoebe's line?"

"On mine. You know how sometimes the phone doesn't ring and you pick it up and there's already somebody on there?"

"Who was it?"

"It was Burghardt Johnson."

He couldn't have looked more surprised if I had said Colin Powell. Agreeing to keep the secret of Phoebe's birth had made it impossible for Louis to maintain their friendship. How could he, with that big lie squatting right in the middle of the proceedings? "B.J.?"

I plopped down on the couch. "The one and only."

Louis came around and sat down beside me. "He didn't get a letter, did he?"

"God, no!" I said. "He's working on a refugee story and some people told him he should call me."

"I wish I could get that Negro to write something for the *Sentinel*," he said. "But I can't afford him."

I looked at him. "That's all you have to say?"

He shrugged. "How's he doing?"

Men are hopeless. "Ask him yourself. He'll be here next week."

"In Atlanta?"

I nodded.

"Where's he staying?"

"The Regency downtown."

"Well, tell him to call me. Maybe we can get together."

Louis was acting like this was the most natural thing in the world, but I knew the potential for world-class weirdness was very high.

"Promise me something."

He looked at me. "Sure. What?"

"Promise me you'll back me up if things get weird."

"Weird how?"

"I don't know. Just weird."

"I promise."

His earlier question was buzzing around my mind like a fly on a horse's tail.

"You don't think Phoebe contacted him, do you?"

"Is he in the diaries?"

"No."

"Then there's no way for her to know. He's telling you the truth. He needs your help."

"Should I give it to him?"

"I don't know."

"That's no kind of advice," I said. "What good are you?"

"I'm sorry," he said, "but this is every man for himself. I need your help, too."

"It never rains but it pours. What's up?"

Louis walked back over to his desk and pulled out an invitation, which he handed to me with a flourish. "Ta-da!"

The card was printed on heavy ivory stock and requested the presence of the bearer at the annual Atlanta Association of Black Journalists dinner in a couple of weeks, where Louis Adams Jr. would accept an award for his father, posthumously, on the anniversary of the *Sentinel's* fortieth year. Miss Iona had been urging people to "do something for freedom" longer than I had been alive.

"Congratulations," I said, and I meant it. Longevity counts for something, even if the glory days are an increasingly distant memory. "But you're already getting the award. What kind of help do you need?"

"I need a date."

"A date? What was all that talk about falling in love? Now you're asking me for a date?"

Louis laughed. "I have fallen, for your information, but my beloved has to go to a conference in Chicago. She's approved you as her surrogate."

My eyes scanned the invitation. "It's formal," I said. "Did she approve my wearing one of her many beautiful ball gowns?"

"We didn't discuss your attire," he said. "I, however, will be wearing a tuxedo."

"You hate tuxedos."

"Which is why I need your support. An unescorted man in formal attire is either a gangster or a gigolo, and I can't let either one of those rumors get started."

"Don't knock gangsters," I said, in deference to my dad. "Are you going to have a real bow tie?"

"Amelia says she couldn't love a man in a clip-on."

I could tie a perfect bow tie in under

thirty seconds. One of my favorite memories of my father is of him teaching me how to tie all manner of knots, from a Windsor to a formal cravat with a stick pin. Of course, he could do it himself, but he said it made a man feel like a king to have a woman tie his tie and that my husband would appreciate it as much as he appreciated a home-cooked meal.

"Then I'll come by early and tie it for you."

"Bless you," Louis said. "You're a woman of many talents."

"And so is my daughter," I said, getting up to go. "Let me know how she made out at Smith."

"You know I will," he said, giving me a quick hug as he walked me out the door. "But tell me this. Would you have called her if B.J. hadn't been on the phone?"

"Yes."

"Then why didn't you?"

"Lost my nerve. How many reconciliations do you think a woman can stand in one night?"

24

They were wearing white. All twenty-seven of the women who had completed their GEDs in the last year while employed as Mandeville Maids were now dressed like participants in a mass wedding. All they needed were enough grooms to go around. But this wasn't a marriage ceremony, so they had to settle on a few bored boyfriends, a baby daddy or two, one embarrassed husband struggling with two-year-old twins, and one very young, very famous R&B star named Busy Boy Baker who had come to support his sister, a recovering crack addict, and was refusing to sign autographs on the basis of this being "her day," not his.

All the other members of the audience of about two hundred were women coming to show support for mothers, sisters, friends, cousins, aunts, and drinking buddies. They sat in the small auditorium, patiently waiting to honor their own. Sam stood in for Ezola and introduced State Senator Precious Hargrove, who congratulated the women and read a letter from the governor. The mayor sent a representative, who also read a letter of congratulations and high praise.

In the midst of all this attention, the brides began to shift restlessly in their seats. They had been promised a day off with pay to attend the ceremony and smile for the cameras. Now these fools were going to talk away damn near the whole morning. The program coordinator, an intense-looking young woman whose braids were swept up in a dramatic mound on top of her head, went on and on about how bright their futures would be now that they had taken the first step. It was all true, but as she kept talking I couldn't help wondering how much difference a GED would really make in their lives. I put that thought out of my mind. This was a day to celebrate one small step. They could figure out the rest later.

Then Sam stood up to make remarks on behalf of his boss and mine. This was my first experience as a speechwriter, and I was curious about how it would feel to hear my thoughts filtered through Sam's beautiful voice. He stepped up to the microphone, dressed, as always, in a dark, expensive suit and with a presence that made him seem much taller than he actually was.

He looked around long enough to focus the crowd's wandering attention; then he spoke slowly, letting each word have its due.

"There is a sisterhood," he said, although at first he had balked at the use of the word as too ideological, "that exists among black women that has sustained us as a people from the first day we arrived on these American shores."

I wanted to just say *America,* but Sam wanted some rhetorical flourishes, so he insisted on *these American shores.* It didn't matter. That voice could caress a cliché until you would swear you were hearing it for the first time. Even the two-year-olds sat quietly on their fathers' laps, and I found myself wishing I had written something worthier of that voice. He deserved better than what I had given him.

"It is a sisterhood of strength and courage and discipline and determination. By your actions over the past twelve months, you have shown yourselves to be full-fledged members of that rare and noble group."

I'm pretty sure I didn't write *rare and noble,* but the audience was loving it, and Sam was giving them just enough of that Sunday-morning sway to get them going.

"You have shown yourselves to be more than meets the eye. You have shown yourselves to be the best of what we have to give to our familes, our communities, our world."

Then he stopped suddenly and looked around.

"Make it plain," a woman said from the back of the room, and several others tittered nervously. It was the voice effect. Nothing we could do about that.

"If you'll indulge me for a moment, I'd like to flip the script just a little." He smiled like he was actually waiting for their permission; then he turned toward Busy Boy, still sitting in the audience, and called him by his legal name. "Mr. Baker, would you come and stand with me, please?"

The audience and the honorees gasped, then squealed and applauded wildly as young Mr. Baker, clad in a giant T-shirt, oversize jeans, and spotless white tennis shoes made his way to the small stage. By acknowledging his presence, Sam had set them free, and fan frenzy was suddenly in full effect. Busy Boy took it in stride, hopped up on the stage to exchange a handshake with Sam, and then turned to face the sudden flash of cameras busily recording the moment to prove that those in attendance had actually been in the presence of a real, live superstar.

"All right, ladies," Sam said gently, urging the women back into their seats. "As some of you know, Mr. Baker is a big supporter of our GED program."

His sister beamed.

"Mr. Baker and I were talking the other day, and I told him how much Miss Mandeville wished she could afford to send all of you girls right on through college."

Ladies? Girls? Sam had sneaked right back to the language of the fifties when I wasn't looking.

"We wish she could, too!" somebody shouted from the back of the room and was rewarded with scattered applause and a few "amens."

"Well, Mr. Baker said he'd like to see that, too. So he's here today to make me a promise."

You could have heard a pin drop. The brides leaned forward en masse.

"Any one of you who is accepted into an accredited college or junior college within the state of Georgia, Mr. Baker and Mandeville Maids will guarantee your tuition and all college expenses paid until you finish!"

There was another gasp and then an explosion of applause. The women jumped to their feet. Their friends and family threw programs in the air. The pop star looked properly humble, and Sam smiled like an indulgent paterfamilias. When things calmed down a little, Sam said Mr. Baker had a gift bag for each of the graduates, including his latest CD, and if they'd join him downstairs at the reception to follow, he'd be happy to sign autographs.

That was all they needed to hear. Sam pumped Busy Boy's hand again and they did that chest-thumping, backslapping thing brothers do that passes for a hug. Bodyguards hovered nearby. Ezola's official photographer recorded every moment, and the media that had come to cover a routine human-interest story found themselves with a celebrity angle that guaranteed a place in the first fifteen minutes of the local news.

Although I admired the partnership, I was a little surprised that Sam hadn't mentioned it to me. He'd asked me to prepare remarks without ever giving me an inkling of the rabbit he was about to pull out of his hat. Not that he was obligated to tell me. It just seemed odd that he didn't.

The auditorium emptied out in record

time as the graduates and their friends rushed down to claim their goody bags and their autographs. Sam handed the star over to one of Ezola's top assistants and two huge bodyguards, who hustled him down a back stairway to avoid the crowd. Another guy with his hair pulled back into a small ponytail hung around watching people leave the room like he had to be sure there were no terrorists present among the excited throng.

I made my way down front as Sam retrieved his notes. "Congratulations," I said. "That was some speech."

"Catherine," he said, smiling, tucking the notes back into his soft leather envelope, and stepping down to greet me. "So glad you made it!"

"I wouldn't have missed it for the world," I said. "That's a pretty amazing commitment you just made."

He chuckled softly as the last of the women hurried down to the reception. "You think so?"

The response surprised me. "Yes, I do."

He looked at me like I was hopelessly naive. "How many women took the test?"

"Twenty-seven," I said, having heard each one's name as it was called aloud.

"Out of that twenty-seven, how many

you think will actually apply to college?"

"Maybe half?" I said, guessing.

He raised his eyebrows. "These women are still working full-time. It's very hard work, and when they get home, they're tired. They've got families and boyfriends and all the things that made them drop out of high school in the first place, except more so. Now, realistically speaking, how many would you say?"

His question took the pleasure out of the moment in a way that seemed unfair, since he had orchestrated it so perfectly. Even worse, he was probably right. Most of these women had extended themselves as far as they were going by finally getting a GED. To assume that meant they were ready for college now was to deny the reality of their lives.

"I don't know," I said.

"Try none," Sam said. "One or two at the most, and those won't finish. The most this kid will have to fork over is tuition for a couple of semesters at some junior college. It won't add up to two grand, all total, and the publicity he'll get will be worth a hundred times that much."

"They'd probably do better if they had some counseling," I said.

Sam nodded, the light playing across his

bald head. "They probably would, but this is a business, Catherine, not a college campus. We're not *really* here to educate the masses and uplift the race. We're really here to make money."

"Miss Mandeville said we were here to bear witness."

His smile never wavered. "And I think we did that today in fine style."

"Yes, I guess you did."

"*We* did, Catherine," he said, turning to look at me as we walked toward the door. "You're part of the team now, and everything we do here is a team effort. You do understand that, don't you?"

He was talking to me like those corporate guys at the ad agency where I had worked once for three months that seemed like three years. The tone was one that always sounded friendly and concerned, but vaguely threatening around the edges. Like they always wanted you to know your job was at stake if you didn't hurry up and get on the good foot.

"I think it would be helpful," I said, being diplomatic, "for us to sit down together and share some ideas."

"That is first on my agenda," he said, all smiles again. "How about next Thursday at two?"

"Fine," I said. "I'll look forward to it."

"Aren't you coming to the reception?"

"I have another appointment," I said, heading toward the parking lot, not the reception downstairs, where Busy Boy's CD could now be heard blasting from the sound system. "Please give my best to Miss Mandeville."

I didn't wait for him to reply. I pushed open the door and headed for my car, repeating the date and time of our appointment so I wouldn't forget the details before I wrote it down. Thursday at two — but where? I had been so busy extricating myself from whatever mind game Sam was playing, I hadn't confirmed a location. My carelessness annoyed me as much as his cynicism, so I headed back inside to complete our business.

When I opened the door to the auditorium, there were only two people left there: Sam and the bodyguard with the ponytail, if that was what he was. They had their heads together and they were talking intensely. When I pushed the big door open, letting in a shaft of light that traveled up the middle aisle and spilled around them, they both turned toward me with a look of annoyance at the interruption.

Sam's face softened a little when he

realized it was me. *A little.* Ponytail's face might as well have been on Mount Rushmore. "Yes, Catherine? Did you forget something?"

"You didn't say where we were meeting on Thursday."

"My office."

"Fine," I said, backing out. "Sorry to have interrupted you."

"No problem."

But Ponytail seemed to think there was. He may not have said anything, but his face sure had the look of somebody who specialized in bringing the bad news.

25

Louis left a message on my cell phone. He had talked to Phoebe and she had asked him to open the letter. "Congratulations," his message said. "You are now the proud mother of a member of the Smith College class of 2009."

Proud is right, I thought, driving through downtown and turning toward West End. She worked hard for this. She organized it and focused on it and presented herself to Smith as the amazing, multifaceted jewel that she is, and they recognized her just like I do. As I turned down Abernathy, I imagined how excited she must be. Of course, there was a part of me that was really pissed off and sad that we were still in a weird not-speaking phase, but the part that was happy and proud was stronger. The part that wanted to remove from her mind any possible question of my feelings at this moment so that when she looks back later, she won't say, "My mother never even congratulated me on getting accepted to Smith." This was a chance for me to insert myself into the narrative of this moment in her memory as "the good mother," even in the midst of what Amelia called madness, but which may just be the way of things between mothers and daughters at certain phases of the moon.

I pulled into the florist shop's reserved space out front and parked. The twenty-four-hour beauty shop was full, as it usually was. I saw Flora waiting and waved through the window. She waved back as I pulled open the florist's door and stepped inside. The bouquet in the window today was multicolored roses. Phoebe never cared for roses unless somebody she knew grew them. Amelia's garden had spoiled her for hothouse roses with perfect petals and no scent at all. Phoebe liked flowers she couldn't grow, and birds-of-paradise topped her list. In this, she shared a passion with the shop's owners, a married couple who had been running it together for fifty years. The roses in the window were an exception. The rule was unruly bouquets of orange and purple and gold, which Baby Doll and I loved to give each other for our mutual enjoyment. But today I was simply placing an order and sharing the good news.

Sandra Hunter greeted me with a smile

when I dinged the bell above the door that alerted her to customers. "Come in, come in!" she said. "Algernon is going to hate that he missed you."

"Me, too," I said. "Is this his weekend in Biloxi?"

She laughed and shook her head. "Two old fools. He and Charlie go down there once a month like clockwork, lose a hundred dollars apiece like clockwork, and come on back."

"Don't they ever win?"

She shook her head. "Never. The best they ever do is break even, but you know what? It keeps them out of trouble and makes them feel a little dangerous, so I can't complain."

"Give him my love when he gets back," I said, keeping to myself the fact that Miss Iona said Mr. Charles was always lucky and routinely came back from the casino with a handful of money.

"You know I will," she said. "Now what can I do for you?"

"I need to send some flowers to Baby Doll," I said. "She got accepted at Smith College."

"Oh, my goodness," Miss Sandra said, coming from behind the counter to hug me. "Congratulations! You must be so proud."

I took the card with Louis's handwriting on it out of my purse and reached for my credit card. "That's exactly what I want the card to say. That I am *too* proud!"

She handed me a pen and a small pad and reached for the phone. "Write it down. I'll make sure they get it right and send her out the prettiest birds in the state of Massachusetts!" She patted my hand, still smiling proudly. She had known Phoebe all of her life.

Congratulations, Baby Doll, I wrote, then stopped and started again. She was about to go to college. She might not feel like *Baby Doll* anymore. I started again: *Dear Phoebe . . .* That was even worse. All I really wanted to say was, *I love you. I miss you. I'm so proud of you. . . . Love, Mom.*

So that's what I wrote, and I told Miss Sandra to get them to underline *love* twice. Just to make sure she didn't miss it.

26

Amelia had agreed to loan me an evening dress, since my meager wardrobe offerings do not include a suitable gown for the AABJ dinner, especially since I was accompanying the son of the evening's honoree. I'm shorter than Amelia by a few inches, and thicker by a few inches, but we're close enough that she pulled six possibilities from her closet, all of which would do the job with no alterations or major pinning. I rejected out of hand anything that required extreme high heels (for me, that's anything over three inches), control-top panty hose, or taping of body parts to ensure that they didn't pop out inappropriately over dinner.

"I can't believe you have all those dress-up clothes."

" 'Dress-up clothes'?" she mocked me gently.

"You know what I mean," I said, sitting on her bed amidst the slippery, silken pile. "Where do you go to wear these clothes?"

"Diplomatic functions still tend to be formal," she said. "I'm getting ready to do some serious international business. These are just some of my costumes."

"That's a good way to think of it," I said. "So are we picking out my costume for the award dinner?"

"Absolutely. Something simple and classy," she said, pulling out an emerald green sheath that would have been at home in Jackie Kennedy's White House.

I shook my head. "Too green."

She nodded and picked up an orange A-line taffeta skirt and a bright pink jacket. It was beautiful, but I didn't have enough pizzazz to carry off orange and pink at the same time. I shook my head.

She frowned slightly, thinking, and I reconsidered the green number. Maybe I could work a kente-cloth shawl draped over one shoulder.

"Hold it!" Amelia said. "I have the perfect thing for you."

That sounded promising. Maybe Amelia had held back on one amazing piece that would look great, feel great, and be comfortable. She reached into her closet and pulled out a wine-colored piece of fabric that looked vaguely like a dress with what I think was a scoop neck, extremely long sleeves, and a hemline that seemed to dip lower in the back for some reason I couldn't determine. On the hanger, it looked a mess.

"This is it?" I said, not even trying to keep the disappointment out of my voice.

"Oh, ye of little faith," Amelia said. "Go into the bathroom, take everything off, and put it on."

"Everything?"

"You know that old-time brassiere and big old granny drawers are not going to work with this dress," she said, pushing me toward the tiny bathroom off her bedroom.

"I don't wear granny drawers," I said.

"Yeah, you do, but that's a topic for another day. Right now, put this on and come out so I can help you drape it."

I let her push me into the bathroom and close the door behind me. "I can't even tell which end of this thing is up," I said, although I had to admit the jumble of fabric felt soft and weightless in my hands. It might not look like much, but it felt terrific.

"Just do it," Amelia said. "We've got to wrap this fashion moment up so you can tell me how you're going to handle seeing your ex after all this time."

"He's not my ex," I snapped, stepping out of my sweats. "We were never married."

"I can see you're handling it beautifully," she said. "Don't forget to take off your bra."

"I'm handling it."

"You need to just relax and go with the flow," she said.

I groaned. "That's exactly what he kept saying on the phone. 'Go with the flow.' "

"I like him already," Amelia said. "Great minds run in the same channels."

"Or are caught in the same time warp," I said, emerging from the bathroom with the wine-colored thing hanging on me with no more grace than it did the hanger. Part of the skirt was dragging the floor, and I shuffled over to the full-length mirror near her dresser and presented myself for our mutual inspection. "Tell me this isn't the way it's supposed to look."

"Of course not," Amelia said, coming over to loop and tie and button and tuck until the thing began to re-form itself around my body in the most amazing way. The neckline flowed into the bodice, which draped itself over my bare breasts like it had known them all their lives. The strangely cut skirt ended up as a softly wrapped cocoon that clung where it was most flattering to cling and skimmed the rest like a skate bug on the surface of a pond. By the time Amelia completed her ministrations, I looked like I had just stepped out of the pages of *Essence* magazine and was on my way someplace *fabulous.* The best part was, it was comfortable as a pair of flannel pajamas and seemingly weightless.

"It's perfect," I said, turning around slowly to admire my artfully covered behind.

"I told you," Amelia said. "It's all in the drape."

I turned away from the mirror. "So who's going to drape it? You'll be in Chicago. Does Louis know how to do it?"

She laughed. "Please! Louis can barely tie his own tie, much less drape anything. But it's not hard. I'll show you how."

"Show me now," I said. "Then if I can't do it, we still have time to pick something else."

"Relax," she said. "I'll talk you through it."

She started taking the dress apart carefully while I watched her like a hawk. A half an hour later, I had mastered the technique and learned not only the formal drape that I'd be wearing to the AABJ dinner, but a more casual, just-below-the-knee/a-little-higher-in-the-neckline version that Amelia suggested I wear when I had my first face-to-face with B.J.

"I don't think so," I said, once I had

changed back into my sweats. "All I need is to pull the wrong thing and who knows what could happen?"

"What do you want to happen?" she said, hanging up my new favorite dress on a padded hanger, where it immediately camouflaged itself by becoming a shapeless mess again.

"I have no idea," I confessed, reaching for another hanger for the also-ran green dress while Amelia zipped a garment bag over the pink-and-orange two-piece.

She looked surprised. "You have to have an idea. How are you going to control the situation if you don't even have an outcome in mind?"

"This from the woman who just told me to go with the flow?"

"I'm serious. When you think of seeing him after all these years, what comes to mind?"

"Other than the fact that I hope he'll be a broken-down old wreck with a scraggly beard and rheumy eyes and his best days behind him?"

She looked at me. "You're kidding, right?"

"Sort of," I said, hedging a little, since it sounded awful when I actually said out loud what I'd been thinking.

"How about some tea?" she said, closing the closet door.

"Was that the wrong answer?" I followed her downstairs to the kitchen and took a seat at the counter.

"That's one way to look at it," she said, filling the teakettle, "but the thing is, who wants to waste time having dinner with a guy like that?"

"You got that right." I laughed at the way she came at it. "Sounds like the reunion from hell."

"Exactly." She turned on the flame and got down two cups. "So why not consider the best case?"

"And what would that be?"

She put a tea bag in each cup and I could smell the cinnamon. "That would be, he's as fine as ever, his career's going great guns, and the only thing he's ever regretted in his whole charmed life is leaving you without a proper good-bye."

She said it so simply that its directness almost brought tears to my eyes, a reaction that was not lost on Amelia.

"It's too late to expect him to explain," I said.

"Then don't. Pick a restaurant you like, make sure they give you a good table, put on your beautiful dress, and leave your expectations behind."

"Along with my granny panties?"

She smiled at me sympathetically. "Did you ever think maybe this is the universe's way of trying to help you answer Phoebe's question?"

"I don't think the universe spends a significant amount of time trying to answer my daughter's questions."

"That will be a real surprise to her."

"One among many," I said. "Just one among many."

27

One of the first things I asked Miriam to do was to make me a copy of her sister's picture from the locket so I could show it around. So far, nobody had seen or heard anything, but I had pinned her photograph to the bulletin board in my office to remind me that this search was about a real person who needed some real help immediately. The sympathetic police detective I spoke to said it was like looking for a needle in a haystack, but he'd do the best he could. That didn't sound very promising, and the more information I gathered about the ways young women refugees were being exploited, the more frightened I was for Etienne. Children as young as seven and eight, boys and girls, were being snatched or lured away from relatives and forced to live in filthy, overcrowded quarters like the one where Miriam had been stashed, with no way to contact anyone they knew once they disappeared. Every kind of intimidation was being used, but the most effective weapons these modern-day slavers had was the fact that so many illegal immigrants didn't speak or read English, and they were terrified of being reported to the INS. Nobody wanted to be identified as a troublemaker, so witnesses to any crime were hard to find.

What wasn't hard to find was the coverage of Busy Boy Baker's partnership with Mandeville Maids. It led all three nightly newscasts locally and was featured on the front of the Living section of the *Atlanta Journal-Constitution* with a photo of Busy Boy in the middle of the women in white. They were clustered around him, grinning like somebody had just said, "Say money." He had one arm around his sister and the other around a woman who looked like she was in the midst of a moment that would last a lifetime. That picture also made its way into *Jet* magazine as a photo of the week, and into the *Sentinel* as community news. I clipped it out and pinned it to my bulletin board next to Etienne.

Looking at the women's excited faces, I wondered how they would feel if they knew how little faith their benefactors really had in them, but they didn't have a clue and probably didn't care. They all agreed it was a great opportunity. Whether they chose to take advantage of it was another question altogether.

B.J. called to give me his date and time of arrival. I took Amelia's advice and told him to meet me at the Pleasant Peasant downtown at six thirty. That would give him enough time to get checked into his hotel and take a breath before dinner. He was staying at the Hyatt Regency, which was only a few blocks from the restaurant, so we wouldn't have any traffic to deal with. Atlanta's legendary freeway snarls are always the wrench in the best laid plans, and I avoid them if I can. Life is too short to contend with other people's bad driving and road rage on the way to catch up with an old friend.

I still had a couple of days before his arrival, which was fine with me. I was busy trying to reprogram myself. Amelia's decidedly more upbeat projections for the evening had grown on me, and gradually I realized I was looking forward to it. Several successful practice sessions had convinced me I could drape the strange dress appropriately for the occasion, so I gave myself the option to wear it if I was feeling particularly bold at the moment when I had to decide.

B.J. had been my friend for almost two years before we became lovers. He knew Louis because they were both journalism majors and the three of us started hanging around together. They were always arguing about whether we needed more local news or more focus on international affairs. I never understood why the two had to be in conflict. They acted like they had never seen that bumper sticker that says, *Think Globally/Act Locally.* Maybe it's just the way men communicate.

When I'd get bored with that discussion, I'd make them go to the movies or listen to some music or talk about my chosen career as a diplomat. It was a good three-way friendship, and B.J. fit into my ongoing life with Louis in a way that we all enjoyed, and then . . . what does the song say? I fooled around and fell in love. I didn't mean to, did not have it in mind, but Louis got an internship in Chicago the summer after our junior year, and B.J. had a project that kept him in Atlanta, where I was working in former ambassador Andrew Young's office and starting to apply for grad school. Our three became two, and left alone, B.J. and I fell into each other's arms like we'd just been waiting for Louis to leave the room.

It was heaven. A friend I could talk to who also made me woozy with the pleasure of our lovemaking. A comrade who would travel the world with me and share my bed and my brain with equal pleasure. It was a dream come true, and sometimes when I'd watch him sleeping or we'd slide into the bath he'd run for us to share, I'd know it was just that: a dream. A temporary and highly transitory state that would have to come to an end. I accepted that, I think, but what I had always hoped was that even if this amazing sexual bubble couldn't last, we could still be friends. It sounds like a classic kiss-off line, I know, but that's only if you've never really had a good friend. B.J. was my friend first, and I missed that part of him as much as anything else.

The doorbell startled me out of my daydream and I glanced at the clock. It was six thirty and the sky was turning pink outside my window. I wasn't expecting anybody, but I was definitely up for an interesting drop-in. If I was lucky, it might even be a hungry friend with an idea for dinner. Not exactly. I opened the door to find Sam Hall standing there in yet another dark blue suit and tasteful tie, smiling apologetically.

"Catherine," he crooned my name like a Quiet Storm deejay. "Is this a bad time?"

I'm glad I always dress for work. Doing business in your sweats is a slippery slope that leads to a day spent in your bathrobe and slippers. Plus, it leaves you at a distinct disadvantage when confronted with impeccably dressed drop-ins. I had on a good pair of pants and a blue silk tunic Phoebe gave me last Christmas.

"I'm not sure," I said. "A bad time for what?"

The smile got a little wider and he held up a bottle of wine. "An apology, an explanation, and a glass of my favorite cabernet."

That made me smile. I'd been thinking about dinner, but this was an infinitely more interesting proposition.

"Come in," I said, stepping aside to let him.

He stopped in the small foyer just inside the front door and looked around. This house was one of the original Victorians that once defined Peeples Street, and it still has all the original wood inside. My mother always took pride in this house and used it as evidence that my father's unconventional and peripatetic lifestyle did not mean he wasn't a good provider. When the property passed to me, I felt honor bound to hold up that same standard, especially since I also do business here. The place looks good, if I do say so myself, and Sam was clearly impressed.

"This is a lovely place," he said, following me into the living room.

"Thank you," I said. "Why don't you have a seat and I'll get some glasses?"

He put the wine on the coffee table and sat down on the couch, still taking in his surroundings with the practiced eye of a professional. I brought back an opener and two red-wine glasses with impossibly slender stems and big, round bowls. They had been a set of six, but I had broken them all, except these two. Louis gives me a set of wineglasses every Christmas, and they rarely make it through New Year's Eve. It's a running joke between us, but these were survivors.

I picked up the wine and started to open it. I could tell Sam was surprised, but if he brought wine *and* opened it, it was too much like a date and this *ain't* that. Not by a long shot.

"I used to be in the real estate business," he said. "This house is in the half-million-dollar range."

"It's not for sale," I said, easing the cork out of the bottle and wondering what he was doing here.

"I'm sorry for dropping in unannounced," he said while I poured us each a glass of wine. "But I thought it was time for us to get to know each other a little better."

I put down my glass. "Is that the apology or the explanation?"

"Okay, cards on the table." He smiled. "Look, Catherine, I'm not a bad guy, but I'm probably not the kind of person you're used to working with, am I right?"

If our conversation after the ceremony was any indication, he should get an award for understatement.

"Yes, I guess you are."

"And you know what's the main difference between me and them? I'm a businessman. Making money is not a crime in my book, and I intend to make as much of it as I can, as fast as I can, before the bottom falls out or somebody blows up the world."

"Is that why you went to work for Miss Mandeville? To make money?"

He sat back and grinned at me. "See how you said that? 'To make money,' like I was doing something sinful because I want to be well paid for what I do."

I took a sip of my wine. "Maybe we should start there. What do you do?"

"That would be the explanation part, but I hadn't finished my apology."

"I'm sorry. Go on."

"Here's the thing." He put his glass

down and leaned toward me. "I'm sorry if what I said the other day offended you. I don't have anything against those girls. . . ."

He must have felt my objection, since the graduates ranged in age from early twenties to mid-forties.

"Those *women*," he corrected himself smoothly. "I want the best for them, in every possible way, but I'm realistic about what they are to me."

"Don't you mean *who* they are?"

"No, because they're not a *who*. They're a *what*. Cheap, available labor to do the jobs nobody else wants to do. That's the only reason I'm interested in immigrants, because they're more of the same, except they'll work cheaper, be more grateful to get it, and not make waves. So I'm sorry if that offends you, but that's where I stand, and the sooner you know it, the more productive our working together is going to be."

I wondered how Ezola could stand to have him around. "How do you figure that?"

He leaned forward suddenly like he was anxious for me to understand. "Because I'm honest. I'm not trying to pretend to be one of those do-gooders you're used to working for who are so busy begging for money they don't know how to make any, but that's what I do. I'm in the business of amassing capital, gathering resources, and if I can help somebody along the way, or *seem* to, that's all right with me. But that's never the goal. It's only a by-product of the process."

I couldn't argue with what he was saying, and as I thought about it, there was no need to. Hiring the women I was helping target for Ezola was going to help somebody along the way. Rewarding a handful of women for earning a GED was helping somebody along the way. And even holding out the carrot of college scholarships would help if anybody took him up on it. What made me mad was his attitude. He seemed so callous toward the women, which is, I guess, the way of the world. Maybe I had just been working around do-gooders too long to admit it.

"That may be the most unrepentant apology I've ever heard," I said. "I can hardly wait for the explanation part."

He sat back then and took a swallow of his wine, smiled appreciatively, and swirled it delicately around in my doomed goblet like he was sampling the best of the harvest at a Napa Valley wine tasting. "I'm a failed romantic," he said, and his beautiful lingering over the word shot down my recent irritation with his worldview and replaced it with renewed curiosity about what sort of person he really was. He wasn't what I'd call likable, but he was very interesting. Plus, we failed romantics are a very exclusive club, despite our tremendous membership numbers, and we usually recognize one of our own. As a failed romantic, Sam was about as convincing as Michael Jackson is pretending to be a guy who really loves kids.

"You don't strike me as a romantic, failed or otherwise," I said. "You're a pragmatist if I ever saw one."

"Maybe you're right, Catherine, but I used to be a lot like you. I was still in business, but I believed in *the people*." His voice put quotation marks around the words to show what he thought of those who still felt that way. "I inherited a real estate company from my father and I embraced the challenge of running it with real passion. My father was old-school, but I had new ideas about how to encourage home ownership in renters. I wanted to use the rehabbing of houses to revitalize poor neighborhoods and energize their residents. I wanted to use home ownership to positively impact everything from health care to public safety."

Those ideas — the ones I endorse so completely — sounded so right coming out of Sam's mouth, spoken in that mellifluous voice, that I couldn't believe he didn't still believe them. "What happened?"

He shrugged, his well-padded shoulders and his perfectly tailored jacket making the gesture look graceful in a self-deprecating sort of way. "Nothing. Absolutely nothing. My tenants weren't interested in anything except drugs and watching TV. Their children tore up everything they touched, and you couldn't fix it up more times than they could tear it back down. Their rent checks bounced, and the crews I hired from the neighborhood sold the tools I gave them and disappeared."

His story sounded like a nightmare. Trying to change poor people's lives is never as glamorous or inspirational as they make it when some do-gooders get the central role in a Hollywood movie. In real life, Sam's experience is probably closer to the truth, a long series of unrewarded sacrifices and thankless tasks that rarely impact the lives of the people you want to rescue. It sounded like Sam had suffered a classic case of burnout. I refilled our glasses, and he took a sip before he continued his story.

"I realized that not only was I not going to be able to make the changes I had dreamed about, but I had invested so much money in the possibility that I was about to lose the business." He shook his head to clear the bad memory. "I needed to evict the deadbeats, fix the rental places up, and get some tenants in who could pay. The sheriff handled the evictions, but the mess those niggers left behind was just unbelievable. Garbage everywhere, diapers, every kind of drug paraphernalia. It was disgusting."

He gave a slight shudder, and a small frown appeared between his eyebrows. I could imagine walking into the houses he had been renting in good faith and finding such a mess. He had my sympathies on that. I've participated in enough clearing-out and fixing-up of abandoned apartments to know how nasty people can really be when they put their minds to it.

"That's when I met Miss Mandeville," he said, his voice a mixture of affection and respect. "I came to her because I needed a crew of maids to come put those hellholes I owned into some kind of order so they'd be fit for human habitation.

When I described the situation, she said they could handle it, but the price she quoted was way over my head. When I appealed to her for a reduced rate, because I was about to lose my business, she offered to buy me out and bring me into her operation as a vice president if I would accept her offer immediately. She told me she needed some assistance and she thought we could do business, but if I wasn't interested, she'd find somebody else. I signed the contract that very day. That was three years ago, and she was right. We've been doing great business ever since."

It was a great story, and it sounded like Ezola. She was not a woman who liked to wait. They seemed well suited: equally determined, equally unapologetic, and equally manipulative. I had never forgotten Ezola's "sorry black bitches" test question. Or forgiven her for it. Sam hadn't been that direct, but his calling his former tenants *niggers* was close enough.

"So what are two hard-nosed businesspeople like you and Miss Mandeville doing pulling in a confirmed do-gooder like me?"

"Because you're the best at what you do," he said. "You're tough and opinionated and not easily bullshitted, even by two masters."

"I'll take that as a compliment."

"I meant it as one. This is all new territory for us, and we don't want to stumble. You'll keep us honest. That means a lot."

This time, when he smiled, I smiled back. "Should I add that to my job description?"

"No need. We'll just keep that between us." And he raised his glass and touched mine lightly.

"Welcome aboard, Catherine. It's going to be a great ride. I promise you."

"I'll fasten my seat belt," I said, paraphrasing Bette Davis's famous admonition to her guests at the start of a long, drunken evening where she cusses everybody out and then staggers off to bed.

"Good enough." Sam laughed and put down his glass. "And now I'm going to get out and leave you to your evening. Uninvited guests should never overstay their welcome, but first I need a favor."

"What can I do for you?" I put down my glass, too.

"I need a copy of those remarks you did for the ceremony. My copy got away from me."

"They were pretty well upstaged by Busy Boy, don't you think? Maybe we should let them just slink away."

"Not a chance," he said. "Just because I never said it, doesn't mean I don't intend to quote it. 'The rare and noble sisterhood.' That was great stuff."

I refrained from reminding him that that particular gem was his own ad lib and not my genius, and stood up.

"I've got a copy in my computer," I said. "I can print one out if you want to take it with you."

He stood up, too. "If it's no trouble that would be perfect, and I would love to see your work space."

It hadn't occurred to me that he could come back to my office with me. I was comfortable sitting with him in the living room, but I didn't really like to have my clients roaming around the rest of the house.

He saw the hesitation and smiled. "Don't worry, Catherine. It's not a test. You can just tell so much about a person by how they organize the place where they work. I mean, all you have to see is that throne to get an idea of how Miss Mandeville sees the world. Or at least her place in it. Do you mind?"

I wondered what my office would reveal. "Of course not," I lied, but what could I do? If I declined to take him to my office now, he would assume I had something to hide. "It won't take a minute."

He followed me down the hall, past the posters of Chinese factory women, Nigerian market sellers, and Jamaican secondary-school teachers. They had been part of a misguided campaign encouraging people to enjoy their jobs by using the slogan that defined the Japanese commandant of a prisoner-of-war camp in the movie *Bridge on the River Kwai*, "Be happy in your work." The woman who designed the poster had never seen the movie, but for anybody who had, the phrase was forever linked to the commandant's barked order to his dying prisoners to be joyful in their forced labor, and the small organization that commissioned the poster was forced to withdraw it from circulation or risk a media and client backlash that could affect their funding and their reputation.

I felt sorry for them and I loved the campaign. The smiling women on the posters always looked healthy and strong and truly happy in their work. I had lined the hallway with them as sort of a positive blast of female energy and imagery for anybody who made it this far. Sam took it all in without comment. I walked into my office and indicated the chair I kept for visitors.

"Can I look around?" he said.

This guy was shameless. It was like asking if it was okay to poke through somebody's medicine cabinet. If you're going to analyze somebody's stuff, it's not fair to make them give you permission.

"Feel free," I said, feeling more boxed by the second, as I sat down behind my desk, opened the Mandeville file, and scrolled down quickly.

Sam was walking slowly around the small room, checking the titles on the bookshelf, noting the CD case and the Keith Jarrett that had been playing softly all day on repeat.

He strolled over to my bulletin board as my printer hummed into action. The two photos I'd pinned up earlier smiled out at him: one of Etienne's sweet, round, open face and the other of the Mandeville graduates surrounding Busy Boy with all that unrequited love.

"I'll bet that picture is up on refrigerators all over town," he said. "At least in the kitchens of anybody who was there, or said they were."

I just smiled.

"This is a lovely girl. Is she your daughter?"

"No," I said, "she's the sister of a Haitian friend of mine. They've lost track of each other."

He was still looking at Etienne. "How do you lose track of a beautiful kid like that?"

Men act like beauty is some kind of safe passage through life. Ask a pretty woman if that's true, and most of them will tell you how much of their girlhood they spent dodging the attention of every man they met, including priests, uncles, cousins, and sometimes dads.

"There's a lot of sexual exploitation of refugee women and children," I said. "Forced prostitution is a real problem."

"That's an important distinction," he said, looking down at the newspaper clippings, photographs, and magazine articles that were part of my educating myself about the problem. A recent story in the *New York Times Magazine* called "Sex Slaves on Main Street" featured a cover shot of a young girl in knee socks and a school uniform. The implications were clear, but the shot was exploitive and creepy. Sam picked it up to look closer as I took the last page from the printer, clipped them all together, and slipped them into a folder. His energy was always weird, but in a space this size, it made me uncomfortable.

"What do you mean?" I switched off the

computer, but he was still eyeballing my research: e-mails from colleagues, possible leads on missing girls, horror stories of searches that turned up bodies or nothing at all.

He turned away and seemed surprised to see me standing at the door, but he followed me out while he explained. "Just that prostitution is a complicated issue. Some women are forced into it, but some women see it as the best available option."

He said it like choosing to have random sex for money could be evaluated right along with being a waitress or a teacher's aide in a day-care center, but I wasn't in the mood to argue prostitution with him. The wine was sitting in my empty stomach, making me feel as queasy as the company. "Which is why we have to offer other options," I said.

He smiled back. "Spoken like a dyed-in-the-wool do-gooder if I ever heard one."

"Guilty as charged," I said, handing him the folder with his speech in it. "Thanks for coming by."

"Thanks for letting me in," he said, "and for hearing me out. We don't have to agree on everything to be a damn good team."

I wasn't sure I believed that at all, but at least now I knew where we stood, and clarity is always power.

"Good night," I said.

"You, too." And he climbed into the silver Lexus that was parked in my driveway and eased off into the deepening twilight. Of one thing I was certain: he thought he was leaving with more information than he offered, but that was only if I hadn't been paying attention, and like I told Ezola, that's not my style. Sam had come offering an olive branch, but something told me it probably had more thorns than a rose and none of the sweetness.

28

The next day Miriam came over to bring me some information that had really upset her. She was very agitated, and it took her a minute to tell me what was going on. The strange wig was practically trembling on top of her head. Amelia explained that Miriam was terrified of being kidnapped by the people she'd run away from, and her wig was part of her disguise. In theory, that was a good idea, but it looked so terrible, it drew more attention than it deflected.

When she calmed down a little, she told me she had met a woman at her citizenship class who lived at a residence hotel and had seen some guys bring in two vans of women a few weeks ago and put them up in adjoining rooms. Almost immediately, the woman said, guys started going in and out at all hours of the day and night. They never stayed long and they didn't make much noise, so nobody bothered them. The women never came out at all.

Except one time when one of them who seemed about fifteen or sixteen came out and begged her to call the police because they were being held against their will. Before she could say any more, one of the other women came out and grabbed her and made her shut up. The older one was really mad, and she kept saying, "You're going to get us all sent back."

Miriam was blinking back tears as she told me that she had asked the woman if she called the police. The woman admitted she had been afraid to, since she didn't have any papers either. Late that night, the guys with the vans showed up, and by morning everybody was gone.

"I showed her the picture," she said, her voice shaky.

"Of Etienne?"

She nodded her head. "She said it wasn't her, but it could have been. What if they have her in a place like that?"

The tears spilled over now, and I put my arm around Miriam's shoulders to steady her. This was our first concrete lead, but it was taking us down a terrible path.

Miriam was clutching the locket around her neck.

"How long ago was it?" I said gently.

"A month. Maybe a little more."

That was a long time, but if we got right on it, talked to some people who were still at that hotel, maybe we could find something. But if I was going to be out playing private investigator, I needed some help on the home front. My work with Ezola was just going to make it more difficult to stay on top of things, and Babylon Sisters had a reputation to maintain. It was very clear to me that I needed an assistant *yesterday,* as Sam would say. Suddenly, I had a flash of inspiration.

"Miriam," I said. "I need your help."

"What can I do?" she said quickly. "I will do anything to find my sister."

"Will you come and work for me?"

She was surprised, and her eyes opened wide under that ridiculous wig. "Work for you?"

I nodded. "If I'm going to be out and about, I need someone to answer the phones, respond to e-mail. The same kinds of things you've been doing for Amelia."

I knew her internship would be over soon and that Amelia wasn't going to be able to keep her. This might work out perfectly. Why hadn't I thought of it before?

"You could start as soon as you're finished at Amelia's."

Her expression told me everything I needed to know, but if it hadn't, she threw her arms around my neck and hugged me so hard, the wig slid over one eye so she looked like a drunken pirate.

"Yes! I would love to work for you!" she said, grabbing the wig and tugging it down to secure it. "Yes!"

"Good," I said, "but there's one thing you have to do for me."

She was suddenly serious. "Yes?"

"Don't wear the wig at work." She looked embarrassed, but I smiled reassuringly. "Amelia told me why you wear it, but most of the time it'll just be me and you, so you can be yourself."

"Thank you," she said with a smile of pure gratitude. "I will."

29

How did I let Amelia convince me that I could manipulate this ridiculous jumble of fabric without her assistance? She was in a meeting at the Chamber of Commerce with Mr. Tanaka, followed by dinner, and wouldn't be back for another couple of hours. I was finally forced to admit that without her, this was worse than a losing proposition. It was also a giant stress inducer, confidence buster, and all around reminder that whatever I might have grown up to be, a fashion plate was not among the possibilities. After draping and redraping for the better part of forty-five minutes, I gave up and retreated to the safety of my own clothes. A pair of easy-cut black pants from Chico's, the busy woman's boutique of choice, and a brightly embroidered blouse from Guatemala I had found at a tiny shop in Northampton when Phoebe and I first went to look at Smith made me feel better immediately. I added a pair of big silver hoops and five or six bangles, and even broke down and brushed on a tiny bit of blush. Eighteen years is a long time. No harm in putting my best face forward.

The stress had rolled off me in a wave as soon as I stepped out of Amelia's dress, so I sat down on the side of the bed to buckle on my favorite little Chinese shoes with the red silk dragon on each toe and tried to conjure up an image of B.J.'s face, eighteen years later, but I couldn't. What changes a face from one thing to another is not just the passage of time, but what's going on as you're moving through it. The lines around your mouth are affected by how often you smile, just like your eyes are affected by how often you cry. The face I remembered when I thought about B.J. was lean and brown and young. I wondered what face B.J. remembered when he thought about me.

I took my shawl from the closet, threw it over my shoulder with no need to drape a damn thing, and looked at myself in the mirror. There I was: healthy, happy, a little nervous about the next couple of hours, but relieved of the need to worry about my dress disintegrating during dessert, nothing I couldn't handle. I had tied my hair up and off my face so there was nothing to hide behind, and that was fine with me. I didn't want him to respond to me for looking like somebody else. I was prepared to stand or fall in this moment based on who I really *be,* as the jazz guys say. And truth be told? I be just fine, thanks. I think I be just fine.

30

I saw him before he saw me. That was no accident. I arrived fifteen minutes early to secure a spot in the window so I could do just that. I ordered a glass of wine and tried to relax. At least I was in familiar surroundings. The Pleasant Peasant is my favorite downtown restaurant, and it has occupied the same location for thirty years. Like many downtown diehards, their current challenge is negotiating safe passage for their customers through the constant flow of homeless men from a nearby shelter. Although they weren't usually aggressive, panhandlers make people nervous, and that's never good for business.

I've made peace with panhandlers by being sure I carry a couple of dollar bills in an easily accessible pocket when I walk around downtown. When I'm approached, I offer a dollar immediately. Nobody's mad at getting any denomination of folding money, so the exchange ends on a pleasant note of common humanity instead of guilt and recrimination. I chalk it up to urban living, and keep on steppin'. I had given a dollar to a guy pushing an overstuffed trash bag in a battered grocery cart on my way into the Peasant tonight. He thanked me profusely, and I told him to take care of himself, and that was the end of it.

But as I looked out the window, waiting for B.J. to alight from a cab out front, I saw the guy again, walking down Peachtree Street with the early-evening traffic whizzing by, engaged in an earnest conversation with a tall, thin man in a black turtleneck and an open trench coat with the collar turned up. Before they parted company, the tall man handed the man with the cart his second piece of folding money in less than an hour. Of course, it was B.J.

I looked at him through that window, and damn if it didn't all come back in a great big rush. All the good stuff and all those last terrible, confusing moments, until I didn't know whether to hug him or hate him, but neither one seemed quite right, so I just sat there watching him walk in the front door and glance around, looking for me. If I wasn't already rattled, his strong resemblance to Phoebe would have been more than enough. Same lanky frame. Same deep-cocoa-brown complexion and big dark eyes. I'd have to be

235

sure he never saw a picture of her. It would be like looking in the mirror.

I waited until he turned in my direction and then raised my hand in case he had trouble recognizing me. Thank God I had on my own little outfit. If I'd waved in that wrap-and-drape dress my breasts would probably have popped out of their own accord. His smile when he saw me was worth the price of admission all by itself. He looked so genuinely happy and excited to see me that I couldn't help but smile back.

"Catherine," he said, "you haven't changed a bit."

Not true. I'm ten pounds heavier and a whole lot smarter. I stood up so he could kiss my cheek, but held on to both of his hands so a hug was out of the question.

"You haven't either." Which was also untrue. He was still as fine as ever, and that smile was still a killer, but there was something so deeply troubled, so absolutely sad in his eyes that I almost looked away.

"It's been too long," he said, folding his coat and resting it on the back of the chair as he slid in across from me.

"Almost twenty years."

He shook his head. "That's when you know you're getting old. When you've had friends for over twenty years."

"Speak for yourself," I said. "I think we're in our prime."

"You certainly are, but I think the jury's still out on me."

Before I could ask him what he meant by that, the waiter came by to take his drink order, and B.J. ordered a cup of espresso. I was surprised. Even in college, B.J. had been a big drinker. He never worried about it, but I did.

"Fighting jet lag?"

"Not exactly. I stopped drinking a couple of years ago. Stopped smoking last Christmas. Caffeine is about the only vice I've got left."

"What made you stop?"

He shrugged and ran his hand over his close-cropped hair. "Being a drunk is an occupational hazard for foreign correspondents. We wear it like a badge of honor. A rite of passage. You spend all day in a war zone or a refugee camp or a guerilla hideout, and then at night you go to the bar in the well-guarded hotel where you're staying and swap war stories with other reporters and the occasional American expatriate who can't remember why he came there in the first place. I saw myself becoming one of those guys, and it wasn't who I wanted to be anymore. So I came home."

The waiter brought the tiny cup of espresso with a curl of lemon on the saucer beside it. There was a lot more to that story, but I was the one who had demanded that we talk in present tenses, so I didn't pursue it.

"Louis sent his regards," I said, trying to sound casual, like I thought they had talked a few months ago. "And told me to warn you he's going to try to talk you into writing something for the *Sentinel*."

"I'm open to persuasion," B.J. said, taking his cue from me as if there had been no twenty-year break in their communication. He took a long swallow of the steaming espresso that practically emptied the cup. I repressed a motherly warning about the dangers of drinking too-hot liquids. "How's he doing?"

"Same as always. He also said to tell you he can't afford you."

"He never could," B.J. said, smiling in spite of his sad eyes. "How's the paper doing?"

"Not good," I said. "Louis writes great editorials, but he can't get any subscribers, and most of the advertising's dried up, too. He's looking for investors, but so far nobody's turned up."

B.J. shook his head. "That's a damn

shame. The *Sentinel* was a great paper. Not just a great *black* paper — a great paper."

I understood his need to make the distinction. It's like the Brother Ruben argument. You never had to love the *Sentinel* because of race pride. You could admire it the same way you would the *Washington Post*. Because it was good.

"It's not dead yet," I said, feeling suddenly protective. "Louis is determined. Will you have time to call him while you're here?"

"Absolutely. I'll be around for three or four days. All my leads seem to take me to Atlanta, so I've got some poking around to do."

Was that too much time or not enough? Too much time for what? Why did I sound so calm and feel so crazy? I took a sip of my wine, glad he couldn't see the insane conversation going on in my head. *Calm down,* I cautioned myself. *Just calm down!*

"Why don't you tell me about your story?"

He polished off his espresso and pushed the delicate cup aside. "Straight down to business, huh?"

I just smiled. *Damn right.*

"My original idea was a long piece about the impact of refugees on African-American urban populations, but that was way too big a topic. No way to get my arms around it."

I nodded. "So you narrowed it down?"

"To women. The experience of being a female refugee is completely different from the experience of being a man. My story will focus on that difference."

"Why?"

If he was surprised by the question, he didn't show it. "Because in any population the treatment of the women and children always reflects the true values of that community. It hits people closest to where they really live."

Great answer, I thought. "I couldn't have said it better myself."

"That's because you said it perfectly the first time." He grinned.

He was right. The summer we became lovers, we had tackled the issue of sexism head-on. Not because he wanted to, but because I had just taken a History of Feminism class at Spelman and I was fired up to spread the good word.

I laughed. "No wonder it sounded so good! You learned your lesson well!"

"That's because I respect the narrative of women's lives," he quoted me again, sounding like a fourth grader about to win the citywide spelling bee. One of the most intense discussions we ever had centered around men's inability to "recognize and respect the narrative of women's lives." B.J. had denied any such blind spot, and it had taken all my powers of persuasion to convince him that his response to the question was proof enough of the truth of my premise.

I raised my glass. "Move to the head of the class."

"Thank you," he said. "Now can I ask you something?"

"Sure."

"How are we doing so far?"

I started to pretend I didn't know what he meant, but it's hard for a woman who's taught a man the intricacies of how not to be a sexist asshole to claim ignorance of the dynamics in a moment as basic as this one.

"We're doing fine," I said, waving at our waiter so we could order. "So far, so good."

31

Two hours later we had eaten everything that was put before us. I'm sure any strict Freudian worth her hourly fee would talk about sublimation of a sexual urge into a more acceptable hunger, but so what? The food gave us something to do while we talked. And did we ever talk! It was as if we had picked up a conversation where we'd left it yesterday. We established that we were both single and unattached. I told him about Babylon Sisters and Mandeville Maids and Amelia's law firm and Miriam's sister going missing. He told me about information he was getting that there was a regular flow of illegal aliens between Miami and metro Atlanta, basically for the big office-park and discount-store cleaning contracts. He was focusing on Haitian women because his contacts told him there were a lot of Haitians being stashed in slum housing all over an economically depressed neighborhood called Vine City. Poor brown people to camouflage other poor brown people. These guys were shameless.

We had each heard the whispers about forced prostitution, but nothing on the record yet. I invited him to take a look through my files Friday afternoon. It was a testament to how comfortable I was by the end of the evening that I didn't feel strange telling him to come by the house. He felt like a friend again, and I relaxed into the moment.

"Louis heard a rumor a couple of years ago that you were writing a book."

B.J. groaned and looked slightly embarrassed. "I'd like to know who started that rumor. People keep asking me about a book that I never said I was writing. Then they feel bad for me because I haven't finished it."

"So I guess that pretty much disqualifies it as pleasant after-dinner conversation?"

He raised his eyebrows. "Is that what this is? Pleasant after-dinner conversation?"

"Absolutely," I said. "We've conducted our business. We've had our dinner. Now we're supposed to wind down with a little neutral chitchat, say good night, and go home."

"You've never engaged anybody in neutral chitchat in your life."

"People can change," I said.

"No, they can't, except to get more like what they already are."

"That's a depressing thought," I said. "What about personal growth, spiritual transformation, sudden bursts of cosmic consciousness?"

"All of that is what makes you aware of who you are." He smiled and sat back. "But getting you closer to your essence doesn't change it."

"So your best advice is to 'go with the flow'?" He was getting so serious, I had to tease him just a little.

"Let me tell you a story," he said, leaning forward again, ignoring my teasing, serious as hell. The restaurant was filling up, and even at our cozy corner table, the buzz could be distracting.

I leaned forward so I wouldn't miss anything. "I'm all ears."

"Right before I came home, I was held hostage in Afghanistan. There were two other American guys, and they took all three of us because somebody had told them we were CIA and they wanted to be sure before they cut our heads off."

He said it matter-of-factly, but the words sent a chill through me. He had been moving around in a part of the world where that had already happened to an American journalist.

"My God! What did you do?"

He shrugged. "We waited. That was all we could do. They took us to a village way up in the mountains and stashed us in their tiny little jail. Nobody even knew we were there. We had never seen these guys before, so all we knew was that they were really young and really pissed off at America."

It was strange to hear what he was saying in the middle of the dinner hour in a popular Atlanta restaurant. We may as well have been on another planet.

"There were some Afghani guys in the other cell, and the guards kept coming in every couple of hours and beating the shit out of them. We could hear it all even though we couldn't see them, and it sounded pretty bad. One of the guys with us completely freaked out. Curled up in the corner like he was trying to be invisible. The other guy kept trying to talk to the guards in English, even though they didn't understand a word he was saying."

"What about you?" I was beginning to understand the expression in his eyes. Did the fear you must feel in that situation ever go away?

"I was hanging in there pretty good, trying to stay cool and hoping for the best. Then one morning, after we heard them beating the Afghani prisoners half the night, everything got real quiet. Then they brought out this guy's body. It wasn't even wrapped in a sheet or anything, and we could see how bad it was. They did everything to this guy. As they dragged him past our cell, one of the guards laughed and pointed at him, then pointed at us. That's when I realized we probably weren't going to make it out either. It looked like we were going to die there."

He paused and took a sip of water, tried to smile, but couldn't pull it off. "You know how people always say when you think you're going to die, your whole life passes before your eyes?"

I nodded.

"They're right, but in my case, it wasn't just a quick flash. It was like watching a full-length feature. I lay there on that hard little pallet and blocked out everything around me and just watched the story of my life play out inside my head. The whole thing, starting with my mother's voice, my father's hands, on through the years, good times and bad, ups and downs —"

The caffeine was kicking in, and B.J.'s words tumbled out in a rush. I wasn't sure where he was going with this story, but I was pretty sure it wasn't going to be in the pleasant-postdinner-chitchat category. He stopped himself suddenly, sat back again, and took a deep breath. He looked lost for what to say next.

"I hear they have great espresso here," I said, to lighten up the moment until he could collect himself.

"I think I've had my limit" — he smiled crookedly — "but this is what I really want to tell you. They held us there for two weeks before they finally let us go — I still don't know why — but lying there, night after night, watching my thirty-plus years rolling by, I realized I wasn't perfect, but I wasn't such a bad guy, except . . ."

He looked at me so hard I had to look away. "Except one time. One terrible moment." He reached across the table and took my hand. "I realized the only time I didn't act like the man I want to be was the last time I saw you."

"B.J., don't." I withdrew my hand, but he didn't stop talking. The truth is, I don't think he could stop.

"I promised myself that if I survived, I was going to make it right."

So I'm the vision that saved his life, sort of like a sepia-toned *Kiss of the Spider Woman.* I should have seen it coming, but I didn't, and it was too late to pretend I hadn't heard the words. They were echoing around inside my head like a gong. Suddenly, I was terrified of whatever he was going to say about that moment all those years ago. Pure panic drowned out my need to know what he was going to say next. I had thought I was ready for this moment, but I wasn't even close. It was time for me to go.

I stood up to go before I knew I was going to, reached for my purse, and took out two fifty-dollar bills, which would cover the meal and be enough for a nice tip. B.J. stood up, too.

"Where are you going?"

"Remember what I said about not looking back?"

"Cat, listen I —"

"No, you listen." My voice was trembling. What was I so mad about? "I meant it, and if you can't respect that, we'd better not see each other again."

His eyes searched my face. "There's so much I need to say, Cat. I don't know if I can promise you I won't try to say it."

That really pissed me off. How was he going to show up after all this time and tell me he didn't think he could play by my rules? "Well, when you decide, you call and let me know. Good night." And I left him standing there and walked out.

32

The eleven-o'clock news was all bad, delivered live and in living color. There were wars and droughts and famines and fatwas, and everywhere you looked, terrified women, starving children, and streets full of angry men with guns. That was the world from which B.J. had returned, looking for understanding or absolution, neither of which I was prepared or obligated to offer him. I curled up in the corner of the couch that belongs to Phoebe when she's home, watched the world go up in flames in one report after another, and tried to sort out my feelings on a story a little closer to home.

If I wasn't prepared to hear his confession or offer solace, what was I prepared to offer him? Some files on a story he could do in his sleep? Dinner once in a while when he came through town? Some kind of fake friendship that acknowledged only the *fact* of its former incarnation, but none of the nuances? How could I even call it a friendship when I had just spent an entire evening making what I myself had identified as *chitchat,* without once finding a way to say, *Oh, by the way, we have an amazing daughter who looks just like you?* At least he had tried to say something real. I had run like a rabbit. And a self-righteous rabbit at that.

On the screen, wailing women in black burkas were huddling in front of a bombed-out shell that had been their house. There were children clutching their mother's skirts, too terrified to cry, and men already shaking their fists at the camera and vowing revenge. Sometimes it seems like an endless cycle of violence and fear and the lies that lead to war. In those moments, the small crises of the heart pale to insignificance in the face of suicide missions and genocide and bombs that can be activated with cell phones, but the pain is still real. And doesn't each small moment of personal truth lead to the next one and the next one until it becomes second nature and you couldn't tell a lie if you wanted to? And wouldn't that change everything?

Maybe that's where B.J. is now. Maybe that was why he wouldn't lie and say he'd play by my rules even when I snapped at him for getting too close. Maybe that's what makes his eyes so sad. He's still trying to get to the truth in a time of lies.

33

I hadn't heard from Sam since he came by, so I wasn't sure what to expect when I arrived ten minutes early for our scheduled meeting. Just as he had done for my first visit, he met me at the elevator with a welcoming smile, but this time, I followed him down the hall to his suite of offices, which seemed to occupy most of the floor below Ezola's throne room. He led me past an attractive, smartly dressed woman whom Sam identified as another Mandeville success story, and into his private office.

"She used to be a maid?" I said, admiring the African sculptures that were placed around the room on small pedestals, each with its own recessed lighting. They were obviously the real thing, and the monochromatic color scheme in the rest of the room gave my eye ample opportunity to admire them.

"Started with us when she was twenty-two, coming off a bad breakup with two kids and no degree. Seven years later, she's working as my secretary." He said it like there could be no higher calling.

"So sometimes people do follow through," I said, taking a seat across from the huge glass-topped table that was as close as he got to a desk. It looked more like another piece of sculpture, especially since there wasn't a sheet of paper on it, or anywhere else. If I had been hoping to snoop around his office like he did in mine, I was out of luck. All his work space told me was that he had very good taste in art and liked well-designed furniture.

He took the cream-colored leather chair behind the desk and smiled to acknowledge our recent exchange. "Yes, I suppose they do, but not enough to change the odds."

Before I could respond, his secretary rapped on the door softly and stuck her head in without waiting to be invited. "Miss Mandeville is on her way down," she said. "They just called."

"Fine," Sam said, getting to his feet immediately. "Go meet her at the elevator."

I was confused. "I didn't know Miss Mandeville was coming to this meeting."

"I didn't either," he said. "You must have made a terrific impression on her."

"Should I have prepared something?"

Sam shook his head. "How could you?

She likes to pop in sometimes, unannounced. Keeps everybody on their toes."

I'll bet she does. When she really gets going, it's probably a regular corps de ballet around here. Since Sam was standing, I stood up, too. I drew the line at a curtsy, but standing up to say hello to the boss was fine.

Within seconds, Ezola opened the door for herself and stepped into the room like a force of nature. She was dressed exactly as she had been when I met her, down to the pearls and pumps, but her face was a storm cloud of disapproval. I hadn't been here long enough to piss her off, so I assumed Sam was the one with the problem. I was wrong. She stalked up to me, put her large hands on her slim hips, and thrust her face much too close to mine for comfort. I took a step back and looked at Sam, who kept his eyes on Ezola.

"Who do you think you're playing with?" she said accusingly, but her voice was so light that it came out more as an indignant screech.

"I don't know what you're talking about," I said. "And I don't —"

I was going to say, *and I don't appreciate your tone,* but she cut me off. "I asked you a question."

And she stepped forward, again closing the space between us. I felt like I was back in the fourth grade, fleeing from my nemesis, the fifth-grade bully, but it was too far for me to run home, so I'd have to just tough it out.

"I'm not playing with anyone," I said, turning toward Sam so he couldn't keep pretending he didn't see my distress. "I'm trying to do my job."

Sam finally came from behind his desk and took Miss Mandeville's arm. "Let's all sit down," he said, indicating a chair across from mine for his boss, who took it reluctantly, still giving me the evil eye. "I'm sure we can talk this thing out."

What *thing*? Every exchange with them was like a trip through the Twilight Zone. I hadn't even sent in my first invoice, and this gig was already working my last nerve. Phoebe had better calm down and make her peace with me or I'd have to reconsider what I was prepared to do for tuition's sake. I want the best for my daughter, but there are a lot of schools that don't cost thirty-eight thousand dollars a year.

I sat back down. Sam sort of perched on the edge of his desk and then turned to me.

"Miss Mandeville would like to ask you

about some of your other clients."

"Is there a problem?"

"No problem," he said. "We just need some information."

That was how she acted when there was no problem? I'd hate to see Ezola's reaction if there ever was one. "I've given you a list of who they are. What kind of information do you need?"

"I need to know what kind of business they're in that has to do with prostitution!"

"*What?*" I was now officially confused.

"You heard me! Prostitution!"

I heard her, all right, but I had no idea what the hell she was talking about. I sat back and looked from one to the other, hoping somebody was going to tell me what was going on.

"It's not the first time," Ezola hissed at me. "Whenever you work with a lot of women, there's always somebody sniffing around them, trying to see who's looking for the high life without the hard work."

"Is that what you think I'm doing?" I said, too amazed to be offended.

"Catherine," Sam said when Ezola just glared at me and didn't answer. "Miss Mandeville got a call this morning about your having dinner last night with a guy who's got a pretty bad reputation."

He was talking about B.J. This was getting stranger by the second. "A pretty bad reputation for what?"

"For trafficking in women." Ezola spit the words at me like she'd just discovered my deep, dark secret. "As if you didn't know. What a coincidence that you start working for me and get spotted talking to a pimp all in a few short weeks, but you know, I don't believe in coincidences. Never have. I think you came here to try to use this organization for . . . God knows what!"

This time I interrupted her. "I came here because Sam called and invited me, and for no other reason. I signed on with you because I thought what you were proposing was a good idea, and I still do, but this is ridiculous!"

Ezola sat back and looked at Sam, who turned to me with that *I'm on your side* voice and a world-class shit-eating grin. "Who was he, Catherine?"

"That's none of your business," I said. "But since it seems to have caused such a high degree of consternation around here, let me put your minds at ease."

I should have said *warped little minds,* but I was still trying to be professional. "I was having dinner with an old college friend of mine, Burghardt Johnson. He's in town re-searching an article about the impact of immigrants on urban communities. At-lanta is one of the places he's looking at, and I thought there might be a place in his story for your project," I said, turning back to Ezola, who was still watching me, but seemed to have calmed down a little. "Your source, whoever it is, is misin-formed."

Neither one of them said anything for a minute, and then Ezola had the nerve to smile. After all that ugly, now she was smiling like a Sunday-school teacher.

She looked at Sam. "I told you, didn't I?"

He nodded. "Yes, you did, Miss M. You certainly did."

She's "Miss M." now?

Ezola turned back to me. "I told Sam I knew it wasn't true. I'm sorry, Catherine, but this is too important to leave anything to chance. I had to know."

"Next time," I said, still pissed, "why don't you just ask me?"

"Maybe next time I will." She stood up then, and so did Sam, but it was my hand she reached for and then held on to. "Sam tells me you're doing some excellent work for us already."

He was nodding, back in my corner, but I had one more question. "Why were you spying on me?"

She patted my hand and let it go. "I wasn't. It was just a coincidence that someone saw you who thought your friend the journalist was someone else."

"I thought you didn't believe in coincidence."

"Every now and then," she said, heading for the door as Sam hurried to open it for her, "I'm wrong."

34

"What was all that about?" I said angrily after Sam put Ezola on the elevator and came back.

He was still grinning like this was the best afternoon of his life. "Don't let it throw you. She's always testing. It's just her way."

"Just her way?"

He nodded like nothing out of the ordinary had just occurred.

"Well, that's not the way I do business, and unless you can guarantee me that scene was an exception and not the rule, you can find yourself somebody else to join the team."

"Calm down, Catherine." His voice was soothing. "She's just nervous because this is a big move for the company and she really needs your help. She's sailing on uncharted waters and it's hard on her. She's used to being in control."

"So am I."

"That makes three of us," he said, smooth as silk. "But you're right. She goes too far sometimes. This was one of those times."

That mollified me a little, but not much.

"And who is this mysterious source that just happened to see me out with a friend and felt the need to report it?"

"Who knows?" he said, still soothing me with that voice. "Miss M. is famous for her spies. What I want to know is how you're going to get us included in that story Mr. Johnson is working on. That sounds exciting."

You have to give Sam credit for being single-minded. I had said B.J.'s name only once, and he was already on it.

"I'll talk to him about it and let you know."

"Is he any good?"

"He's the best," I said without hesitation.

Sam nodded his approval. "I'll take your word for it. Is there anything else?"

Miss Ezola's tantrum had obviously eaten up all the time Sam had for this project today.

"Nothing that won't wait," I said, gathering up my things.

Sam stood behind his desk, but didn't move to walk me out, which was fine with me. I'd had enough of both of them for one afternoon. When I stepped outside, the success-story secretary brushed by me without a word to usher in Sam's next appointment, a hard-eyed man in a dark blue suit with his hair pulled back in a small ponytail.

Ezola isn't the only one who doesn't believe in coincidence, I thought, after I had tipped the valet and was headed home. I flipped open my cell phone, dialed the Regency hotel, and asked to speak to Mr. Burghart Johnson.

He answered on the second ring, and I could hear CNN on the television. "Hello?"

"B.J.," I said. "It's Cat. Is four o'clock tomorrow still good for you?"

35

In less than an hour, B.J. was going to walk through my front door, and I was in a panic. He had been gracious about not bringing up my dramatic exit from the Peasant on Wednesday night, and agreed to meet me here so I could tell him about my bizarre exchange with Sam and Ezola. I had no idea why someone would be watching B.J. I didn't buy Ezola's coincidence explanation for one second, and I knew no one was watching me. The least I could do was let him know we had been observed and reported upon. What to do about it was up to him, but if somebody was accusing him of being a part of the very thing he was investigating, he had a right to know.

The problem was, to quote Miss Iona, he didn't need to know everything. But if he set foot in this house, he'd be surrounded by images of his look-alike daughter, and I wasn't ready for that yet. I may have had to let him make his confession, but I didn't have to jump ahead by making mine. So I had to de-Phoebe this house before he gets here. Starting with the living room.

I grabbed the photographs off the mantel, the one framed on the wall by the bookcase, and the one in the silver frame from New Mexico. Where to put them? I already felt guilty, so I couldn't just toss them in a closet or hide them in the pantry. She was my secret, but she's still my Baby Doll and she deserves some respect. *Upstairs!* He wouldn't be leaving the ground floor, so I'd put them in my bedroom for the time being and after he left, I'd put them back. I took the stairs two at a time and deposited the photographs gently on my bed, avoiding eye contact with the bright, open-faced images of my daughter. Why hadn't I ever realized how much she looked like B.J.?

Back downstairs in the kitchen, I stripped the refrigerator, which was crowded with snapshots from last summer. Here she is working in Louis's garden. Now she's back at the beach with Amelia trying to fly a kite. Here we are grinning outside the Fox Theatre on our way to see Erykah Badu work her magic, and again at a book signing with our arms around E. Lynn Harris. I took them all down, leaving the fridge looking strangely naked with only grocery coupons and a to-do list that was already two weeks old without one task checked off.

In my office, there were framed snapshots chronicling our journeys to places she'd pick from the map and then study, so when we got there she knew everything and could teach me as we went along without realizing how much she was learning, too. There were still a few baby-in-the-bath pictures that I kept for my own pleasure, although they make Phoebe groan when she sees them. My favorite of them all is the one we took on the day she got on the train to Fairfield. She wouldn't let us drive her, and she didn't want to fly because she wouldn't be able to see what it looked like on the ground between here and there.

Louis and Amelia and I took her to the train station and handed her over to the smiling attendant, who assured us he would deliver her safely to her destination and agreed to take our picture to commemorate the occasion. We are all smiling like maniacs, and in the middle Phoebe stands with her arms around me and Louis, holding up her fingers in two pairs of rabbit ears behind our heads. I didn't know it until I got the pictures back, and it still makes me smile. I took that one down, too, and then carted the whole lot upstairs with the others and laid them gently on the bed.

Okay, I thought, closing the door behind me like the minute I turned my back they might rise up and follow me back downstairs. *Weird mission accomplished.*

36

By the time I pulled together the things I'd promised B.J. before our dinner chitchat took a wrong turn, and made some tea to share, it was five minutes to four. I put the pot of peppermint tea and a couple of mugs on the coffee table and scanned the room for any signs of Phoebe. There were none. I glanced out the front window to be sure B.J. wasn't already heading up the front walk, and when I determined the coast was clear, I dashed down the hall to pee before he got there.

Good thing I did. What greeted me when I walked into the downstairs bathroom, which was always the one to which I directed company, was my daughter's smiling face sitting on Little Blackie, the sweet-tempered black horse with three white feet who helped her fall in love with riding. Framed and placed over the commode, it would be simply a backdrop for a woman using the facilities, but an eye-to-eye experience for a man once he assumed the required stance.

Jesus! I thought, taking it down immediately. *Have I missed any more?*

There was no time to consider the question. While I stood there, wondering where to stash Phoebe and Little Blackie, the doorbell rang like Big Ben precisely at four o'clock. There was no way to get upstairs unseen to place this photo among the others in a respectful pile on my bed, and it was too big for the medicine chest. The only thing to do was to prop it under the sink in the small cabinet that held extra toilet paper and a can of Comet. I hated to do it, but B.J. was standing on the front porch, so I slid the photograph carefully between two rolls of Charmin, closed the cabinet's double doors gently, and turned out the light behind me, not realizing until I came down the hallway that I had forgotten to pee.

He greeted me with a hug that didn't linger too long and stepped inside. He had been here many times before. My mother always liked B.J., and before he got an apartment our junior year, he spent as much time at our house as Louis did, which was considerable.

"This place never changes," he said, "except for the better."

"Thanks," I said, leading him into the

living room. "Come on in."

I sat beside him on the couch, telling myself it wasn't to get closer, but just to make it easier for me to pour the tea. He looked more relaxed than he had Wednesday night. He was wearing a creamy white sweater, a brown leather jacket, and a pair of perfectly distressed jeans that had gotten that way in the real world, not by being bleached by a designer.

B.J. wasn't handsome in a conventional way. If you took his face apart, none of the pieces would seem to fit together, but I think that's why he was so strangely appealing. His beauty is so unexpected that by the time you realize what a rare and lovely creature he is, you have already fallen in love with him. At least, that's how I think it happened to me. Lord knows where we'd be today if I had taken him to a Sweet Honey concert.

"I'm really happy that you called me," B.J. said. "I spent all night trying to figure out a way to call you."

"Nothing's changed about that," I said quickly, like I hadn't been obsessing about it ever since; rethinking my position, rewriting my exit line, looking for a way around the truth and not finding it. "But I wanted to tell you about an exchange I had with one of my clients yesterday afternoon."

"All right," he said, leaning over to pour his own tea and a cup for me. "Tell me everything."

Funny how when you're in the midst of a lie, everything sounds like an accusation. I took a sip of the steaming tea and tried to pull my thoughts together. "I told you I was doing some work for Mandeville Maids."

He nodded. When I had mentioned Ezola the other night, he was familiar with her work. Seemed *Miss M.* was already nationwide.

"I had a meeting over there yesterday. What I thought was going to be a routine exchange turned out to be an intensely weird session with the big boss that focused on somebody seeing us at dinner and reporting to her that I was fraternizing with a well-known pimp."

"*What?*"

"That's what I said, too. Seems that one of her spies identified you as Mr. Big in a thriving underground trade in women for sex. She accused me of being your mole inside the organization to recruit women."

He groaned. "These guys are unbelievable."

"I don't know what guys you're talking

about, but I told them you were a respected journalist and an old friend."

"Did they believe you?"

"Of course. It's the truth. She even apologized, after a fashion, but she was so aggressive when she came in, I thought we
were going to come to blows."

He looked at me and shook his head. "I
can't believe she would accuse you like
that. She must have had people making
end runs before."

"She said she had."

"How'd you get hooked up with them in
the first place?"

"They called me out of the blue. Admired my work and needed some help
reaching out to the international community, especially women. She's strange, and
her top guy is pretty weird, too, but her
program is great."

"Who's the guy?"

"His name's Sam Hall. His father was a
terrible slumlord back in the sixties. He
had a really awful reputation."

"I remember the father," B.J. said slowly.
"He was pretty old by the time I got here,
but one election there was a story about
him in the *Voice* because he was so notorious none of the candidates would take
his money."

I nodded. "That's the one. His son is out of the real estate business now and working for Mandeville Maids. He's over-seeing the project they hired me to work on."

"Is he a good brother?"

He was using the term *brother* to mean someone whose actions defined them on the side of the race. "Can't tell yet. I think he's okay. Not my kind of guy, but com-pletely committed to Ezola. Neither one of them has any reason to spy on me. I think somebody's keeping tabs on you. Any idea who?"

He stood up and walked over to the window. I took a sip of my tea and waited for him to tell me what he knew.

"Ever since I started working on this story," he said, "somebody's been trying to get me off of it. I'm close to whatever it is that can blow the lid off all these modern-day slave traders who seem to be using At-lanta as their home away from home out-side of Miami. At the very least, I can shine some light on what's happening to these women."

"Who do you think it is?" Etienne's face floated in front of my mind's eye like a spirit guide or an angel.

He shrugged and came back to sit beside

me. "I'm not sure, but I know nothing happened until I started asking questions about prostitution. Half the leads I had dried up or disappeared. People stopped calling me back, and the ones who did developed amnesia whenever I asked them a direct question."

It didn't make me feel good to realize that whoever was trying to shut down B.J.'s information pipeline had contacts who knew who I was and where I worked. How determined were they, and how far were they prepared to go?

"Are these guys dangerous?"

He looked at me, then reached into his jacket pocket, pulled out that ever-present reporter's notebook, flipped to a blank page, and wrote *10 for 10* at the top.

"What's that mean?"

"Ten dollars for ten minutes," he said. "That's what they charge."

"That's what *who* charges for *what?*"

"These guys are taking girls as young as twelve or thirteen and charging people a flat rate of ten dollars for ten minutes alone with them. Let's say they've got ten girls who are seeing four customers an hour."

"Four an hour?"

"They give them five minutes in between."

This was making me sick. "Five minutes? That's not even enough time to wash!"

He looked at me. "They don't wash."

The full magnitude of what he was saying began to dawn on me. I had been looking for contacts to take me into that world and help me find Etienne, but the specifics of what I would find there hadn't fully taken shape in my mind.

B.J. was still scribbling numbers. "Ten girls seeing four customers an hour at ten dollars apiece."

It sounded like a question on the SAT test from hell. "If they work five hours a day, that's two hundred dollars a day."

"Per woman," B.J. said. "So it's two thousand dollars a day. Let's say they have one day off for traveling to the next stop, so they work an average of six days a week."

Six days a week at twenty men a day? How long could they survive it? How long would they want to?

"That's twelve thousand dollars a week, at fifty-two weeks a year."

He wrote down a figure and turned the notebook in my direction. "They stand to make over a half million dollars a year."

The figure sounded unbelievable. "All

that from ten women? What if they could find a hundred?"

B.J. looked at me, closed the notebook, and put it away. "They're working on it," he said. "That's why they're dangerous. In the meantime, they don't need me shining a lot of light in their direction, especially here."

"Why especially here?"

"Because black women run this town. From what I hear, they took care of the pimps over on Stewart Avenue, and once they see what's going on here, they'll take care of this, too."

It had been a long struggle to get it done, but several years ago Atlanta women took on a group of notorious, homegrown pimps who were shamelessly recruiting girls as young as eight and ten years old. Pimping was still a misdemeanor then, and the profits were always high enough to outweigh the risks, or they used to be. But after a while, the pimps got so bold that a black woman judge couldn't stand it anymore and she started talking publicly about the baby prostitutes who were showing up in her courtroom every week. Politicians got involved; so did mothers, social workers, doctors, feminist activists.

The pimps, being pimps, refused to take

low, and pretty soon, it became all-out warfare for the future of these little kids. Finally, even the state legislature and the churches had to get involved, and when the dust cleared, pimping had been reclassified as a felony and the most notorious lawbreakers had been sent away for twenty-year sentences that left them visibly shaken, and left the women who had taken them on one step closer to reclaiming the streets their daughters walked to school every day.

"Should I be nervous?"

"No," he said. "Just be careful."

"How careful?"

"I'm going to Miami. I've got a source down there who's still willing to talk. By the time I get back, I'll have a better idea of what I'm up against."

It hadn't really occurred to me that he'd be back so soon. I wondered how long he'd be around then, but couldn't think of a way to ask him. "Maybe while you're gone I can get Sam to tell me who Ezola's source was for the rumor about you."

"I don't want to get you involved in this."

"I'm already involved in it," I said. "Whoever is spying on you is also spying on me."

"You've got a point there," he said slowly. "Maybe I'll ask him myself. You told them I was a hotshot journalist?"

"The hottest," I said.

"Then tell him I'd like to have an interview so he can tell me all about his new project."

That made me smile.

"What?"

"He'll be delighted," I said. "In fact, I already told him I was going to try to get you interested."

B.J. smiled, too. "Can you set it up for when I get back?"

"Consider it done," I said. "It really made me feel strange to know we were being watched. I'd like to know who it was."

"Me, too."

There was a short silence between us, so I filled it. "I've pulled some information together for you," I said quickly. "Would you like to take a look at it?"

"It's been a long day. How about if I take it with me?"

"All right," I said, wondering if his "long day" comment meant he was getting ready to go, and realizing that I wasn't ready to let him.

"This isn't the part where we have to

make chitchat again, is it?" B.J. said, smiling at me as I cast around in my brain for a way to make him linger.

"No," I said, suddenly inspired. "This is the part where we go look at the sunset."

"That's the best offer I've had in ages," he said, and his face told me it was true. "As I recall, the top step of your back porch is the best seat in the house."

I had been watching sunsets from that top step all my life, almost like a meditation, and B.J. used to like to sit with me sometimes. Louis didn't have the patience for watching sunsets, but B.J. knew how to enjoy the way the light changes from golden to pale pink at the same moment the sky goes from blue to shades of orange, and you know it's only a matter of time before the moon appears and changes that same light to silver. If you've got a loving friend nearby, that's when you probably lay your head on his shoulder or touch his hand, just to say, *I see it, too.*

"You've probably seen some sunsets that put this one to shame," I said, lifting the hook on the back screen door and stepping outside.

"I've seen some spectacular displays, that's for sure," he said, following me out and taking a seat on the step beside me.

"Those beaches where rich kids go to spend their parents' money have some that you can't believe. They make a whole ritual out of watching it, but it always ends up in some kind of beer-drunk bacchanal, so that takes away from the overall experience."

"I'll bet," I said, loving the smell of Amelia's roses and the softness of the breeze that blew by us like a kiss. "Kind of like Mardi Gras at the beach."

"Afghanistan has some amazing sunsets, too, especially up in the mountains. The air is so clear that the colors are almost too vibrant. It's like looking into the sun. You want to, but your eyes can't stand it."

We were sitting close enough to touch, but we didn't. We had sense enough just to watch the sky for signs and be glad we had stayed alive long enough to find ourselves here again with another chance to get it right, whatever *it* was, or is, or is gonna be. So we sent out a thank-you to the universe, or at least I did, and the universe sent a sunset worthy of the rich kids, which must have been the sign B.J. was looking for, because he leaned over and touched my hand gently. When I didn't object, he picked it up and kissed my palm, his lips soft against my skin.

"I'd better go," he said.

"All right." The silence and the sunset had weakened my defenses to the point where I was afraid that if I started talking, I really would tell him everything.

The neighborhood was in that quiet moment just before dinnertime, and when I walked him out front, we were the only people on the street. B.J. turned to me, and if he had asked me a direct question, there was no way I wouldn't have answered, but he didn't.

He just leaned down and kissed my cheek. "I'll call you."

"All right." Just a few more seconds and he'd be gone.

"Cat?" He had started down the stairs and then doubled back.

Remain calm! "Yes?"

"I'm sorry."

"Sorry for what?"

"For whatever I did that kept you away from me for the last eighteen years." The pain in his eyes matched the pain I felt when he said it. Eighteen years is a whole lifetime, and for what?

"I'm so sorry," he said softly. "And if you let me try to make it right, I swear to you, I will."

He didn't wait for me to answer. He just

turned around and walked down my front steps, out onto Peeples Street, and turned right toward the MARTA station. I watched him until he was about to disappear into the shadows of the huge weeping willow that dominates Amelia's yard and droops its branches over the sidewalk like a lace curtain at your grandmother's bedroom window. At the very last minute, he turned around, raised his hand, waved once, and was gone.

37

I guess I could feel worse, but I don't know how. I let him apologize like he had done me wrong, when I made my choices all by myself. Back inside, I looked around at all the places where Phoebe's picture was supposed to be and all I saw were empty spaces. It didn't even look like my living room, which only reminded me of how deep in this lie I had managed to plant myself and how hard it was going to be to dig myself out. There was no way I could keep lying like this. It was exhausting, and he deserved better. We all did.

I went upstairs, gathered up all of Phoebe's pictures, and put them back where they belonged. B.J. would never be able to fulfill that promise to "make it right" if he didn't even know what was wrong. Every picture I put back in place seemed to accuse me through my daughter's innocent eyes, and she was right. Her father was a good man, trying to get better. Who was I to deny her a place in his life?

I replaced the picture in the bathroom

last and it made me feel worse. Phoebe didn't deserve to be stashed away under the sink like a mildew repellent. All the perfect rocking chairs and creative homeschooling in the world couldn't make that anything but wrong. There was a lump in my throat the size of Stone Mountain, and I realized I was closer to tears than I had been in a long time. There was only one person who could understand. I straightened the picture back into its usual place, sent a mental apology to Baby Doll, and went to call Louis.

The phone rang four times, and I was about to hang up and go in search of him in Amelia's garden when he picked up the phone. He barely had time to say hello before I started babbling.

"This isn't working," I said. "I thought I could take it, but I can't. It's just too much to deal with right now. I love my daughter, but this is driving me crazy!"

He waited until I stopped to catch my breath, the same technique he always uses when Phoebe's ranting about one thing or another. Was I ranting?

"Are we talking about your new job or your old boyfriend?" he said calmly.

"My job is fine," I said. "It's B.J. who's driving me crazy."

"I talked to him this morning. He sounded pretty sane to me."

"You're not listening to me." I moved effortlessly from ranting to whining. "He's not crazy. *I am!*"

My voice tried to go up at the end, which would definitely have qualified as wailing, so I brought it back by sheer force of will and took a deep breath.

"You're not crazy," Louis said. "Highstrung, maybe, but you are one of the sanest women I know."

"Which doesn't say much for your lady friends."

"What lady friends? You're it, so you can't go crazy on me."

"What about Amelia?"

"She's in another category," he said. "You are, as always, in a class by yourself."

He was so sweet. He could probably hear the craziness in my voice. "What am I going to do?"

"Tell me what happened."

"He . . . We . . ." What could I say to make Louis know what I was feeling? "I think I still . . . like him."

Louis was waiting for more, but that was pretty much it. "You still *like* him?"

"Yes." That lump had taken up permanent residence in my throat, so I swallowed hard around it. "More than I thought I would."

"I see." Louis was hedging his bets.

"I don't think you do," I said. "He apologized."

"For what?"

"For all crimes, real and imagined."

"Did you accept his apology?"

Why did the question finally make me cry? I wiped away the tear with the back of my hand. "He didn't even know what he was apologizing for." I sniffed loudly.

"Sweetie?" Louis's voice was so gentle. "Do you want me to come over?"

"No, I'm okay."

"You don't sound okay."

There wasn't much I could do about that, so I didn't say anything. I just sniffed again.

"Are you still up for dinner with the four of us at Amelia's on Monday?"

It had seemed like a good idea at the time, but now the thought of spending another evening with B.J. seemed like torture. Louis and Amelia would just make it harder to sustain the lies and evasions. I could just see the three of us, who had no history of lying to one another in any combination, trying to talk with Phoebe's phantom presence hovering over the proceedings, waiting to be invited to sit down.

"I really don't think I can handle it."

I waited for him to try to talk me into coming or to tell me how disappointed Amelia would be, or, worst of all, to say that I was just being silly, but he didn't do any of those things, which is why I love him.

"Today is Friday," he said like he was checking his calendar to be absolutely certain. "Monday night is a long time from now. Why don't you wait and see how you feel then?"

"What's going to happen in a couple of days?"

"Who knows? What have you got to lose?"

"My *sanity?*"

"An overrated commodity, at best," he said. "You'll never miss it. Now forget about your troubles and come on over here and watch *The Hulk* with me on pay-per-view."

To test his theory, I did just that, and you know what? Two glasses of wine and a bowl of microwave popcorn later, I didn't miss my sanity at all.

38

Miriam reported for work on Monday. Amelia's letting her finish up her internship on half days so she can start spending mornings over here, since I'm swamped and could really use the help. She arrived with a large newsboy cap pulled low over her eyes, but when she took it off, her hair was neatly braided in cornrows that circled her head like ribbons. Without that awful wig, her beauty was even more obvious. I tried not to think about all those numbers B.J. had written in his notebook: *10 for 10.*

"Bravo," I said, as she patted her hair shyly with her long, slender fingers, waiting for my reaction. "I love your braids."

"Bravo," she said, smiling happily. "I love them, too."

We went over her duties — answering the phone, answering routine e-mails, helping with research, and, of course, keeping up with our search for Etienne. But I didn't have to tell her that. Then I gave her a quick tour of the house, since she was going to be working here and I wanted her to be comfortable. I told her she was welcome to anything in the refrigerator. She was still painfully thin and I was already making plans to fatten her up.

We finished up in the kitchen, and when I asked her if she had any questions, she pointed to the refrigerator door.

"Is that your daughter?"

I nodded. "That's Phoebe. She's away at school."

We stood there looking at Baby Doll's laughing face, and Miriam smiled, too.

"You must miss her."

"I do," I said. "She's all the way up in Massachusetts."

I might as well have said, *She's summering on Mars.* Massachusetts was another world to Miriam, who had never even seen snow.

"But you talk to her on the telephone?"

"Sure," I said, "but she's mad at me right now, so I haven't talked to her lately."

I heard myself speaking in a tone that made light of the situation, but Miriam looked confused and concerned.

"Your daughter is *mad* at *you?*"

She couldn't get her mind around the idea of it. How could she? With her own mother so far away, maybe even dead, the idea of such an estrangement was inconceivable.

"Not really," I said, trying to gloss it over. "She just thinks she is. I'm sure we'll talk soon."

"And then she will be happy again," Miriam said softly. "It is hard for a daughter to be so far from her mother."

It dawned on me that I had been so busy with how hard it was on me, I hadn't really focused on how hard it must be for Baby Doll.

"Yes," I said. "I know."

My new assistant had a way of saying things so simply sometimes that you couldn't get around them. The question was, Why would you even try?

39

On Monday afternoon, I called Louis and told him I'd see him tonight at dinner. Not because suddenly I wanted to, but because there was no way I was going to tell Amelia I was blowing off dinner at her house because I was afraid to sit at the table with B.J.

Afraid of what? she'd say in typical Amelia fashion, and what could I say? *Of telling the truth? Of not telling the truth? Of him asking why I haven't returned any of his three phone calls so far? Of not being the full-grown, in-control, in-demand, always-on-top-of-things free woman I know myself to be?*

None of those reasons would strike a chord in Amelia, who seems to lack the gene for lying. That will immediately endear her to B.J. They've never met, but I have no doubt they'll like each other. Louis already likes him, so he and Amelia will be busily tele-graphing their approval of allowing him into Phoebe's life while I try to figure out whether to let him into mine. Their combined positive psychic energy will be a powerful challenge to me as I try to be myself without being my *real* self. Whatever that means.

It took me forever to get dressed. It was like picking a costume for a character I was agreeing to play. Eliminate all colorful ethnic clothes and unique jewelry that might draw the question that must be answered with these words: *My daughter gave it to me for my thirty-fifth birthday.* Or *My daughter and I bought identical ones in an outdoor market in Sri Lanka.* Those were unnecessary lies that would sap my energy, distracting me from the one lie that had to be maintained a little longer. So I finally settled on a green silk tunic and a black satin skirt that was cut perfectly for a person like me with a small waist and hips to spare. I put on my chunky turquoise necklace, more for luck than for looks, and enough Jamaican silver bangles to scare off the evil eye with their jangling, and a pair of sandals with just enough heel to make me feel like a grown-up. Turning around in front of the mirror, I finally liked what I saw. The pile of discarded pants, skirts, tops, and a dress or two that lay scattered on every available surface seemed a small price to pay for looking like I wanted to look — cool, calm, and collected. None of which I was, but presentation was half the battle, and I had a date for dinner.

40

When I walked up on the back porch and slipped out of my shoes in deference to the house rules, I could see Amelia in the kitchen taking something out of the oven. I waited until she set the hot pan down on the top of the stove before I tapped on the back window and waved.

She waved back, her hands encased in big, yellow oven mitts, and motioned me inside.

"Hey, neighbor," she said, extending her cheek for me to kiss while she basted a beautiful peace of steelhead trout topped with slices of lemon and Amelia's own special blend of herbs. It smelled as good as it looked, and it was immediately obvious that even if B.J. and I were going to have another couple of hours of sublimating sex drive for appetite, the evening still wouldn't be a total loss.

"Hey, yourself," I said. "What can I do to help?"

She was wearing tight black pants and a white sweater that draped a little on one side to reveal a perfectly toned shoulder and create a flattering angle for her graceful neck. Her little Afro was newly cropped, and her skin was glowing like the pearl earrings that were her only jewelry.

"Nothing," she said. "This trout has another twenty minutes, and everything else is just about done."

She spooned a clear, buttery broth over the fish where it rested on a rack. Amelia loves to cook and her kitchen is the biggest room in the house, with the stove anchoring one end and the breakfast nook at the other.

"You met B.J.?"

She nodded. "I like him."

"I knew you would."

"Cute, too." She slid the pan back in the oven and closed it. "Also seems to have some sense, although I just met him, so I don't know how much is substance and how much is charm."

"He's a good guy," I said.

"With an abundance of the aforementioned charm." She took off her oven mitts, hung them on a hook beside the stove, and turned back to me with the barest suggestion of a frown. "So tell me again what the problem is?"

She was already lobbying, and I hadn't

even gotten in the door good.

"Timing," I said, having anticipated her question and the answer most likely to satisfy her, and me, until I could figure this out. "It's all about the timing."

"Is that it?" Her face brightened immediately. "Timing?"

I nodded.

"All right, then. *That* I can understand. How do you like the table? Those are the last of the sunflowers."

As usual, once Amelia had an answer that satisfied her, she moved on. The round table in the breakfast nook was set for four of us with Amelia's bright blue Mexican dishes and a tall vase full of sunflowers that seemed unaware that they were the last of the lot. Two thick, red candles and boldly designed, brightly colored linen made things look friendly and festive. I relaxed, realizing nothing weird was going to happen in my girlfriend's kitchen. These were not just my friends. They were my best friends. How safe could I be?

"It's lovely," I said. "I can't believe you did all this without my help."

"B.J. is the one who needs your help," she said, peeking into a pot on the stove and releasing a fragrant promise of something spicy into the air.

"How do you figure that?" I said, hoping he hadn't confided in her about his blanket apology the other night.

"Louis is trying to talk him into coming to work for the *Sentinel*."

"What?" He couldn't live here. Where was I supposed to stash his daughter?

"Go on in there and see for yourself. He's been lobbying like crazy ever since B.J. walked in the door."

"Aren't you coming?" I sounded like a kid on the first day of school who just realized Mommy was leaving.

She grinned at me. "I think you know everybody. Go on! I'll be in there in a minute."

She was back at the stove, and I didn't want to distract her in the last few minutes, when the meal comes together or falls apart based on the skill and focus of the cook. I patted my turquoise necklace for luck and headed down the hall in a house I know almost as well as I know my own. Amelia is a hard-nosed lawyer out in the world, but her house is a soothing space where rooms seem to flow into each other as effortlessly as she moves through her pool. Jason's upstairs bedroom remains his domain whenever he comes to visit his mother, but the rest of the house is all about white rugs, floor pillows, white couches, and candlelight.

Tonight was no exception. The cozy living room was lit with white pillars on mirrored trays, and their mild vanilla fragrance mixed with the smell of the roses wafting through Amelia's open windows. They were probably the last of the season, too. Even in Atlanta, fall has to finally come into its own. Beside the front door, Louis and B.J. had obediently left their shoes. As I walked into the room to greet them, my bare feet didn't announce my arrival. From where they sat at opposite ends of the couch, their backs were turned, and they were so focused on their discussion neither one saw me.

I took two steps in and stopped. Should I clear my throat? Go out and come in again? I was definitely going to have to work on my entrances. This one was undeniably underwhelming.

"I'm already working on a story," B.J. was saying. "I can't just drop it because your reporter can't find the thread."

B.J. had heard Louis's thread lecture almost as many times as I had.

"Then give me the one you're working on!"

B.J. sighed. "I can't do that."

295

"Why not? You said yourself nobody's waiting for it. You're doing it on spec, hoping somebody will bite on the basis of your reputation, but it's a new world, brother. Nobody much cares about real news except me and you. All the black newsmagazines except *Jet* are out of business, and even if you get it published in one of the white ones, they'll bury it. At the *Sentinel*, I can promise you page one."

"Right next to your editorials?"

He was actually considering this. Were they both crazy?

"In the prime spot," Louis said. "Above the fold."

B.J. didn't reject the offer outright, so I used the moment to announce myself and hopefully change the flow of this conversation until I could get Louis alone. "Am I interrupting something?"

They leaped to their feet like the gentlemen their mamas and daddies raised them to be and turned to me in tandem.

"How could you?" Louis said, coming around to kiss me on the cheek.

I smiled at B.J. "Amelia said you might need some help in here."

He smiled back with no hint of annoyance at my ducking his phone calls since we'd watched the sunset. "She got that right."

B.J. was wearing dark pants and a well-cut black shirt. His bare feet were long and slender, with perfect toes that had never been squeezed into cheap shoes. Burghardt's people traced their family to the same tree that produced W. E. B. Du Bois, which is where B.J. got his first name. They couldn't remember when they hadn't had money.

Louis was dressed in a white linen shirt from Mexico that I know for a fact to be a gift from his goddaughter. The man may be a saint, but he's still clueless. He poured me a glass of white wine from the bottle resting comfortably in a silver ice bucket on the coffee table.

"I'm the one who needs help! If I can get this Negro to write for the *Sentinel*, people might buy it, or even better, *subscribe* to it. We'll be back on our feet in no time."

"Back in the black?" I said.

"Exactly," Louis said. "Talk to him!"

"How am I supposed to live in the meantime while we're still in the red?"

B.J. said "while *we're* still in the red." Not "while *you're* still in the red." Louis heard it, too. His lobbying was working, so he upped the ante.

"You know I'm not going to let you starve, brother," he said. "Six months is all

I'm asking. I've got a great big house and plenty of room. We can pay enough to feed you and pay any expenses associated with this story, including" — he paused dramatically — "underwriting your trip to Miami *and* a round-trip ticket to L.A. when you get back to take care of things there until you relocate."

Louis was speeding right along. How did he get from one story to relocating the man permanently before Amelia had time to serve dinner? Phoebe's shirt was working its spell, and it was all too fast for me. Louis was looking at B.J., waiting for an answer, but B.J. was looking at me.

"I won't need to go back to L.A.," he said. "I brought everything I need with me."

"Travelin' light?" I said, since the intensity of his gaze required some response, although that was probably not it.

"Old habits are hard to break."

"So is that a yes?" Louis said. "Tell me that's a yes."

"What's a yes?" Amelia said, walking into the room before B.J. could answer.

"I think the *Sentinel* has a new star reporter," Louis said. "Ask him."

Amelia turned to B.J. "Are you sure you want to do this? I've heard the editor over there is impossible."

"He's worse than that," B.J. said. "But I can handle him."

"So is that a yes?" Louis said again. "Or are we still negotiating?"

B.J. looked at Louis and then back at me, sipping my wine and staying under radar. "We're done negotiating. I just need to see if it's okay with Catherine."

Louis and Amelia both turned toward me, as surprised as I was. For my part, I choked on my wine, which wasn't very cool, but what kind of question was that? I hadn't even had a chance to adjust to his being here for a few weeks. Now he was ready to move into Louis's house, right around the corner, and put down roots. My so-called friends were boxing me in on all sides, and I didn't appreciate it. Not only that, I didn't know how to get out of it. Three pairs of eyes were trained on me like I had the answer to the last question on *Who Wants to Be a Millionaire?*

"You okay?" Amelia said when I stopped coughing. She looked concerned, like I might jump up and run out the back door before she could talk me out of it.

"I didn't mean to scare you," B.J. said apologetically.

"You didn't scare me; you surprised me. What do I have to do with it?"

He shrugged his shoulders. "I wouldn't want to do it if you didn't think it was a good idea."

He didn't say *why* I might not think it was a good idea. He didn't have to. Phoebe might as well have been curled up on those floor pillows, hugging her knees and waiting to see what I might say next, but Amelia stepped in and saved me like the good friend she is.

"Well, whether she does or whether she doesn't, I've got dinner on the table," she said, slipping her arm around my waist. "And around here nobody has to agree to anything on an empty stomach."

41

Dinner was wonderful. There was no more discussion about where I stood on the *Sentinel*'s star reporter, but I can't deny that my brain was busily considering the question like there was going to be a pop quiz between dessert (a wonderful lemon tart) and coffee (a strong Cuban blend that we drank from little white cups like B.J.'s espresso the first night we had dinner). Amelia and Louis kept the conversation light and lively, with occasional, more substantive forays into world events and local politics.

For his part, B.J. was a good storyteller. All of his adventures weren't as harrowing as the one he'd told to me. His descriptions of the swarms of golden butterflies he encountered in Colombia were like something out of a novel by Gabriel García Márquez, and his time spent with Buddhist monks in a place outside of Paris called Plum Village made me wish he actually would write the book people kept asking him about.

"You've been in such beautiful places,"

Amelia said. "I envy you your travels."

"The sad thing is," B.J. said, "that most of the time I was there to cover some kind of conflict. At first it was disconcerting. I couldn't get used to the juxtaposition of so much beauty and so much violence. Then one day my editor got tired of me going on and on about it, and she said, 'Would you like it better if the place where they were fighting was ugly?' Which is the real question, I guess. Not *where* the war is, but *why* there are wars at all."

Nobody said anything to that, since we knew it was a serious, but rhetorical question. There are always a million answers — the generals and the rebels make sure of that — but when you really think about it, there's no good reason to try to kill as many people as you can, for as long as you can, until the ones who are left surrender their lives, or their resources, or their culture, or their self-respect, or their ancestors, or their spirits, or their oil, until they get strong enough to throw you off their backs and the whole cycle starts all over again. Thinking about it can make you feel powerless and scared, and that was no way to end an evening that had evolved into one of the best I've had in too long.

"Do you remember that old song," I said

to Louis, "where the guy has a dream about all the soldiers refusing to fight another war? My mother used to sing it."

Louis shook his head, frowning. "I don't think so."

"I remember it," B.J. said. "She sang it to me when I was interviewing all those Vietnam vets."

"That's right. She was talking about the march on the Pentagon."

"Sing it," said Amelia.

"I don't remember all the words," I said. "What's the first line?"

B.J. grinned a little sheepishly. "I'm a better writer than I am a singer."

"My mother said it's the spirit that counts when you're trying to end a war," I said. "Not whether or not you sing on key."

He took a deep breath and started singing in a strong, clear baritone voice that would have guaranteed him regular solos in any church choir in Atlanta. " 'Last night I had the strangest dream . . .' "

He might as well have handed me the sheet music. In just those few words it all came back like a childhood memory, including the harmony, which my mom always sang in her lovely alto. I looked at him and fell right in.

" '. . . I've never had before. I dreamed the world had all agreed to put an end to war.' "

Our voices got stronger as we went along, and the words I forgot, he remembered, until we got through the whole thing, and by the last note of our impromptu duet, whatever defenses I had left were gone. I loved this man and always would. I loved his mind and his heart and his stories and his secrets and his promise to *make it right*. I wanted that to be my promise, too. I might not be able to stop a war, but I can sure declare a cease-fire until we get some peace talks going.

"It's all right with me," I said to B.J., as if he had just articulated his relocation question. "About you coming to work for the *Sentinel*, I mean."

I could practically hear Louis holding his breath and Amelia sending up a little prayer.

"Well," B.J. said softly, "can I take that as a yes?"

42

Once Louis and B.J. shook hands to seal the deal, Amelia opened a bottle of champagne and another of sparkling cider, so we could toast this new partnership that was going to drag all of us, some kicking and screaming more than others, into the next phase of our lives. Sure, I was nervous, but I felt strangely relieved, like when you finally break down and go have a physical. You're still worried at some level about the outcome, but once you hop up on that table, you've set things in motion and there's no turning back.

It was getting late and B.J. had an early flight. He declined Louis's offer to take him back to his hotel, since our favorite editor was above the legal limit, but acquiesced to Amelia's request that he not take the train so late at night. The compromise was that Amelia would call a cab and I would walk B.J. past the pool so he could see the restoration and then wait with him out front until the cab came.

Of course, this was Amelia's way of giving us a moment to ourselves, and we took it, wending our way down the path through Amelia's rose garden until it opened out into the mermaid's domain. The people who sold the house to Amelia had neglected the pool for years, and the last time B.J. saw it, there were leaves and fetid water in the bottom, a ripped canvas hanging over the top, and many missing tiles around the edges. Now he stopped at a beautiful little oasis where swimmers and supplicants could pay homage to the mermaid and renew themselves.

The lights were on in the pool, but not around it, so the rippling water gave off an almost otherworldly aquamarine glow. B.J. walked slowly to the pool's edge and looked down. I stood beside him, but not too close.

"I remember you talking about this mermaid," he said. "She looks exactly like you described her."

"Amelia and Jason did a great job. They did it all themselves over the better part of a year."

"He sounds like a good kid."

"He's great," I said, bragging like I was his mother and feeling a sudden, almost overpowering urge to tell him about his own great kid. I repressed it, watching the mermaid listening to her shell and hating my own cowardice.

"Correct me if I'm wrong," B.J. said. "But I think I still make you a little uncomfortable."

I looked at him. "Things have been moving pretty fast around here since you showed up."

"Shall we slow them down just a little bit?"

"That might be a good idea."

"All right," he said, and turned toward me with a little bow and a smile. "May I have this dance?"

I was totally up for some romantic role-playing. "Is it a slow dance?"

"The slowest."

"But there's no music," I said, moving into his arms, but keeping my distance. The nuns used to tell my Catholic girl-friends to always leave room for the Holy Ghost between them and their dancing partners. I left enough space for the Holy Trinity.

He looked down at me and grinned. "Then I guess we'll have to sing."

"Okay. Pick a tune."

We were already doing a little swaying thing to the music in our heads, so it didn't really matter. Pretending to dance gave us an excuse to be in each other's arms at the end of a long, strange night. He could have said "America the Beautiful," and I would have hit it.

"I think I've done all the singing I can do in one night."

"No problem," I said. "I'm a world-class whistler."

He raised his eyebrows and looked at me around the Holy Ghost. "That's something I didn't know about you."

"There's lots of things you don't know about me."

"That's part of your charm," B.J. said softly. "You're a woman of mystery."

You have no idea, I thought. We were moving around in perfect sync, although we hadn't named a song yet. Even after all these years and all these tears, we were still so physically in tune with each other it was like slow dancing with your shadow. I hoped he wouldn't hate me when I told him the truth. All I could do was hope for the best, but for right now, I disregarded the nuns like a true mermaid-worshiping pagan and laid my cheek on B.J.'s chest so he could kiss the top of my head like he always used to, which, of course, he did immediately. We stopped moving then and just stood there looking at each other.

"Can I come in?" he said softly.

"No," I whispered. "Too many ghosts."

"I'm not a ghost, Cat."

He didn't feel like a ghost. "I know."

From out front, I heard the cab blow its horn.

B.J. smiled at me. "Saved by the bell."

I smiled back and we stepped away from each other.

"Can we get together when I come back?" he said as we walked together down the front walk where the big yellow cab was waiting.

I nodded. "Of course."

"Good," he said, opening the door as the bored-looking driver smothered a yawn. For us, this could be the start of something. For him, it was just the end of another long night. "I'm sure there's a ghost-free zone around here someplace."

"I'll keep my eyes open," I said, stepping back from the curb as the cab pulled off into the darkness. I watched it until it turned the corner, and in the quiet I began whistling just loud enough for me to hear.

Last night I had the strangest dream, I never had before. . . .

And you know what? I might not be world-class, but I wasn't half-bad.

I dreamed the world had all agreed, to put an end to war. . . .

43

The next morning, the phone woke me up early, and I found myself hoping it was B.J. to tell me he'd enjoyed our dance last night as much as I had. "Hello?"

"Am I speaking with Catherine Sanderson?"

The man's tone, an unappealing mixture of nervous and imperious jolted me awake. I didn't know anybody who routinely spoke like a disapproving potentate.

"This is Ms. Sanderson. To whom am I speaking?"

The only time I ever say *to whom* is when I'm trying to be snotty. This guy's voice brought that out in me immediately.

"My name is Robert Mayson, and I got a letter asking me to take a . . . a test . . . to establish —"

Oh, no! I had thought my interaction with Phoebe's fantasy fathers was over, but apparently this one had been lollygagging around and was just making contact. Robert Mayson's name didn't ring a bell, and I didn't want it to.

"Excuse me for interrupting you, Mr. Mayson, but I can spare us both any further embarrassment," I said, talking over his sputtering. "I know you are not my daughter's father, and pretty soon she's going to know it, too, so you won't be hearing from her again."

He let out a sigh of relief. "Thank God! You have really taken a load off my mind."

"Sorry for your inconvenience," I said.

"Inconvenient is what it would be, too," he said. "I'm getting ready to go into politics, and I can't afford to have any skeletons rattling around in my closet, if you know what I mean."

"I understand. Well, good-bye then and —"

"Hold on a second," he said, sounding less nervous and more bossy. "I need to ask you a couple of questions, if you've got a minute."

My heart sank. I felt like Al Pacino in *The Godfather* scene that guy on *The Sopranos* likes to imitate. *Every time I try to get out, they pull me back in.* "Yes?"

"Why did she think it might be me? Forgive me if this sounds awful, but I don't even remember you."

I didn't remember him either, so we were even. "It doesn't matter. You won't hear from us again."

"I have no reason not to believe you," he said.

There was a *but* hanging in the air like a birthday piñata.

"But I'm still going to have to ask you to sign a notorized statement to the effect that I am not your child's father."

"A what?"

"My campaign manager says it's the only way to be sure I'm not vulnerable to any kind of blackmail. Politics is a rough business."

"You're kidding, right?"

"I couldn't be more serious."

If I was looking for a sign, this was it, as big as Halley's comet. "Listen, what's your name? Robert? That won't be necessary. I'm not a blackmailer and I'm not a politician."

"Then you refuse to sign?"

He wasn't listening. "The only way this is going to be a problem for you is if you ever call this number again. Do I make myself clear?"

I only say *do I make myself clear* when I'm being *really* snotty, and I was. This guy could go ahead and be elected president, for all I cared. The only thing I knew for sure was that the next time I laid eyes on Burghardt Johnson, I was going to tell him about his daughter. *Enough is enough.*

44

The Atlanta Association of Black Journalists'
annual awards dinner is always a glittering,
formal affair, held in the ballroom of a
downtown hotel, where the black press turns
out en masse to honor their own. It also
draws a lot of politicians, advertisers, entrepreneurs, and community leaders. In addi-
tion to being a gathering where you are
certain to run into lots of old friends, it is
also a hotbed of gossip and innuendo where
rumors are disseminated and dissected with
lightning speed. Anyone who wanted to get
the word out about any- and everything
could simplify the process by coming to this
event and dropping a few exclusive tidbits
into a few attentive ears. There are usually at
least two or three hot items making the
rounds before the cocktail hour is over, and
another three or four by the time everybody
gets situated at their assigned tables. But tonight there was only one thing buzzing
around in every conversation: Burghardt
Johnson was writing for the *Sentinel*.

Louis had lost no time in recasting his

front page to announce B.J.'s refugee series, and folks were dying to know the details. B.J. was an AABJ success story. He had joined the group as a freshman journalism student and done freelance work for the *Atlanta Voice* before he graduated. He maintained his membership while he was in West Africa and for several years after that. As his byline began to appear in more and more national and international publications, AABJ's membership kept up with his work with the pride of an extended circle of uncles and aunts.

When he dropped out of sight several years ago, they assumed the rumor about the book was true and didn't worry until they realized several years had gone by and no book had appeared. Their excitement over Louis's announcement was heightened by their relief that B.J. was still a part of their small but intensely loyal family. The fact that he had resurfaced on the staff of tonight's honoree only served to underscore their good judgment in recognizing the *Sentinel* with their Pioneers Award.

Handsome in his tux, and sporting a perfect bow tie, Louis was shaking hands, sharing hugs, and accepting congratulations with equal aplomb. Wisely forgoing another attempt at Amelia's wrap-and-drape concoction, I had spruced up my long, navy blue, *almost* formal dress with my mother's real pearls and let the stylist at Roots International twist my hair into a lovely cascade of braids that she pinned on top of my head like a crown.

I felt glamorous and really happy for my friend. Louis, always Mr. Cool, was so excited when I went by to pick him up that he almost couldn't stand still long enough for me to tie his tie. You'd never know it now as he leaned down to hug Miss Iona and whisper something in her ear that made her throw back her head and laugh out loud. Then he was shaking hands with Blue Hamilton, kissing Flora Lumumba, and hugging her husband, Hank. Behind them, I could see Precious and Kwame Hargrove on either side of a very pregnant Aretha, who was due any day now. Precious was shaking hands like a good politician, but Kwame was totally focused on guiding his wife to their table so she could sit down.

From where I was standing, I was out of the flow of people to and from the bar and I could sip my wine and watch the crowd gathering. Amelia had admonished me to observe and remember all details, serious and superficial, so I could give her a complete report when she got back. I was on my j-o-b.

Sam spotted me at the same time I saw him entering the ballroom. He raised a hand in greeting and headed my way. There was an attractive young woman on his arm who looked familiar, but I couldn't quite place her.

"Catherine!" he said, leaning over for a quick peck on my cheek. "I was hoping you'd be here."

"Louis Adams is a good friend," I said. "I wouldn't miss it."

"Maybe you can introduce me," he said. "I've read the *Sentinel* from time to time, but I've never met its illustrious editor."

"I'd be happy to," I said, but I wanted to add, *as soon as you introduce me to your date.* The woman was standing silently at Sam's elbow like a doll, but she didn't look happy to be there. Maybe that was why he was ignoring her. Or maybe that was why she was looking that way. I couldn't tell yet.

"That's quite a coup for such a small paper," Sam said. "Is Mr. Johnson around tonight, too?"

"He's in Miami," I said. "But I mentioned the project to him before he left, and he'd like to talk to you when he gets back."

Sam looked pleased. "That is good news. From the buzz that's greeted the announcement, I think we're guaranteed some significant exposure."

He didn't look any closer to acknowledging the woman beside him, so I turned to her and held out a hand. "Hello, I'm Catherine Sanderson."

"Desiree Williams." She sounded more pissed off than she looked.

Sam looked surprised at my introduction. "You met Desiree at my office. My secretary, don't you remember? She's our success story."

"Of course I do." I was embarrassed that I hadn't recognized her, but that was such an insane moment, I didn't really look at her face. Besides, tonight she looked so elegantly and expensively pulled together in a strapless black gown and diamond drop earrings that she bore little resemblance to the working woman I'd barely glanced at the other day.

"I apologize," I said. "You look so different."

She didn't smile. "No problem."

"Can I get you ladies something to drink?"

"I'm fine," I said.

"Vodka and tonic," said Desiree. "With lime."

Sam moved to the bar and left us standing rather awkwardly together. I smiled at her. "Sam's very proud of your accomplishments."

"I owe it all to Mandeville Maids," she said, but something in her tone was a little sarcastic. "Where would I be without them?"

I tried a change of subject. "Are you from Atlanta?"

She shook her head firmly like the idea was absurd. "I'm from Fairfield, Connecticut."

Her diction was perfect. Her outfit was easily worth a grand, not to mention the jewelry. Her makeup was flawless and her manicure was professional. She seemed to have risen like a phoenix from the ashes of whatever disaster had left her doing janitorial work and emerged on the other side unscathed. I wanted to ask her to tell me her story, but Sam was back with her vodka and there wasn't time to pursue it before Louis broke away from his well-wishers to materialize at my side.

"Sorry for abandoning you," he said, smiling from me to Desiree to Sam.

"Louis Adams," I said. "Let me introduce you to Desiree Williams and Sam Hall."

Sam and Louis shook hands. Desiree inclined her head and sipped her drink, but she didn't say anything.

"Congratulations on your award and your new series," Sam said.

"Thank you," Louis replied, grinning happily. "The *Sentinel* is going to shake things up good around here, and you know what? It's about time!"

The AABJ president was at the podium urging people to settle down so the program could begin. Sam said he hoped to have a chance to talk with Louis again soon and guided Miss Williams to their seats. Louis took my hand and we headed for table one, where Miss Iona and Mr. Charles, Blue and Regina Hamilton, Hank and Flora Lumumba, and Precious Hargrove were already seated. Kwame and Aretha were sitting in the back in case they had to leave in a hurry. Babies on the way couldn't care less about where their mama's water broke. They were still on eternity time.

"So that's your boss, huh?" Louis said.

"I'm my own boss," I corrected him. "I'm an independent consultant."

"His girlfriend looked a little distant."

"That's his secretary. A former Mandeville Maid."

Louis raised his eyebrows. "I thought that kind of transformation happened only in the movies."

"Sometimes Atlanta will surprise you," I said as our tablemates spotted us and stood up for another round of hugs before the program actually got under way.

"Atlanta always surprises me." Louis smiled, giving my hand a little squeeze. "That's her great charm."

"Just like me." I smiled back.

"Exactly like you," he said. *Exactly.*

45

We talked and laughed our way through dinner as Louis greeted a stream of well-wishers. The timing of the announcement of B.J.'s series couldn't have been better. The *Sentinel* was back in a big way, and anybody who thought this evening was going to be a fond farewell to another fallen soldier would have to think again.

Louis headed for the stage after a glowing introduction that recounted the founding and history of the *Sentinel*, the selfless dedication of Louis Adams Sr., and his unsung role in the local and national communities of black journalists. He accepted the plaque from AABJ's president and waited for the applause to die down before he said his thank-yous. When he spoke, his voice was low and intimate, like it would have been if he had been talking to us over drinks in his favorite booth at Paschal's. We leaned forward as if pulled by an invisible string so we wouldn't miss a word.

"My father published the first issue of the *Sentinel* on August thirtieth, 1964, because he wanted to do something for freedom. He wanted to be the voice of a community in transition. A community that was realizing that its future depended on its willingness to come together and refuse to go along with business as usual. My father wanted us to get our news filtered through our own African-American eyes, because he knew that was the best chance we had of getting to the truth. Our truth. The truth of who and what and why we are."

"Take your time, brother!" said a man from the back of the room.

"His mission was to tell the truth no matter what the consequences for himself, or even for his family, because he believed that without the truth, men and women are powerless to take control of their communities and their lives. Well, I still believe that, and the mission of the *Sentinel* was then, is now, and always will be, to tell the truth to the people. No matter who tries to silence us. No matter who would counsel that it's better not to stir things up, or tell us the pursuit of truth is just a sixties dream that gets batted around every now and then by old radicals who can't figure out what to do next. The pursuit of truth is not a black history moment. It's a living, breathing quest, an endless journey that requires us to rise to the challenge by re-dedicating ourselves to the things that made the black press great — courage, clarity, and convictions."

He was interrupted by applause. Miss Iona was looking at him with her hands clasped under her chin and tears sparkling in her eyes. Mr. Charles was her favorite escort, but Louis Sr. had been her soul mate.

"So I accept this award on behalf of my father, and I know if he were here tonight, he'd want me to tell you to do three things. Tell the truth to the people. Subscribe to the *Sentinel*."

He looked over at Miss Iona beaming at him. "And do something for freedom today!"

People got to their feet in a standing ovation as Louis made his way back to our table, but before he sat down, he did one more thing for freedom. He stopped in front of Miss Iona and handed her the plaque, right in front of everybody, acknowledging for the first time what folks had been saying about her and Louis Sr. for years. Relieved at last of the need to pretend, the crowd roared its approval. I could see that Miss Iona was crying.

That's the thing about the truth, I guess. Once you start, it feels so good, you just can't stop.

46

There were two messages waiting when I got home. The first one was from B.J. to let me know he had some strong leads about Miriam's sister and saying he'd call me as soon as he got back. The second one was from Phoebe. She had called at nine o'clock, knowing I'd be at dinner with Louis, leaving no chance for me to pick up. Her voice sounded the same way it always did when she was asserting herself against the *mother.* Determined, but a little shaky.

"Hey, Mom, it's me."

Like I didn't recognize her voice from the first syllable of the first word. Like I didn't hear the air moving before she spoke. "I wanted to say . . . I just . . . I don't want to talk to you yet, but I just wanted to let you know the flowers got here."

Then there was a long pause, and I heard my daughter sigh.

"Thanks, Mom."

Then there was another long pause.

"Okay. I guess that's all. Good night."

I played it back twice to enjoy the sound of her voice. I wanted to call her and say, *That's not all*, Baby Doll. *This is only the beginning.*

47

The first story in B.J.'s series was a passionate overview of the refugee problem and an equally passionate promise to make it real for readers by putting a face on it. To illustrate what he meant, B.J. had written about a family of six from Guatemala, none of whom spoke English, who rented a broken-down house in Vine City and paid three times what they would have paid anywhere in the city because of an avaricious landlord who took advantage of them in every possible way. He showed the tremendous profits being made off of people's misery and named the absentee landlord, a well-known local businessman. The article was an eye-opener, and it achieved Louis's main goal: it got everybody talking. The issue sold out on the newsstands in two days. B.J. was due back from Miami tomorrow with the second installment, but tonight I was taking myself out to dinner alone.

Dusk was already turning into dark, and the streetlights flickered on as I walked down Oglethorpe. Chanterelle's Restaurant is a well-kept West End secret. Tucked away on an unassuming side street with Laundromats, union halls, and the new Krispy Kreme as nearby neighbors, the small storefront establishment serves up what can only be described as *gourmet* soul food. While the offerings may resemble the menu familiar to anyone who frequents black-owned restaurants — macaroni and cheese, baked chicken and dressing, barbecued ribs, collard greens, and candied yams — the skill of the owner/chef is such that in his hands, they become something succulent and special.

The chicken is perfectly tender and delicately flavored. The corn bread dressing smells of celery and sage and practically melts in your mouth. The vegetables are never soggy, the collards are spicy without being too hot, and the banana pudding and red velvet cake are tied for best dessert *ever.* On busy afternoons, the chef himself is likely to be standing behind the steam table, pointing out to newcomers that it's *sauce,* not *gravy* he's spooning onto that creamy mound of mashed potatoes they're holding out in his direction. He was as demanding and temperamental as any chef in a French five-star restaurant, and his clientele as patient as any long-suffering Parisians, and for the same reason: the food was just that good.

The streets were full of people shopping, heading home, hanging out. Traffic stopped at a pedestrian crosswalk to let an old woman cross without rushing, and the open door of the barbershop I was passing released the voices of laughing black men into the street. A young couple passed by dressed in the strange combination of skintight and supersize that defines their generation's fashion sense, and two women wearing the red and black colors of the Shrine of the Black Madonna greeted me with a friendly "Good evening, sister," as they hurried toward their destination. I felt so content and pleased to be where I was, I almost broke out into Mister Rogers's tune about *it's a beautiful day in the neighborhood.*

I didn't see Louis sitting on the other side of the room, deep in conversation with B.J., until I had picked up my order, found a table, put my napkin in my lap, and reached for my fork, which I promptly dropped into my mashed potatoes. What were they doing here? I didn't even know B.J. was back. Didn't he say he would call me? Did he call me? He didn't say *when* he would call me, but all that dancing in the dark and talking about *ghost-free zones* at least implied a call when the plane touched down, or while he was walking through the concourse at the airport, maybe even waiting at baggage claim, which always takes a while, but not after dinner at Chanterelle's. Plus, it's right up the street, so a call to say, "I'm back, and would you like to join us for dinner?" wouldn't have been out of the question.

But none of that had happened, and because it hadn't happened, I couldn't just take my tray and squeeze in at their table. Even worse, for some weird reason, it was suddenly embarrassing to be caught having dinner alone. What had been a perfect evening of enjoying my own company now seemed vaguely pathetic, even in these postfeminist years when everybody knows *it's okay*. As I sat there trying to decide if it was too late to get my order to go, Louis looked up, saw me, and waved. B.J. followed his eye and smiled with real pleasure.

I waved back and smiled with real confusion that I hoped was invisible to the naked eye. I had no reason to act like a petulant high school girl who had just busted her steady at the malt shop. B.J. and I were in the process of figuring out who and what we were. The old rules did not apply, and the new rules weren't even in place yet. All

I could do was try to stay in the moment and remain calm.

Louis left B.J. to hold their table and came over. I stood up to hug him before we cleared the aisles and sat back down. Chanterelle's fills every available space with chairs and tables. The crowded aisles between them don't permit much table hopping and hovering.

"Hey, sweetie," Louis said. "Eating alone?"

"Yep," I said. "When did B.J. get back?"

"Last night," Louis said. "We've been working nonstop. This new piece is going to blow them out of the water."

"Last night?" He'd been here all day and never called me? This couldn't be a good sign, but if it was a bad sign, what was it a bad sign of?

"Around midnight. I picked him up so you couldn't make him a better offer."

Louis was grinning, but I knew he wasn't kidding and I grinned back. Why was I already keeping score? It was *still* a perfect evening.

"Well, do you plan to keep him out all night, too?"

"I'll try not to," he said.

"I'd appreciate it. How am I ever going to be absolved if I can't get a minute to make my confession?"

"Point well taken," Louis said, leaning over to kiss my cheek. "I'll send him right over."

Like I was going to tell all over baked chicken and collard greens.

B.J. waited for Louis to return to their table before he came over and sat down in the empty chair. "Hey, Cat."

"Small world," I said. "How was your trip?"

"Better than I hoped. I've got a guy down there who remembers Miriam and her sister. He was the one who made the arrangements with their mother."

"Are you sure?"

He nodded. "I need to talk with Miriam to confirm some things as soon as possible, but it looks legit. The people who took her sister seem to have really strong ties to Atlanta, and she may be scheduled to come through here again in a few weeks as part of some kind of circuit."

"A circuit?"

"My source says you can tell when they're bringing in women because they secure the houses differently."

"So nobody can get to them?"

"So they can't get out. They board up the windows and redo the locks so you can

331

only open the doors from the outside."

"They lock them in?"

"Ten or fifteen at a time. If they start making trouble, the guys who are guarding them threaten to set the place on fire."

I resisted the impulse to ask him what kind of man would burn women alive for being *troublemakers,* but there was no answer to such a question, so I didn't waste our time pretending there was. "Miriam will be at my house tomorrow," I said. "Can you meet her there around four?"

"Sure. Will you stick around so she'll have someone there she knows?"

"Of course."

"Great," he said, glancing over at Louis, who was conceding their table to two people hovering nearby with fully loaded trays and hungry expressions on their faces. "I guess we're being evicted."

Was that it? "Welcome back."

He looked at me and smiled again. "We've got some last-minute stuff to do down at the paper, but Louis swears we won't be long. Would you like to have coffee or something later?"

This "remaining calm" thing works like a charm if you can just remember to do it. "I'd love to."

"I'll call you when I'm headed back this

way." Then he kissed the same cheek Louis had previously bussed, and they headed out the door.

Louis's mother may have been her husband's wife, but the *Sentinel* was her husband's dream, and he had passed it to his son along with those long legs and that lopsided grin. There was no way to compete with that, and I wasn't even going to try. Why should I? I had dreams of my own to think about, and a little plate of heaven to sustain me while I did. And when you think about it, if that isn't a perfect evening, I can't help you.

48

This time, I had decided to leave Phoebe's pictures around in their usual places. He would have to ask me who she was, and, surrounded by her smiling face, I'd be powerless to deny her. Even if I did, all he'd have to do was look at her to know the secret I'd been keeping all these years, and then I'd have to break down and let it all out.

It wasn't that I didn't want to tell him. I literally couldn't find the words. I needed an opening line to introduce the subject in a gentle, nonconfrontational way that *eased* us into the conversation. I needed a few short sentences that would state the facts, take my best shot at an explanation, and offer him the option of a face-to-face meeting with Phoebe, but only if they both wanted it.

The fact was easy: *We have a seventeen-year-old daughter.* The offer of a meeting was easy because unless they both agreed, it never had to happen. It was the explanation part that was, as my father used to say, kicking my ass like I stole something. I knew I had to explain, but how? For a long time, I thought it all went bad when I decided not to have the abortion and I didn't tell B.J., but I think now it was before that. It was when I tried to make the decision not to have her based on who I *thought* he was and who he *expected* me to be. I don't remember asking myself what I *wanted* until they called my name at the clinic, and I couldn't step forward.

Having Phoebe was something I did because of who I really was, and I've never regretted it for a single second, but still needed an introduction to the subject at hand. I looked at Phoebe's picture on the freezer door as I took the coffee out to make a fresh pot and tried to imagine the exchange.

Him: What a lovely young woman. Who is she?

Me: Oh, that's our daughter, Phoebe. She is lovely, isn't she?

That was no good. I tried again.

Him: What a lovely young woman. Who is she?

Me: You remember that procedure you

couldn't go to with me? Well, I couldn't go either.

That was even worse.

Him: What a lovely young woman. Who is she?

Me: B.J., we need to talk.

The worst opening line in the history of relationships. This was what I got for not watching soap operas. Those girls know how to confess every possible transgression, from extramarital affairs to switching babies at birth, without even breaking a sweat. How do they do it?

The phone rang as I took down two cups from the cabinet over the sink. "Hello?"

I was glad to hear B.J.'s voice on the other end. It was almost ten thirty. After eleven is too late for coffee and true confessions on a weeknight.

"Cat? I'm sorry to be so late calling."

"That's okay. I just put the coffee on."

"That's the thing," he said. "Louis just reworked the whole front page."

Phoebe's photograph smiled back at me from the refrigerator door, and I felt a wave of frustration. *Damn!* It was harder to tell this secret than it had been to keep it. But B.J. didn't know that. He thought he was just coming by for coffee, not to be a major player on *Days of Our Lives.*

"How much longer do you think he'll be?"

"There's really no telling," he said. "Can we get together tomorrow?"

Tomorrow and tomorrow and tomorrow . . .

"Sure," I said, as the smell of coffee I wasn't going to drink filled the kitchen. Now *that* was pathetic. Amelia's question bounced around in my brain: *What do you want to happen?* I knew exactly what I wanted to happen. "How about dinner? I'll cook."

"You don't have to do that," he said.

"I want to," I said. "Besides, how else can we be sure we won't run into any more of Ezola's spies?"

"Good thinking," he said. "Am I still meeting Miriam at your place at four?"

"Absolutely," I said. "She's expecting you." She had been so excited to hear that there were new leads on her sister.

"Thanks, Cat," he said. "I'm sorry I couldn't make it tonight."

"Tell your boss I'm going to send a union organizer down there if he doesn't stop these terrible hours you're working."

"I'll be the first one to sign up."

I could hear the smile in his voice, and I was glad I hadn't been petulant about his change of plans. I wondered if it was possible to be in love with a man and develop a vocabulary free of the responses that make every conversation a minefield of hurt feelings, half-truths, and dashed expectations. The more I sidestepped all that and went right to the truth, the better I felt.

"Good night," I said.

"Good night."

There was no need to waste a whole pot of coffee, so I poured myself a cup. It wasn't until I went back to the refrigerator for the cream that I realized I was going to have to take Phoebe down one more time. B.J. was coming here at four to interview Miriam. I couldn't leave the pictures around for that.

Him: What a lovely young woman. Who is she?

Me: That's our daughter, Phoebe, but go on and do this interview and I'll fill you in later.

That would never do. I'd have to put

them away, find some reason for him to leave the house for a little while after he talked to Miriam, put them back up, and then greet him for dinner like they'd been there all the time, or confess I'd been taking them down and putting them back like a set designer who couldn't make up her mind. Neither option particularly appealed to me, but I figured Miriam deserved B.J.'s undivided attention tomorrow and de-Phoebe-izing the house one more time was the only way to guarantee she got it.

So I put down my coffee and apologized to my daughter one more time with the guilty parent's favorite rationalization: *This hurts me more than it hurts you.* She didn't believe me for a second.

49

Sam called to say he was looking forward to talking to B.J. and to complimenting Louis on the big splash the series was already making.

"It's all anybody's talking about," he said in the admiring tones of a man who recognizes a creative use of the media when he sees it. "Davenport can't show his face in public."

Quincy Davenport was the businessman whose slum property B.J. had featured in his story. After it appeared, Channel Two Action News had sent a film crew to interview the family B.J. had featured, and while they were on camera, a rat scurried across the walk behind them.

"He ought to show his face in public by cleaning up those houses he's renting," I said.

"That's the bottom line, I guess," Sam agreed. "Maybe what he needs is a cadre of Mandeville Maids to put it right. Think there might be a story in that?"

I could see it now. A cadre of white-uniformed women descending on Davenport's little shotgun houses and emerging a few hours later, leaving behind a spotless new environment for some family other than their own.

"There might be a human-interest story if you're going to donate their services," I said.

"*Donate* their services? Did you forget everything I said the other night about being in business?"

"That's exactly my point. If it's about doing good, they might run it for free. If it's about making money, they make you pay for it."

I could hear him chuckling, and it sounded seductive, although I don't think he meant it to. "Point well taken. It was just a thought."

"Don't worry," I said, glad he had backed off a bad idea so easily. "I'll give you some talking points before you meet with B.J."

"*B.J.?*"

I blushed even though he couldn't see me. "Burghardt Johnson. We used to call him B.J. in college. I'm sorry."

"I see," Sam said. "Well, tell *B.J.* I'm raring to go, and if slumlords are what he's chasing, I've got some stories that'll curl his hair. Is he still looking for leads?"

"I don't know. You can ask him when you two talk."

"I just might do that," he said. "Make sure I have those talking points the day before I need them, will you?"

"I will," I said, but he was already gone.

50

When Miriam arrived at the house for her interview, she immediately noticed the absence of Phoebe's photographs and it completely freaked her out. She was neatly dressed in a dark skirt and a white blouse that made her look like a schoolgirl. Her awful wig had been traded for a gray fedora during an afternoon excursion to my favorite vintage clothing store, but when I commented on it, she barely acknowledged the compliment.

"Where's your daughter?" she said, her voice full of worry.

"She's fine," I said, kicking myself. Why hadn't I thought about Miriam's reaction to my sudden housecleaning? "It's just that . . ." *Just that what?* "It's just that when I have business appointments at the house, I like to keep things strictly professional."

She looked even more confused. "You don't want them to see her picture?"

"It's not so much that I don't want them to see her picture. It's just that I like to keep my personal life separate from my professional life."

This from a woman whose office was nestled in a back bedroom so she could look around her computer and see her collard greens growing. Miriam was unconvinced, and there was a little worry wrinkle between her eyebrows.

"Don't worry," I said. "As soon as you're finished with your interview and Mr. Johnson goes home, I'll put them all back where they were. You can help me. Okay?"

She nodded with her first smile of the day. "She reminds me a little bit of my Etienne. Not the way she looks, but the way she smiles. When I walked in and she wasn't where she always is, all of a sudden, just like that, I guess I just didn't want her to be gone, too."

Too.

"She's not going anywhere," I said. "Trust me."

I'd be glad when all this subterfuge was over. I'm not cut out for it, and trying to learn on the job was truly working my nerves.

By the time B.J. arrived at a house with plenty of newly empty wall space, and I introduced him to Miriam, she was enviably poised, considering how stressful the situation must have been for her. I had told her that B.J. was a friend, as well as a great reporter who wanted to help us locate Etienne. She had read his first piece in the *Sentinel*, and even looked up some of his older work online.

"Thank you for agreeing to talk to me," B.J. said as we gathered in the living room. I sat next to Miriam on the couch, and B.J. took a chair and flipped open his notebook.

"You have written about my country many times," she said quietly. "That makes it easier."

He smiled. "Good. Can we start with the night you and your sister left Haiti?"

Miriam looked at me. This was not the first time she had told her story, but did it ever get easier to conjure up a nightmare? I took her hand and held it tight.

"Take your time," B.J. said. "If you need to stop, we'll stop."

"No," she said, firmly. "I will tell you everything I know, and you will tell me everything you know so we can find my sister. Are you ready?"

B.J. nodded, and Miriam took a deep breath. "My mama told us not to be afraid. . . ."

51

For the next two hours, B.J. guided Miriam through a telling of her story that included details I'd never heard her share before. Her voice trembled a few times, and once she choked up just a little when she talked about the day her sister didn't come back like she was supposed to, but she never broke down, and B.J.'s gentle questions never pushed her too hard or too far. When he finally closed his notebook, Miriam hugged him like a favorite uncle and with a little coaxing, even agreed to have her photograph taken holding the locket picture of Etienne to run beside the story.

From what he'd discovered in Miami and what Miriam had told him, B.J. knew there was a good chance someone had seen Etienne the last time this group of women came through. All it would take was for one person to come forward, but that worked both ways. Somebody could come forward who didn't want the information to get out, too, so we decided that Miriam would move in with me for a couple of weeks after the story ran. She'd be safe in West End in case the story flushed out some bad guys.

The session had run longer than we thought it would, and when Miriam realized what time it was, she was in an immediate panic at the thought of arriving late for her citizenship class. She wasn't even sure she wanted to be a citizen. In spite of everything, she still loved her own country, but she wanted to know she could pass the test if she took it. B.J. offered to give her a ride, since he was driving Louis's car, and she gratefully accepted.

I walked B.J. to the door as she gathered up her things. Watching him work, seeing how compassionate he was as he questioned Miriam so gently, made me feel like I could tell him anything and he would understand. "Are we still on for dinner?"

"Absolutely," he said. "I'll drop Miriam, take Louis his car, and be back in an hour."

That was all the time I needed. I hugged Miriam, closed the door, and started upstairs. Dinner preparations could wait until I put Phoebe back where she belonged. I still didn't know what I was going to say, but I figured something would come to me.

An hour later, Phoebe's photographs had

been returned to their usual places. Nothing had come to me yet, so I poured myself a glass of wine and went outside to wait for B.J. on the front porch. When I spotted him coming down the street, my mind couldn't have been blanker. I finished off my wine in three big gulps. He was walking up the front walk and still *nothing*, so I just smiled.

"Did she make it on time?"

"We had five minutes to spare." He put his foot on the bottom step and smiled back. "And she wanted me to apologize for her leaving so quickly that she didn't have a chance to help you put your daughter's pictures back up."

The smile froze on my face. B.J.'s expression never changed, but his eyes were watching me intently. "She said to tell you she'd help you first thing tomorrow."

And there they went, right out the window. Eighteen years of lies and evasions, all gone in one fell swoop. The weird thing was, I wasn't scared or nervous like I thought I'd be. The conversation I'd been dreading had begun without any help from me at all. There was nothing to do now but tell him the truth. I stood up.

"That's all right," I said. "I've already taken care of it."

Then I reached out and took his hand, opened my front door, and walked him inside to take a look at his daughter.

52

There was no need to say anything, or if there was, neither of us knew what. I didn't try to explain. I just kept hold of his hand and walked him around the house like we were in a museum on Sunday afternoon, pausing before each piece, silently observing, then moving on. When we got to the kitchen and I stopped in front of the refrigerator, where the photographs were of a full-grown woman, he let go of my hand and ran his fingers delicately across Phoebe's face as if he could read her thoughts like Braille. I could see that he was trembling slightly. Then he closed his eyes and turned away from her and from me.

"I'm so sorry," I whispered, feeling the inadequacy of the words even as I said them.

He just shook his head without turning around. "Thank God," he said, and his voice sounded strangled and raw. "Thank God! Thank God!"

He just kept repeating it over and over, real quietly, like he couldn't have stopped himself if he'd wanted to. I just stood there, not knowing whether to go to him or not. Finally he took a deep breath and turned back to me. His eyes were shining and his face was wet with tears he was trying to wipe away on his sleeve like a kid on the fourth-grade playground.

"You didn't do it," he said.

I shook my head. "No, I didn't do it."

"Why didn't you tell me?"

There was no anger or accusation in his voice. Just the need to know *why*. This question was very familiar to me. It was the one I asked myself.

"You were on your way to Africa," I said. "I thought you needed your freedom."

Tears were still running down his cheeks and his voice had a choking sound. *"I needed you."*

He pulled out a chair at the kitchen table and sat down like the weight of his own thoughts was too much to carry. I sat down across from him.

"Then why didn't you tell me not to do it?" I whispered.

He looked at me and shook his head slowly. "Because I thought you needed your freedom," he said, so quietly I almost didn't hear him. "I never wanted you to do it. That's what I was trying to tell you that night I got so drunk, but it didn't come out right."

My heart was beating so fast I thought it was going to come through my chest. He never wanted me to do it? "You weren't making any sense."

His eyes looked so sad that I wondered if the sorrow I had seen there on our first night at dinner was something he had taken with him across all that ocean, not something he found when he got there. "I didn't know how to talk you out of it. I didn't even know if I had a right to try."

In the process of figuring out what we wanted, needed, and had a right to, women had talked men into and out of their paternity rights so many times, nobody knew who had the right to do what when, much less why.

"Is that why you left?"

He reached across the table and took my hand, stroking it gently. "I knew I couldn't go to the clinic and not try to talk you out of what you had already decided. Leaving seemed like the best thing to do."

This was beginning to sound like that short story we had to read in high school where the poor husband hocks his watch to buy his beloved wife a comb for her beautiful hair, not knowing that she has cut and sold her hair to buy her beloved a chain for that same prized pocket watch. On Christmas morning, each one recognizes the other's love reflected in their sacrifice. Except her hair will grow back and he can buy back his watch from the pawnbroker's window. What we had offered each other in the name of love and freedom was something much more precious and irreplaceable.

B.J. looked across the table at me. "But I was wrong."

"I was, too," I said. "And we could sit here trading apologies all night, but you know what? In this case, we're really lucky. Two wrongs turned out to make something that's not just right. It's absolutely perfect."

I stood up and went over to the refrigerator and removed a smiling photo of our daughter and handed it to him. He had no choice but to smile back.

"Her name is Phoebe," I said, "and she's been looking for you."

53

Sometimes things are harder than you think they'll be, but sometimes things are so much easier that you can't figure out why you waited so long. This was one of the latter times. B.J. and I started out by going back through the house so I could tell him the story behind the photographs he'd seen when we walked through earlier, tongue-tied. It was like a documentary film called *The Life and Times of Phoebe Sanderson: The Story So Far.* I had years of stories to share with him, and he had as many questions as I did answers.

Did she really look like him, or was he "just trippin' "? (She really did.)

Did she feel like a citizen of the world? (Absolutely. Already spoke Spanish and French and was working on Arabic.)

How old was she when she started walking? (Ten months. Never crawled at all. Just got up one day and walked across the room.)

What did my mother say? ("My mother is the one who started that Baby Doll stuff, so you tell me.")

Was she a good rider? (She can jump a four-rail fence with her eyes wide-open.)

I took him upstairs and let him see her room. He was careful not to touch anything, but there were her dolls lined up on the shelf above her complete collection of *The Diaries of Anaïs Nin* and every book Alice Walker ever wrote. There was her closet, with last year's assortment of clothes that didn't fit this year's style requirements. On her wall was an Outkast poster and one of a smiling Audre Lorde with her famous quote about not having time to be afraid when she was using her strength in service of her vision.

There was her bulletin board and her desk. There was her old computer that she had replaced with a sleek new laptop, and a spray of dried roses from Amelia's garden. There was a framed picture of her in Jamaica last summer, standing next to a tiny Rastafarian woman whose dreadlocked hair was so long it dragged the ground behind her like so many snakes in the dust. Amelia had briefly tried to grow dreads, hoping to match the woman's Rapunzelian length, but she was too vain to survive the Buckwheat stage, when everybody kept asking when she was going to get her hair done.

When we arrived back in the kitchen, I put on a pot of coffee while B.J. stood in front of the fridge, still studying the snapshots.

"How much does she know about me?"

"Nothing," I said. "She thinks I don't know who you are."

He looked at me. "How would you not know who I was?"

"I told her she was conceived during my wild college days, and her father could have been any one of a number of old casual lovers."

"You never had any wild college days."

I put sugar and cream on the table for me, since he always took his coffee black. "She didn't believe me either."

"Smart girl. Why would you tell her something like that?"

It seemed so ridiculous now, I could hardly remember. "Seemed like the best way to make sure she never came looking for you."

He ran his hand over the photograph of Phoebe holding a fistful of Louis's sunflowers and smiled at his daughter. "But she came looking for me anyway, didn't she?"

He laughed out loud when I told him about Phoebe's futile quest for DNA samples from strangers, and I realized it was already becoming a funny story to illustrate a rocky moment just before everything turned out fine.

"She's stubborn," I said, pouring two mugs of coffee and coming to stand beside him. "Gets it from her father."

"I've never kept a secret for eighteen years in my life!"

"That wasn't because I was stubborn. That was because I was scared."

"Scared of what?"

In the picture, Phoebe's bright eyes were twinkling at the sight of us standing there together.

"I don't remember," I said. "It was so long ago."

He turned toward me. "You really are a woman of mystery, you know that?"

Before I could agree or demur, Amelia appeared at the back door and tapped on the window.

"Hope I'm not interrupting anything," she said when I opened the door and she spotted B.J. standing beside the refrigerator, both of us grinning like Cheshire cats.

"You're right on time," I said, taking her hand and drawing her inside. "I want to introduce you to Phoebe's father."

54

To say Amelia and Louis were happy that I had told B.J. about Phoebe doesn't do justice to all the kissing and crying and back-slapping and storytelling that consumed the rest of the evening. They were beyond delighted. B.J. was still a little overwhelmed, but he pored over the scrapbooks I lugged out as if he were in search of the secret of life, and maybe he was. By the time he left at midnight, we were both exhausted and exhilarated. There were no more ghosts in sight, but Phoebe was now a tangible presence in both of our lives, and until we got adjusted to it, our shadow dancing was on hiatus. That was fine with me. One step at a time.

The good thing was, our schedules were going to impose a brief cooling-off period whether we wanted to or not. B.J. was on a flight back to Miami this afternoon for an overnight trip to tie up a few more loose ends. He knew he was onto something when somebody left a message for him at the paper saying this wasn't the sixties and he wasn't Martin Luther King, so he'd better back off. B.J. said it was probably Quincy Davenport's supporters, but Louis said that wasn't their style. Whoever it was, both of them were fired up, and Miss Iona said it felt like the old days.

I had so much work to catch up on, I didn't have time to worry about it. Miriam arrived bright and early, happy to see Phoebe's pictures back, and full of praise for B.J. I didn't tell her he was Phoebe's father. It was okay for Louis and Amelia to know, but before I made a general announcement, I wanted my wild child to hear it from me. Along with my apology for making her wait so long. Thanksgiving seemed to me the perfect time to make the introductions. It was only a couple of weeks away, and she was coming home whether she was speaking to me or not. They could meet face-to-face.

I wanted it to be a special moment for them. I wanted it to be a moment they would always look back on with joy. A moment we could share as a family for the very first time. This was important, and it had to be *perfect*.

Miriam was on the computer, so I answered the phone absentmindedly as I flipped through a stack of folders in search of a long-lost invoice that was way overdue.

"Babylon Sisters. Catherine Sanderson speaking."

"Catherine," said that unmistakably high pitched voice that always surprised me. "Ezola Mandeville. Do you have anything to do with those articles the *Sentinel* is running about using refugees?"

She was abrupt as always, but she didn't sound annoyed.

"I know the reporter and the publisher, but I don't have any direct involvement in the stories themselves. Why do you ask?"

"Because if you had, I was going to offer you a bonus." Her voice was practically lilting, it sounded so genuinely pleased.

"A bonus? Why?"

"Since that story said some companies are using illegal aliens as maids, I can't find enough maids to fill all the jobs I've got! Everybody's scared of getting busted for hiring illegals, so they're coming to me because they know I'm legitimate. It's been great for business!"

She sounded more like Sam every day. "That ought to help us in recruiting, too. Once people know that you're treating people like human beings and paying them decent wages, the word will spread."

"It already has," Ezola said. "The phone is ringing off the hook. Come have lunch with me so I can thank you in person, and maybe I'll give you that bonus after all. How soon can you get down here?"

I looked around at the mess on my desk. "I'll be there in forty-five minutes."

"Don't be late," she said. "Bonus or no bonus, I still expect you to come on time."

55

When I arrived at Ezola's office exactly forty minutes later, she had the nerve to look at her watch before she got up from behind her desk and came around to greet me.

"Thank you for coming on such short notice," she said, shaking my hand. As usual, she was wearing a dark dress, sensible shoes, and a string of pearls. "Please sit down."

Lunch was already laid out, but hidden under silver covers for the moment. Ezola liked to talk first and eat later. She ushered me over to one of the love seats and sat down beside me. I was surprised to see the large throne chair covered with a piece of plain black drape that obscured its bright gold and tufted red presence.

Ezola saw me notice it and smiled. "That chair is ridiculous."

I looked at her to see if this was another test, but I couldn't lie. I smiled back at her. "Completely absurd."

"I watched you the first day you came here, me in my great big foolish chair and you in that sawed-off one that made you have to look up to me even if you didn't want to."

The woman never failed to surprise me. Of course she was conscious of what she was doing, but I never expected her to admit it.

"You didn't need all that to impress me."

She sat back and fingered her pearls with her stubby fingers. "I wasn't interested in impressing you, Catherine. I intended to intimidate you."

"Why?"

"Because I used to be a maid, re-member? Every person who walks in that door for the first time thinks they know more about *everything* than I know about *anything*. If I'm ever going to disabuse them of that notion, I have to make them understand that there's a whole lot of things that I know better than they do, and the sooner they realize that, the better."

"I knew that before I walked in here. All that big chair made me do was wonder whether you knew it, too."

She stood up and walked slowly over to her glass wall and looked out at the atrium, where her beautiful building was showing off its skylight with random rainbows.

"And what did you decide?"

"I decided that you did."

"Good. It's always dangerous to under-estimate me."

"I never do." And that was the truth. I thought she was strange and eccentric and smart and clearly extraordinary. Once she really trusted me, I thought, working with her would be a once-in-a-lifetime adventure.

She came back to sit beside me. "I'm talking about Sam."

That came out of nowhere. "What about Sam?" Last time I checked, Sam was her personally designated eyes and ears and de facto favorite son.

"I know it's hard to believe," she said, her voice sad and light as a feather. "But some information has come to me that Sam may be all up in this business with Quincy Davenport."

"With the slum houses?"

She nodded.

"Are you sure? He has always spoken of you and the work you're doing here with great respect. I can't imagine that he would jeopardize it for something like that."

"I have considered him like my own," she said, getting up again and pacing around the room a little, but not in a quick, agitated way. More like an angry lion in a cage. "He's helped me build the business to what it is today. He brought you in when we needed someone like you to help us."

She came back and sat down again. She was really upset about this and she couldn't seem to light anywhere. "And now I need your help again."

The expectant look on her face required an answer. "What can I do?"

Her whole body relaxed and her face softened immediately. "Oh, thank you, Catherine. Thank you!" She leaned over and took my hand. "I knew I could count on you."

"What do you want me to do?" I said, feeling like my generic response had been received with a lot more enthusiasm than it deserved. I hadn't agreed to anything yet. Her thick little fingers felt strong and strange around my own, and I willed myself not to wriggle my hand out of her grasp like a restless child forced to talk to old people.

"I want you to keep an eye on Sam."

My hand withdrew of its own accord. "You want me to spy on Sam?"

I wondered if she usually recruited her spies this directly, and why she didn't just give the job to whoever had been keeping an eye on B.J.

"I want you to think about what it would do to our project and our credibility, mine *and* yours, if it turned out that the man we put in charge of our project was a part of all the things we're fighting against."

She got up one more time and walked back over to the throne and pulled the black drape off. The chair looked even more ludicrous than it had the first time. She tossed the drape to the floor and sat down slowly, regally, her physical presence lending the chair a bit of dignity it did not deserve.

"What if it turned out Sam was a con man, or worse, and even though we talk a good game, neither one of us was smart enough to see it lying there stinking right under our noses?"

The image was effective, and she was right. That was the last thing we needed. We would lose all our political supporters, not to mention the nonprofits and social service agencies.

"If that happens, I would have sat on this throne and made a fool of myself for nothing. Trying to stare down the white folks and scare the hell out of my own people, so I could build a business and save some women from taking the stuff I had to take from everybody just because I was a poor black woman with nothing to say and nobody to listen. My business will never be able to survive something like that, and it all will have been for nothing. My reputation and my word are all I've got, and Sam Hall isn't going to take them from me without a fight."

She was working on my sisterhood, but I needed some specifics. "What can I do?"

"Just tell me what you hear."

"What I hear about what?"

"About Sam." She hesitated.

"And?"

"And let me know if his name is going to be in the paper."

This was making me very uncomfortable. "I don't know if I can do that."

"Why not?"

"Because that's not my job."

Ezola leaned back in her throne and looked at me. "Then think of it as a favor."

She sounded like the Godfather, but this was different. There was nothing she could do to force me to spy, but was it really spying? I didn't want Mandeville Maids to get burned because Sam was more interested in profits than people. This was a great project, and I wanted it to happen as much as Ezola did. I hadn't come to work here because of him. I'd come because of her. Because as crazy as she was, she was doing something positive for some hard-working women who needed all the help they could get.

"I'll keep my ears open."

"Good." She stood up immediately, her smile back in place to show that the conversation was officially over. "Now we can eat."

56

Sam sent me an e-mail telling me how much he had enjoyed the interview with B.J. and promising to call when he got back from a two-day trip to Columbus. I wondered what he would say if he knew Ezola had such serious doubts that he was who he said he was. He didn't really seem capable of that kind of duplicity, especially since he was next in line at Mandeville Maids, but money makes people do strange things, and my ears were still ringing with his *greed is good* lecture, so who was I to doubt Ezola's instincts?

Louis and Amelia had gone to see another big, bad Hollywood movie, and I had just put my work problems out of my mind and was curling up with last Sunday's *New York Times* when B.J. called from Miami to ask me when I was going to tell Phoebe he was her father.

"Thanksgiving," I said. "She'll be home from school, and you can spend some time with her then."

"Do we have to wait that long?"

He sounded so disappointed, I almost

said, *We'll call her as soon as you get back,* but that's not the way I wanted to tell her. It made me feel good that he was anxious to establish contact, and I was even more determined to make that first meeting a magic moment.

"She's wanted this for a long time," I said. "I want to make it special for her."

"Sort of like the father holding his baby up to the heavens at the beginning of *Roots*?"

"She's a little too big for you to hold her up over your head," I said, not ready to be teased. Everything was too new for me to laugh at us yet. I was still trying not to cry. "I just want it to be *perfect.*"

"It is perfect."

I smiled at the love already in his voice — and he hadn't even met her yet. "You know, she thinks that getting to know you can protect her from getting her heart broken."

"What do you think?"

There was no reason to lie. "I'm hoping it can do the same for me."

And he answered my truth with one of his own. "I love you, Cat."

"I love you, too, B.J. Good night." And I clicked off before he could say more.

It was important for me to understand

that his love for me right now was all tied up in his love for Phoebe, and that was a good thing. It was even more important for me to be able to distinguish between his *father love* and *mother-of-his-only-child love,* and that other kind that exists between a man and a woman just because they are a man and a woman, not because they share a child.

But I wasn't required to do all of that tonight. How and why we loved each other would be a mystery we'd have to work on. Tonight, the fact that we did was good enough for me.

57

The issue of the *Sentinel* with B.J.'s Miriam story on the front page sold out before noon the day it hit the stands. People were moved by her story, outraged by her sister's plight, and anxious to help. Louis was printing another full run that he planned to have on the street by midnight. If pimps needed the cover of darkness to thrive, the *Sentinel* was about to put some people out of business. The phones at the paper were ringing nonstop, and Miss Iona drafted one of the interns to help her field the offers that were pouring in for everything from free clothes to free housing.

Miriam had generated an outpouring of attention and outrage, but she didn't want to talk to a lot of curious strangers, so two days before the story appeared, she moved some of her things into the upstairs bedroom next to Phoebe's. Staying with me for a couple of weeks would put her in a safe zone without making her feel like she was under house arrest. She had the run of this place, and Amelia was right next door.

Louis and B.J. lived around the corner, and Blue Hamilton's presence guaranteed her safety on the streets anywhere in West End. She had come a long way from the days she spent hiding behind that horrible wig, and she was getting stronger by the day.

Tonight we were going to Miss Iona's for a dinner in Miriam's honor. I hadn't seen B.J. for more than a few minutes since he got back from Miami, and I was looking forward to seeing him and to toasting the *Sentinel* for reclaiming its place as Atlanta's most-read newspaper. I had just changed clothes and persuaded Miriam to shut down the computer and go upstairs to get ready if she didn't want to face Miss Iona's wrath for being late, when the doorbell rang.

"Fifteen minutes," I said, heading downstairs. "We've got to be walking out that door or Miss Iona will want to know the reason why!"

"I'll be ready." She laughed, and I heard the shower splash into life.

I opened the front door to find Sam standing there with a scowl on his face. The man never tired of arriving unannounced. This time he didn't have a bottle of wine tucked under his arm. He had a copy of the *Sentinel*, which he held up as if he were showing it to me for the first time.

"Have you seen this?" His voice was one loud boom of indignation.

"Of course I have. Come in."

He stepped inside, but stayed near the door like he was too pissed off to come in and sit down. "Do you see any reference in here to Mandeville Maids?"

"Of course not."

"Then please tell me why I spent two hours with your friend B.J. talking about our expansion project and our refugee outreach plans and our scholarship program."

He must have forgotten that he had already told me the scholarship program wasn't all it was cracked up to be.

"This is a multipart series, Sam. This is not the last one that will appear. The programs you talked about will probably fit in a story that runs later."

That calmed him down a little, but he was still annoyed. "Then why did he talk to me now?"

"Because they have to work ahead," I said, not feeling nearly as patient as I sounded. "I told you that, remember?"

He looked at me. "I guess you did."

I didn't know what to say to that, but I remembered my meeting with Ezola, and the word *spy* might as well have been tattooed across my forehead.

"Is there anything wrong, Sam?" *Other than that the boss thinks you are a slumlord and is probably getting ready to cut you loose?*

He ran his hand over his bald head. "No sense pretending, Catherine. I'm feeling some distance between me and Miss Mandeville."

"Distance?" Now I felt as though my *spy* tattoo was flashing like a neon sign.

"Nothing I can put my finger on. She's just not confiding in me like she used to. Like I'm out of the loop." He paused again, then looked up at me sharply. "Did you see her while I was in Columbus?"

Too late to lie. "Yes. She invited me to lunch to tell me that the *Sentinel*'s story had been good for business."

That drew a smile. "I showed her the figures. She couldn't believe it."

"Well, then," I said. "What's the problem?"

He shook his head. "It's a matter of trust, Catherine. I don't feel that she trusts me like she used to."

"I'm sure you're wrong," I said, not knowing what else to say.

"I was hoping Mr. Johnson's story would project me in a positive light and put me back in her good graces. When that wasn't the case, I guess I was just disappointed." He gave a little bow and tucked the *Sentinel* back under his arm. "My apologies for interrupting your evening, and thank you, as always, for your wise counsel."

"You're welcome," I said, opening the door for him and wondering if I was supposed to report this to Ezola as I watched him get in his car and drive away.

It was too late to report anything now. Miss Iona said eight thirty sharp, and she'd blame me if the guest of honor was the last to arrive.

"Miriam!" I called from the front of the stairs. "Time to go!" I listened, but she didn't say anything.

"Miriam?" I called again. The shower had stopped and she hadn't come downstairs. Where would she be?

I took the stairs two at a time and called her again as I peeked into the open bathroom door, glanced in my room, then Phoebe's, then the one where she was staying. Her dress was still laid out on the bed. "Miriam?"

Nothing. Something was wrong, and I had no idea what, but it was making the hair stand up on the back of my neck. I leaned down and looked under the bed, then behind the big chair in the corner. Finally, I opened the closet door slowly, suddenly, sickeningly, unsure of what I might find, and there she was, sitting in the corner, curled around her knees in a tight little knot.

"Miriam, what happened?" I said, going to put my arms around her. "What's wrong?"

She was shaking like a leaf. "It's him." Her voice was a whisper of wind through dry grass.

"Who?"

She nodded, rocking back and forth in my arms like it was all she could do not to run over to the window and jump out. "The man downstairs."

"Sam? He's gone. Do you know him?"

"His voice," she whispered. "I remember his voice."

"When?" Now I was whispering, too.

"The night before they took Etienne."

58

It took me half an hour to talk Miriam out of that closet, into her clothes, and then into the car so we could go to Miss Iona's, where Louis, Amelia, and B.J. were already waiting anxiously. Miriam was still terrified. When she heard Sam's voice — *how could she forget it?* — she had immediately assumed he had come looking for her.

"When did you hear his voice before?" B.J. said, when we had settled into Miss Iona's neat little living room like a protective shield around Miriam, who sat between me and Amelia on the couch.

"He came in with the others who took us to work every day, but they were shining a light in our faces so we couldn't see him," she said. "Only his voice."

"Could you hear what he was saying?"

She nodded miserably, as though somewhere in her brain, it would be playing over and over on an endless loop until we found her sister. "He was saying 'that one,' and 'that one,' and 'that one,' like he was picking out the ones he wanted. The next day, they took Etienne off with two others from our group and then she was gone."

Louis walked over to the fireplace, where Miss Iona kept several pots of bright green ferns; then he turned back to B.J. "Tell me what you've got on this guy."

B.J. already had something on Sam? I was surprised. He'd never mentioned it.

"He's been on the housing end for a couple of years. Quincy Davenport is just a front, and he's so scared now, he's telling everything he knows."

It dawned on me that B.J. must have known about Sam's involvement when he got here. Then an awful thought popped into my brain. Was he just using me to get a story? Had I believed all that dancing in the dark was one thing when it was really just a good reporter following a lead?

"We used to have to worry about white folks riding up in here with sheets over their heads," Miss Iona said, wearing her company apron over her pale blue sweater and skirt. "Now they just send a brother."

"Is there anything that ties him to the prostitution?" Louis said. Over his shoulder on the mantel, there was a picture of his father sitting at his desk in his shirtsleeves, putting another issue of the paper to bed.

"Nothing on the record. These guys are

making so much money, they're ruthless. Nobody wants to be the one who told." B.J. looked at Miriam. "Are you absolutely sure that was the voice you heard?"

Miriam nodded. "Oh, yes. I remember thinking, How could someone with such a beautiful voice use it to bring us such misery? I'll never forget it."

Why hadn't it occurred to B.J. that it might be dangerous for me to be so close to Sam without knowing he was about to show up in a story? Now I was a dupe for B.J. and a spy for Ezola. All because I was trying to pay my child's tuition. Committed motherhood can sure make for some strange bedfellows, especially when you're used to sleeping alone.

B.J. looked back at Louis. "I need another couple of days and I'll have what I need to corroborate what Miriam's telling us. If what I think I'm hearing is true, Sam Hall is the one who's supplying women to the guys from Miami who started this whole circuit. Now he's ready to go out on his own, and to do that, he needs a steady supply of girls to keep it going."

"How long are we —"

Miriam shuddered a little bit, and Amelia put her arm around the girl's shoulders and shook her head almost imperceptibly at Louis. *Too many details.* He stopped in midsentence. "Should we talk about this later?"

Amelia rewarded him with a smile. "I've got an idea. Listen, Miriam, why don't you and me and Miss Iona go out there and hook up some dinner while these folks figure out what we're going to do next?"

Miss Iona stood up immediately and held out her hand to Miriam. "Come on, little bit. You still gotta eat."

Miriam followed them out to the kitchen and left me and B.J. alone with Louis, who was trying to process this new information. So was I.

I turned toward B.J. and he smiled, oblivious. I took a deep breath. "Did you suspect Sam was involved when you asked me to set up an interview?"

Louis looked surprised. "You already interviewed this guy?"

B.J. nodded. "His name had already shown up a couple of times, so he was on my list when I got here. When I realized Cat was working for him, I took her up on her offer to put us together."

When he got here? He suspected Sam the whole time and never said a word? "That night at the Pleasant Peasant, when I was rattling on about my new client, you al-

381

ready suspected Sam in all this?"

"Not at this level," B.J. said quickly. "I thought he was in the housing end because of his father. Not the prostitution."

"That's not the point," I said. "The point is, you didn't tell me! I'm working for these people, and the whole time you suspect them of absolutely awful crimes and you never say a word?"

"Not the whole company. It's just him," B.J. said. "There's nothing that points to Ezola Mandeville in any of this."

He was still not listening. I looked at Louis, who clearly wished he could join Amelia in the kitchen. "Did you know about this?"

B.J. jumped in. "I hadn't had a chance to share it with him yet. It's all coming together pretty fast."

Louis didn't say a word.

"I think Miss Iona needs some more help in the kitchen. What do you think?"

"Miss Iona's wish is my command," he said, easing out of the room like Cab Calloway at the end of a long evening at the Cotton Club.

B.J. looked confused. "What's wrong?"

"You should have told me!"

"I thought it was better not to," he said calmly. "I didn't want to make you uncomfortable at work."

Like he was looking out for me. *Uncomfortable* was an understatement. This job was probably over. "Not until you got your story, anyway."

He looked hurt at my accusatory tone. "I would think you'd want me to find out everything I could about this guy. Look at what he's doing!"

That wasn't fair and he knew it. Or he should have. "Did you think I wouldn't cooperate if you told me the truth right up front?"

He looked at me, and his voice was almost defiant. "I didn't know how much the contract meant to you. I couldn't take a chance that you'd tip them off before I had a chance to check it out."

He didn't even feel like he owed me an apology. "What makes you think I won't go tell them now?"

His tone softened, and he smiled at me like we were friends again. "Because I know you better now."

I was too mad to be distracted by that nonsense. He had used me. Now I had to look out for myself. *Just like always.* "I need to ask you something, and I want you to tell me the truth."

"Of course."

Of course. "Is there anything at any level that points to Ezola Mandeville? Anything at all?"

He shook his head firmly. "No. Not a thing."

"Have you looked specifically for her?"

"I've looked harder for her to show up than I have for Sam."

"Why?"

His voice was gentle, but unapologetic. "She would make a better story."

I stood up. "I respect her. I respect the work she's doing and why she's doing it."

"I know."

He probably never even heard of Bessie and what she did for Bigger and what she got back in return. Did I owe him more than I owed a black woman trying to do business on behalf of other women?

She was strange, but she respected me in a way that B.J. didn't seem to at all. Sam was on his own, but Ezola deserved better. "I have to tell her."

That got his full attention. "You can't tell her. What if she tells Sam?"

"She won't."

"How can you be sure?"

Because, I wanted to say, *she wants him busted as bad as, if not worse than, you do. Because if she has a little advance warning, she can do some damage control and not lose everything she's built and is still building.*

"Trust me," I said. "She won't tell him."

I sat back down and B.J. came and sat beside me. "This story is very important to me, Cat. If I do it right, it can make up for all those years I spent drinking and talking and wasting time."

It sounded like the chorus of a country song. *Just drinkin' and talkin' and wastin' time.*

"My professional relationship with this woman is important to me," I said. "I can't let her get blindsided like this when she's not even implicated."

He stood up and started pacing. "Don't take this the wrong way, Cat, but if it's about the money, I can help."

"What are you talking about?"

His voice was still very gentle, like he was afraid I might bolt, as I had done in the restaurant. "Louis told me you only took the Mandeville job to pay for Phoebe's college. I want you to know, I can help."

Now he was my knight in shining armor? "Louis was wrong for discussing my finances with you, and you are wrong for trying to discuss them with me. I don't want anything from you, and Phoebe's tuition payments are not your problem."

"I'm sorry," he said. "It's just that this story is important for all the right reasons. I don't want to risk it by tipping our hand."

"I'm not interested in tipping anybody's hand," I said, stepping back outside of that *our*. He still hadn't apologized for withholding information, placing me in a highly volatile position with my clients and exposing Miriam to a fright that really shook her up. "But until we spend a little more time together, I don't think you should assume you know me as well as you think you do."

"What does that mean?"

Miss Iona stuck her head out of the kitchen door and waved us in for dinner. "Come on to the table before it gets cold!"

"It doesn't mean anything." I stood up and looked down at B.J., knowing there was no way to explain how it felt to know he hadn't trusted me enough to tell me the truth about Sam. Or to wonder if that was the way he felt when I told him about Phoebe. "Let's eat."

59

After dinner, Louis and B.J. went back down to the *Sentinel* office to meet with the police detective we'd talked to a few weeks ago. We had more information than they did, but it was important to keep them in the loop. Amelia suggested that Miriam move her things from my house to Miss Iona's. That was still close enough to walk to work without leaving West End, but she wouldn't have to worry about another drop-in visit. Miss Iona said Sam didn't know her from Adam's house cat. It was a good suggestion, but it left me alone to consider the events of the last couple hours. B.J.'s almost casual revelation about Sam had thrown me for a loop, but his complete inability to see why it bothered me really made me feel frustrated and powerless, a dangerous combination for someone like me, who prides herself on being in control.

This was exactly what Ezola had been talking about. Being misled by men we thought we could trust. Looking foolish or careless or both because we had misjudged B.J. and Sam. The things they had been doing behind our backs were coming back to haunt all of us in different ways, but I knew she wasn't going to like it any more than I did. B.J. had said her name didn't show up in his investigations, and I knew better than anybody that her loyalty to Sam had seen its best days. I flipped through my Rolodex for Ezola's private number and picked up the phone. She had a right to know, and I had a responsibility to tell her.

She answered before the second ring. "Yes?"

"It's Catherine," I said, feeling suddenly not quite sure about where my loyalties should lie. B.J. and I were on the same team, but Ezola and I were in the same sisterhood. "I have some bad news, but I thought you should hear it from me."

"Go ahead."

"The next story in the *Sentinel*'s series has Sam's name in it. Quincy Davenport was just a front. Those slum houses all belong to Sam."

"I was afraid of that." Ezola's voice had sharp edges around its always strangely girlish tones. "What else?"

"They think he might be involved in prostitution."

"Are they sure it's Sam?"

She didn't want me to have it right. She wanted to believe her spies had been off again. They had been known to make mistakes.

"Someone recognized his voice."

She gave a dry little chuckle that didn't find a damn thing funny, but had to acknowledge the irony. "I always told him it would get him in trouble."

I didn't say anything. Like most spies, even though I had done the job I had been asked to do in service of a righteous cause, I didn't like myself a whole lot for doing it.

"Was there anything else?"

"No," I said, suddenly wishing all this were over. "Except that I'm going to take a few days off until you make some decisions about how Sam fits into the future of the company and whether or not I do. It would be awkward for me to try to pretend nothing has changed."

"Sam has no future at this company," Ezola said firmly. "My search for a new vice president starts now. I'd like to announce the appointment before the story breaks."

"The story will be out in a few days," I said, surprised at how fast she intended to move. "Do you already have someone in mind?"

"Of course, dear," she said. "You."

60

In my dream, B.J. is like he used to be, but better. His arms are as strong, but his lips are sweeter. His eyes are as sad, but his heart is truer.

In the dream all I want to do is open up every part of me that's been closed for so long and pull him so far up into where all the real mysteries meet all the real magic that he'll never want to leave and I'll never want to let him.

In my dream, he is lover, father, friend, family, forgiveness. In my dream, the past is prologue, the present is a precious jewel, and the future stretches out before us like a ribbon of promise.

In my dream, we are like we used to be, but better.

61

At one a.m. my dreams woke me up from a sleep that wasn't as sound as I wanted it to be. I lay there for a minute trying to figure things out, but all that kept coming back to me was that B.J. and I still hadn't had an exchange where all the cards were on the table. I was holding back about Phoebe. He was holding back about Sam. We were both holding back about each other. Half the truth is no easier than an all-the-way secret, and if we were going to have any chance at all of being friends, or something more, we had to come clean once and for all. Just because he hadn't told me about Sam didn't mean I got to lie about spying for Ezola. What's that great Gandhi quote? *An eye for an eye leaves the whole world blind.*

I knew he was probably still down at the paper. He told me he still liked to write really early in the morning, or really late at night, depending on how you looked at it, and Louis's office had become his favorite spot. He said he did his best thinking stretched out on Louis Sr.'s big old leather couch, and that was exactly what I needed now — his best thinking, and mine. Not to mention the truth, the whole truth, and nothing but the truth. He'd be disappointed that I had already spoken to Ezola, but I trusted her, and in a few days it wouldn't matter anyway. Everybody would know all about Sam.

I filled a thermos full of hot coffee and headed over to the *Sentinel* to make peace before my fantasies drove me crazy trying to make love. I eased into a spot near the front door. It was so late that the other businesses around were closed for the night, and since we were out of West End, I had to be careful, but I could see a light in Louis's office. He had blown up a picture of Etienne to poster size and prominently displayed it in the front window. Underneath the photo, it said: *Where am I?* Her face was so alive and happy that you had to smile when you saw it. You had to stop and see what the words meant. During the day, there were always a couple of people standing there, staring at it, or reading B.J.'s story that was posted nearby.

"Hang on," I thought, trying not to think about where she was or where she'd been. "Just hang on a little longer."

I rang the bell. The light went out immediately, leaving me bathed in the security spots, and everything inside the office a dark mystery. I stepped back involuntarily, and the light came back on as suddenly as it had been extinguished. B.J., in his shirt-sleeves, opened the door to greet me.

"There is a god!" he said, giving me a quick kiss on the cheek. "Tell me there's coffee in there."

"I figured whatever you were drinking by this time of night would probably not be suitable for an innocent bystander."

"You got that right," he said as we walked past Miss Iona's desk and into Louis's office. Louis had left the mock-up of the front page on his desk, since he was still fiddling with it. All of this could now be done on computers, of course, but Louis is old-fashioned. He likes to actually touch his newspaper before he puts it to bed. "Sit down. What are you doing here so late?"

"Looking for you," I said, sitting on one end of the couch while he took the other. "We can't seem to stop keeping secrets from each other. Why is that?"

"Bad history?"

"Maybe."

"Look, Cat, I'm sorry I didn't tell you about Sam."

"Me, too," I said, "but that's just part of it."

"What's the other part?"

I took a deep breath. It was important to get it right. "I love you, B.J.," I said, figuring context was everything and truth was the light. "Always have, probably always will."

His face lit up so beautifully that I almost got distracted and threw myself into his arms, but I'm not a kid anymore. I've *got* a kid, and this has to be done right, for her and for me, or I'm not doing it at all.

"But that doesn't mean I've just been waiting around for you all this time." That sounded more defiant than I wanted it to. "What I mean is, you can't come back into my life after eighteen years and start offering to take care of me. I'm taking care of myself and I'm taking care of Phoebe, and I'm doing a good job, too. Even when it's not perfect, we do all right."

Was I making any sense at all?

"Go on."

"Listen, B.J., I don't need you to take care of me. I don't need you to do it *for* me, whatever *it* is. I need you to do it *with* me. I don't need you to think you know better about what's best for me, whether it's about Sam or sex or where to go for dinner."

What was I talking about now? Time to wrap it up.

"Okay," I said, stalling for time. "I think that's all I have to say right now, except I think we should take a moment and make sure we're current on everything. Is there anything else you want to tell me?"

B.J. looked startled. The question caught him by surprise. "About Sam?"

"About *anything*."

"There are a million things I *want* to tell you," he said, smiling, "but if you mean do I have any more secrets, no. No more secrets."

I smiled back at him. "Good."

"How about you?"

"Just one more," I said, "and I'm ready to let it go."

"Well, fire when ready." He reached for the thermos with no idea what I was getting ready to tell him.

I tucked my feet up under me and got ready to confess that I had called Ezola, when all of a sudden B.J. grabbed my wrist and put his finger to his lips for silence. I nodded to let him know I understood, and he got up and turned out the lights just as he had done when I arrived unannounced, but nobody had rung the bell, and as hard as I was listening, all I heard was silence. B.J. reached under Louis's desk and quietly withdrew a double-barreled shotgun. My heart was pounding so hard I thought B.J. could hear it, but he was standing perfectly still, listening intently for whatever he had heard.

The whole scene reminded me of that photograph of Malcolm X standing at the window with a shotgun after somebody firebombed his house, where his family lay sleeping. Then I heard the sound of male voices outside. B.J. heard it, too. He gave me the *keep silent* gesture again and stepped out of the office, leaving me alone and terrified in the semidarkness. I crept to the door and peeked out after him. Who would be coming here this late, and why did Louis have a weapon under his desk? I heard B.J. open the door, and the faint smell of gasoline drifted in from the street.

"You brothers looking for something?" B.J.'s voice was cold.

They saw the shotgun and raised their hands involuntarily. A shotgun will make you do that. "Aw, man, you ain't gotta come to the door with your shit in your hand," said a young voice that was trying to sound aggrieved. "We come in peace, brother."

"You always carry a can of gasoline on your peace missions?" B.J. said. "Step away from the building."

"We got car trouble," said a second voice. "Can't you —"

"Step away from this building," B.J. interrupted him. "Or I'll blow your brains out, if you've got any."

B.J. was standing in the half-open door with the shotgun aimed at two young black men who were backing up toward a black Cadillac Escalade idling at the curb. This couldn't possibly be the car they claimed had trouble. Right in front of the window was one of those red-and-yellow gas cans, and the smell of the fumes was strong.

"See, that's the problem niggas got," said one young man who was dressed all in black and looked about eighteen.

"Yeah, they don't trust nobody," said the other kid, also about eighteen and all in black, like they were a pair of amateur commandos.

"Get in your car," B.J. said. "And get going before I call the police."

At the mention of the police, the driver's-side door of the Escalade opened and a thickly built man in a dark suit got out and walked around the car. He was wearing sunglasses in spite of the hour, but even though they couldn't see his eyes, the two younger men froze as he approached them. Something about him looked familiar, but I couldn't make him out clearly from where I was standing.

"Get the fuck in the car," he hissed, and the two guys scrambled over each other to obey. He waited for the door to slam behind them and then turned toward B.J., who hadn't moved a muscle or lowered that shotgun.

The man spread his arms wide. "I'm not packin' nothin'. I just want to deliver a message."

"I'm listening."

"You better figure out what time it is and stop askin' so many questions all over Vine City."

The voice wasn't familiar, but something about the profile was.

"Are you finished?" B.J. said coldly.

"Yeah, I'm finished, and you better be finished, too."

B.J. didn't respond to that, so the guy got back in the car and squealed his tires as he pulled away. Through the window, I could make out what looked like a ponytail. B.J. brought the gas can inside before coming to check on me, still shaking in the office. He leaned the gun against the wall.

"You okay?"

I nodded. He went to the supply room, grabbed a big jug meant for the water cooler, ripped off the top, and headed back outside to slosh it over the gasoline they had started pouring around the base of the building before B.J. interrupted them. I wanted to help, but I figured the best thing I could do was stay out of the way. I went to the tiny unisex bathroom that Miss Iona always kept spotlessly clean, splashed cold water on my face, and tried to calm down.

I had never seen B.J. in a situation like that before. I had never seen *anybody* in a situation like that before, but I knew he had handled it like a grown-ass man, and for that I was grateful. I'm an independent woman, but when you're in a war zone, you want to be standing with a soldier, and it looked like I was.

"Amateur arsonists," B.J. said, after he had finished outside and locked the front door. "They'd have probably set themselves on fire before they figured out how to toss the match."

"I think I've seen that guy before," I said. My voice was trembling, and I cleared my throat to steady it.

"Which one?"

"The older one."

"Where?"

"With Sam," I whispered. "I think he works for Sam."

62

The police arrived five minutes after Louis came over with two of Blue Hamilton's guys with him in a big black Lincoln, in case we had some more uninvited company. One officer looked around outside while the other one took a statement from B.J. and a shorter one from me. I couldn't tell them what I was really worried about. Not until I talked to B.J. first. Did this happen because I told Ezola what I knew? Did she activate Sam, who sent Ponytail to take care of the problem? The thought of what might have happened made me feel sick at my foolishness. We were at war and I had called the enemy with our battle plan.

The police sergeant was talking to Louis in his office, but I couldn't hear what they were saying. I sat at Miss Iona's desk and listened to B.J. tell the police officer that the Escalade they were driving had no plates in the front and a vanity plate in the back that read simply SMOOTH.

The cop shook his head. "That shouldn't be too hard to find."

"Is that it?" B.J. said, glancing over at me. I wondered if I looked as miserable as I felt.

"That's it," said the officer. "Are Hamilton's men going to be out here the rest of the night?"

B.J. nodded. "Tomorrow, too."

The *Sentinel* office wasn't in West End, but Blue was a friend.

"Good. Then call us if you need us."

"We will."

Louis and the sergeant had closed the door, so B.J. sat on the edge of Miss Iona's desk and looked at me. "You okay?"

"I think this is all my fault."

He shook his head. "How can it be your fault? We've been getting threatening phone calls all week."

"All week?"

"Ever since Miriam's story came out. Somebody's onto us, and they want us to know it."

"I told Ezola."

He looked at me, surprised. "You told her?"

I nodded. "I'm so sorry! Don't ask me why. I couldn't tell you now if you paid me. I was mad at you for not telling me about Sam. It was just stupid. I'm so sorry!"

"Listen, Cat," he said, breaking in when

I choked up in the middle of my apology. "It doesn't matter. All this means is that Sam's the one who's onto us. It doesn't mean Ezola told him anything."

I wanted to believe him. "How do you think he found out?"

He shrugged. "How did they find us at the restaurant? It doesn't matter. It's Sam who's got something to lose, and burning up this building is probably not all he's prepared to do to shut us up."

"What are we going to do?"

He pointed through the glass cubicle wall, where we could see Louis and the sergeant shaking hands. "I think we're about to find out."

Louis walked him to the door and they shook hands again.

"Twenty-four hours," said the sergeant. "Then we'll have to move on it. Arson is a serious crime."

"I hear you," said Louis. "Twenty-four hours."

"Twenty-four hours for what?" B.J. said.

Louis glanced over at me. "You look like hell."

"I feel like shit," I said. "Are they going after Sam?"

"I got them to give us twenty-four hours. That's it."

"Twenty-four hours for what?"

"To see what he'll do next," Louis said. "If B.J.'s source is telling us the truth, Sam's borrowed money from some people in Miami and he can't pay it back."

"He's had to shut down some of their operations," B.J. said. "Now his name is in the paper, and that makes them very nervous. It's bad for business. They haven't been able to move the girls through here as easily as he told them he'd be able to."

Those pictures of Miriam and Etienne were doing their job. Miriam was still lying low at Miss Iona's, but the problem was no longer abstract. It had a face and a smile and a big sister who would never stop searching.

"My contact says Sam offered them some girls he's been holding back as collateral," B.J. said softly. "I think Etienne is one of the girls he's going to use to buy himself some time."

I stood up and looked at him and then at Louis. This was Atlanta, Georgia, a place where B.J. said black women *rule* and people were coming here to trade in human beings like slavery was still legal as long as nobody saw it except the slaves. "Tell me that's not going to happen."

"We've got twenty-four hours to make

sure it doesn't," Louis said. "If I'm guessing correctly, he'll lead us right to the girls. Then we've got him."

"Isn't there anything we can do?" I said, suddenly exhausted.

"Yes," Louis said. "Go home and get some sleep. Something tells me tomorrow is going to be a very long day."

63

Louis wanted me to stay at his house, but I wasn't ready to go into hiding yet, so B.J. had volunteered to spend the night, and I had agreed to let him. If Sam knew where I lived, that guy with the ponytail probably did, too, and I'd had enough excitement for one day.

"I'm going to bed," I said, after I locked the front door behind us. "There's plenty to eat if you're hungry, and there are clean sheets on the bed in Phoebe's room if you want to get some sleep."

He smiled at the specificity of my invitation to sleep over, but seduction was the last thing on my mind, and I didn't want to send any mixed messages. "I can just stretch out down here on the couch."

"Suit yourself," I said, heading for the stairs, "but it's not nearly as comfortable as the one in Louis's office, so don't be shy if you change you mind."

"I won't. Good night."

"Good night," I said, but I could feel him still looking at me, so I turned around.

"You were great tonight."

"I specialize in scaring off first-time arsonists," he said, refusing to play hero.

"I don't just mean that part. I mean the part right before that, where we promised to always tell each other the truth. That means a lot to me."

"I like that part, too," he said, "but there was one other part I liked even better."

"What was that?"

"The part where you said you loved me."

"That's one of my all-time favorites, too," I said, but I was too exhausted to surrender. Inside my house, there was peace, but outside we were still at war. "Good night."

"Good night."

Around four, his footsteps on the stairs woke me. He passed my half-open door without slowing his steps and turned into Phoebe's room. I heard him turn on the lamp and I heard the bed creak a little under his weight. It made me feel good to know that he was sleeping in her space to protect her mother. I knew it would make her feel good, too, and I needed a visual so I could describe this moment for her later. I got up before I lost my nerve, slipped on my big white terry-cloth robe and my Tweety Bird house shoes so he wouldn't think I was trying to lure him into a predawn tryst, eased out into the hallway, and looked through Phoebe's open door.

B.J. was sitting on the side of her bed reading a book I recognized as one of Phoebe's favorites, Alice Walker's *The Temple of My Familiar*. I remember discovering that book at Spelman, loving it, and begging B.J. to read it, but he never did. Now here he sat, twenty years later, wide-awake at four a.m., hunched over it like there was no place else he'd rather be.

I tiptoed back into my room without letting him see me and closed the door quietly. I didn't even need to look at the grubby little card Louis had given me that I'd been carrying around for days with Phoebe's cell phone number on it. The number was a permanent part of my memory bank. I picked up the phone and dialed up my daughter in Massachusetts. Her lovely voice clicked on instantly.

"It's Phoebe. Leave me a message and don't forget to do something for freedom today."

That made me smile the same way I bet it made Louis smile every time he called her.

"Hello, Baby Doll," I said. "It's me. I miss you more than you know." I took a deep breath so I wouldn't start getting all sentimental. "I'm sorry I lied to you about your father. There is never a time when you deserve anything less than the one hundred percent truth from me. That's always been our deal and it still is. We'll talk when you get here for Thanksgiving, and I promise, no more secrets, *ever!*" Then I got a little sentimental in spite of myself. "I love you, baby. Good night."

I hung up before my voice got all weird and she could hear it, although I think she would forgive me a little quavering. Her message said I had to do something for freedom. It didn't say I couldn't get a little emotional while I was doing it.

64

When the phone woke me up again at seven thirty, I hoped it was Phoebe, calling me back, but it was Louis. He didn't even say good morning.

"Is B.J. there with you?"

"Yes, what's wrong?"

"You two need to get over here as quick as you can."

"We're on the way."

The neighborhood around the *Sentinel* office was coming alive. The stores were opening for business. Blue's guys were still sitting out front. People who were headed out to work gave them a wide berth. In West End, we knew they were on our side. Over here, it was still every man for himself, and two well-dressed, unknown gentlemen in a big black car were nobody you wanted to mess with unnecessarily. B.J. and I spoke to them as we hurried inside, and they tipped their hats to acknowledge the greeting.

Louis was in his office drinking coffee with a young woman who was eating a take-out order of pancakes and sausage from Thelma's restaurant next door like it was her last meal. When we walked in together, she stopped with her fork halfway home and looked at Louis.

"It's okay," he said. "Finish your breakfast."

She did, with a single-mindedness of purpose that was either a testament to Thelma's ability to burn, or to the girl's extremely healthy appetite.

"Good morning," Louis said, coming out from behind his desk. "Let's get you two some coffee. I'll introduce everybody in a minute."

He shooed us out the door and over to the coffeemaker where it sat behind Miss Iona's desk to discourage anyone else from trying their luck with the ancient machine.

"Who is she?" I said as B.J. poured two mugs and handed me one.

When I had gotten up to tell him Louis wanted us at the *Sentinel* ASAP, he was still sitting on the side of Phoebe's bed reading. He hadn't been to sleep at all. We hadn't taken the time to make coffee before we left the house, and I breathed in the rich aroma gratefully.

"Her name's Celine Hudson. She works for Ezola Mandeville."

"She's a maid?"

"She's Ezola's personal maid, hired by the woman herself and sworn to secrecy with a thinly veiled threat of great physical harm if she ever told anybody what she saw."

My heart sank. Ezola was all up in this madness. How could I have been so naive?

"Go on."

"Miss Mandeville has three or four houses," Louis said, "but this girl has been working at the one where they've been keeping Etienne."

I almost dropped my coffee. "She's here in Atlanta?"

Louis nodded.

"This woman has seen her?"

"According to Miss Hudson, she sees her several times a week."

"Where?"

"She doesn't know. They blindfold her before they take her to the house. She said it must be in the country, since she hasn't seen any other houses around it, but it only takes about twenty minutes to get there."

That wasn't much to go on, but there wasn't a lot of country left within twenty minutes of Atlanta. She was probably being taken to some kind of subdivision.

"What kind of place is it?" B.J. asked.

Louis sighed deeply, like he wished he

411

had a better answer to the question. When he spoke, his voice was flat and sad, or angry, I couldn't tell which one. "They've got four women there. All under twenty. All beautiful. All virgins."

B.J.'s surprised face mirrored my own. "What do you mean, all virgins?" I said. "What are they doing with them?"

There was no way to make the words sound any nicer, so Louis didn't even try. "They're keeping them for sale."

I leaned against Miss Iona's desk. "For sale to whom?"

"Probably to these guys from Miami who loaned Sam the money."

"What are they going to do with them?"

"Keep them for their own or sell them again, probably. There's always a market for virgins." B.J. spit out the words with more than a reporter's outrage. He had been sitting in his daughter's room all night. What I heard in this voice was a father's cold fury.

"Can I talk to her?" I said.

"Come in and let me introduce you," Louis said. "She should be done with her breakfast."

Celine Hudson was wiping the corners of her mouth delicately, like she had just finished tea with the queen. This time when we walked in, she smiled nervously.

"Miss Hudson, these are my colleagues, Ms. Sanderson and Mr. Johnson," Louis said. "Will you tell them what you told me?"

She looked at each of us, then back to Louis. She was a short, fat woman who was probably ten years younger than she looked. It wasn't just the extra thirty or forty pounds she was already lugging around. There was something in the way she carried herself that made her look like she had already given up. Like she had looked around and food was the most interesting and reliable option, so she took it. She was wearing the same uniform that the maids wore in the main Mandeville building, and her short, dark hair was neatly pressed and curled. She looked old-fashioned, solid, and very nervous.

"Where do you want me to start?"

"Tell them why you came here this morning."

"It was that picture," she said, pointing at the issue of the *Sentinel* on Louis's desk with Miriam holding the picture of Etienne on the cover. "When I saw that picture of her and her sister in the window, I knew it was her. That's all she ever talked about was her sister. I wasn't supposed to be talking to 'em no way, but she was so nice. She was always askin' me stuff. She begged me to tell her where they were — you know, what city — and even though I wasn't supposed to say, I told her they were right near Atlanta. What did I say that for? After that, she was always asking me would I smuggle a note out so she could contact her sister. Asking me would I call the police for 'em. You know, stuff like that."

"Did you ever take a note out for her?"

Celine shook her head. "No, ma'am. They search me when I come in and they search me when I go out. They real paranoid about somebody comin' to get those girls. If I help 'em, I'll lose my job for sure."

"Didn't you ever wonder what was going to happen to them?"

She shrugged. "I sorta knew they was keepin' 'em for some men."

She knew exactly what they were keeping them for, but she had decided to keep quiet anyway.

"They wasn't livin' bad. They up in that nice house. They got they own clothes and cable TV, and they let 'em do each other's nails sometimes. They even did mine once, but I had to take it off before I went home.

They ain't payin' me to be out there getting my nails done."

The fact that they were being held hostage until they could be sold or bartered off didn't seem to bother this woman at all.

"What were they paying you for?" B.J. said.

"Nothin' bad," Celine Hudson said quickly, sounding a little defensive. Maybe she did feel a little guilty after all. "Just regular maid work. Cleanin' up, washin' clothes. It's not bad, and once she trust you to work at the house, Miss Mandeville pay real good."

Tell me about it, I thought, but she still hadn't answered the first question. "If you're not prepared to help them, why are you here?"

She raked her fingers through her hair and then looked at me. "Damn if I know," she said. "I just kind of like that one whose picture y'all had in the paper. She always tryin' to help me clean up or do their wash, even after I told her if she do my job, what they need me for. They sure ain't gonna let me do hers."

She chuckled to herself at the idea, but we just looked at her. "So yesterday, she came up to me and she was crying. I ain't never seen her cry before, so I thought one of the guys they have watchin' 'em had got after her, but she said no. They told them they were having company this weekend and to fix themselves up nice."

"What kind of company?"

"Some men comin' to buy 'em," she said softly. "That guy with the sexy voice told 'em to get ready to move by tomorrow night."

Sam's voice was better than a fingerprint.

"Why was she crying?"

"She don't wanna go. She said if she have to leave Atlanta, her sister will never find her." She looked down at her hands clasped tightly in her lap. "I think she scared, too, you know, of what they gonna do after savin' 'em up all this time. She ain't never had no man before."

I took a deep breath. "So what did you tell her?"

She looked straight at me. "I told her I had to worry about keeping my own job and I was sorry I couldn't help her, but when I went home yesterday, I kept thinking how scared she was and how keepin' 'em like that to sell 'em wasn't nothin' like what Miss Mandeville says when you read about her in the magazines, and how would I feel if that was my baby

416

sister, if I had one, you know? I used to be proud I worked for her, but how can I be proud of doin' this?"

She frowned a little and shook her head. "Then when I went to Thelma's for my pancakes this morning, I saw that picture in y'all's window and it just . . . I couldn't go past her, so I come inside and told him."

She pointed at Louis, then looked back at me and B.J. again like she hoped the three of us could do what she didn't know how to do by herself.

"Thank you, Miss Hudson," Louis said. "You did the right thing."

"So what y'all gonna do about it?"

"We're going to go get her," I said.

She raised her eyebrows and her eyes looked surprised. "For real?"

I nodded. "For real."

"The rest of 'em, too?"

"Every last one," I said. "I promise."

She grinned at all of us then, like the way I said it, maybe it was true. I could tell she hoped it was, and I forgave her for being so indecisive about coming forward. She wasn't ready for the complicated questions her situation had presented to her. The choice between helping a stranger and feeding yourself is always difficult, and acting like it wasn't devalued the courage of what she had done.

"Can I ask you a few more questions?" B.J. said.

Celine Hudson shrugged her shoulders. "Go ahead. I ain't got to worry about getting to work on time. Soon as they see I didn't show up for work this morning, I'm fired anyway."

"What you did is really important," I said, trying to take the sting out of the hard times she probably had ahead.

"Yeah, I guess so," she said, "but that's not why I told on 'em."

"Why did you do it?" I really wanted to know.

"Because some stuff is just wrong," she said. "And if you know it and you don't do nothing, you wrong, too."

"Couldn't have said it better myself." I stood up and headed for the office door. "Excuse me, please."

I left Celine Hudson talking to B.J. and went out to Miss Iona's desk and picked up the phone.

Louis followed me out. "Who are you calling?"

"I'm calling Ezola Mandeville," I said, punching in her private number. "She has to answer for Etienne."

65

Of course, Louis tried to talk me out of it, but I wasn't listening. Etienne was in Atlanta, and Ezola knew where. It seemed pretty simple to me. We had to make Ezola take us there, and nothing Louis had to say was going to change that.

When he realized I wasn't listening to him at all, he stopped talking and took the phone out of my hand before I could finish punching in the number. "And how exactly do you plan to do that?"

"Call that sergeant who was over here last night. Send the police over there."

"Is that why you're calling her? To tell her the cops are on their way?"

Why was I calling her? Because I was angry, the same reason I had called her the last time after B.J. asked me not to. That one worked out so great, I was going to do it again. Bad idea.

"We've got to do something," I said. "They've moving them tomorrow night."

"We're going to do something, but calling Ezola half-cocked won't be it."

He was talking to me hard, trying to bring me back to the question at hand, which was how to find and free these girls, not my having a chance to tell Miss Ezola Mandeville all about her sorry, fake-sisterhood-spouting self. This wasn't about *me*. This was about *us*.

"I'm sorry. What do you think we should do now?"

Since cussing out Ezola was out of the question, I was open to suggestion. Louis started pacing up and down like he always does when he's thinking. "They don't want us to publish B.J.'s next article because it's going to mess up their deal with these Miami guys and bring everything into question, legitimate and illegitimate. That's what brought them over here with those gasoline cans last night."

"Are you going to hold the series?" It was inconceivable to me that Louis wouldn't run the story — he'd been looking into Etienne's eyes on that poster all week just like the rest of us.

Louis shook his head. "I won't have to hold it, but you're going to tell Ezola I'm not only going to hold it — I'm going to kill it."

"I am?"

I could see B.J. closing his reporter's

notebook. Louis saw it, too.

"Hang on a second," he said. "B.J. needs to hear this, too."

Miss Hudson stood up and walked with B.J. out of Louis's office. She was still deep in conversation with B.J., and at the front door she smiled shyly, shook his hand, and headed back to Thelma's. Confession must be as good for the appetite as it was for the soul.

"Her story is airtight," he said. "All we have to do now is find the house."

"Damn the house," Louis said. "We don't have time for that. We need to get them to bring us the girls."

"Tell B.J. what you want me to do," I said as we filed back into his office. We were all too agitated to sit down, so we just sort of stood around while Louis outlined his plan.

"We're going to offer Ezola a trade. We'll kill the story in exchange for the girls."

"Do you think she'll go for it?"

"She's got to come up with something to buy some time with these guys. She's worried enough to burn us out. What's she got to lose?"

B.J. frowned. "Everything?"

"Exactly," Louis said. "But only if that story comes out linking her and Sam to the missing girl. Nobody's looking at her operation except the *Sentinel*. Without the light you're shining, she can go back to business as usual, pay off the Miami boys, and expand her operation just the way she intended to do all along."

He turned to me. "She trusts you, Cat. That's why you have to make the call."

"I thought you didn't want me to call her."

"Not to cuss her out — to schedule a meeting."

B.J. immediately looked concerned. "A meeting with who?"

"A meeting with Cat. She has to take her our offer and make the arrangements."

"No way," B.J. said. "It's too dangerous. These guys aren't playing."

"So let's tell her we have to meet in a public place so I'll be comfortable. How about Paschal's?"

"What makes you think they won't snatch you out of the restaurant? Then we'll be looking for you, too."

"Because," I said calmly, "I'm going to get Blue's guys to drive me over and wait to bring me back."

"Perfect," Louis said. "Ezola will know who sent them and won't try anything. Once she goes for it, you set a meeting place, and I'll tell Sergeant Lawson to stake the place out. As soon as you walk out with the girls, they'll move in."

B.J. was still worried, but I wasn't concerned about Ezola snatching me. The only thing I was scared of was that they'd whisk Etienne and the others away before we had a chance to stop them. I picked up the phone again, and this time Louis didn't stop me.

Ezola answered before the first ring was complete. "Yes?"

"It's Catherine."

"I've been expecting your call."

Celine Hudson was too valuable an employee not to be missed immediately.

"Then we won't have to waste any time pretending," I said. "You have something I want as badly as you don't want that *Sentinel* story to run. I think we can do business."

"Now you sound like one of us," she said in that wispy voice that covered so much evil. "What kind of business?"

"The kind you don't do over the phone. Meet me at Paschal's on Northside Drive at noon."

"I'll be there."

And I took her line to show her I wasn't kidding. "Don't be late."

66

Paschal's is always crowded at lunchtime, and today was no exception. I had gone home to shower and change and sit still for a minute to get ready for this exchange. Ezola was a kind of evil I hadn't encountered very often: a black woman who had no special feeling for other black women. I'm sure she's not the first; she's just the first one I've seen in a long time, and it's always weird. It isn't that I think black women are perfect. It's just that I always think, deep down, there's a little spark of sisterhood that binds us together, no matter what. Sometimes we don't nurture it like we should, and sometimes we let other people abuse it, but I always think it's in there, waiting for the right moment to leap out, warm your heart, feed your soul, and save the day.

But maybe I'm wrong. Maybe sisterhood doesn't always survive everything intact and come out unscathed. Maybe it can be twisted and warped to the point where you think you deserve a throne and everybody else is just a *sorry black bitch* who can't — and won't — do better. Maybe Ezola had looked around at her sisters and said, *Who wants to join up with a powerless group like that? Who wants to spend a lifetime trying to play catch-up with a bunch of females who don't even know enough to tell the difference between love and abuse, rape and reciprocity?*

Maybe that was when Ezola decided it was easier to cash in on our misery than try to correct it, and that choice always belongs to the woman who makes it, since nobody has to be Condoleezza Rice if they don't want to, but it's still weird. The protective coloration that makes us fight so hard for *Brother* Ruben after he already won the prize is the same thing that made me believe working for Ezola could somehow bring some balm to Bessie's long-suffering soul, but I was wrong. That was why I was here to make it right.

Blue Hamilton's guys drove me over without requiring conversation. One stayed with the car and one took a seat at the bar inside, where he could see me as well as all other entrances and exits in the room. I was fifteen minutes early, and Ezola was already there when I walked in. She was seated in a booth in the back. The man with the ponytail was at the bar, four stools away from my guy. Neither one acknowledged the other.

When I slid in across from Ezola, she gave me a tight little smile. She was dressed in her usual dark dress and pearls, but she looked much smaller out of the environment she controlled. Smaller, but still dangerous. This was no time to underestimate her.

"I've told the waiter not to bother us," she said. "One of those is for you."

There were two glasses of ice water on the table. I didn't touch either one.

"Our business won't take long," I said. "Etienne St. Jacques's sister is a friend of mine. I know you're holding her and three other girls. My friends are prepared to kill the series of articles you're concerned about in exchange for the safe return of those girls."

Her lips curled in a mean little smile. "I told Sam that girl would be trouble. Her sister, too, but he wouldn't listen to me, and now look where we are."

"I want to pick them up tomorrow, and if I do, those stories you're concerned about will not run."

She narrowed her eyes. "For how long?"

"Forever," I said. "The *Sentinel* is prepared to stop the series."

"What makes you think that hotshot reporter will go along with this?"

I had anticipated the question. "He's leaving town. He took a job at the *New York Times.*"

She sneered. "White folks got more money, huh?"

"White folks always have more money, but we've still got the last two stories he wrote. The one about Sam and another one all about you."

I said it as threateningly and nastily as I could, and she knew I wasn't kidding.

"What if I give these girls to you and that editor changes his mind and runs the stories anyway?"

"He won't."

"But he could."

"Why? So you could burn his office down?"

She was looking at me trying to decide whether or not to take the deal I was offering. I laid it on a little thicker.

"Or maybe so you can send Sam back to my house to remind me of the terms of our deal?"

She didn't really have much choice. If I was lying, she'd know soon enough, and then all bets would be off. "All right," she said, finally. "Tomorrow morning the office will be empty. Meet me there at seven a.m. Come alone and don't try anything. If

I see any evidence of cops around, Sam coming to your house won't be what you're going to have to worry about."

"Anything else?" I said.

She looked at me. "My secretary will meet you at the door; then I'll send her home and it will just be the two of us. That's the only way this is going to happen."

She was trying to intimidate me, as always, but I wasn't a scared refugee a long way from home. I knew exactly where I was and who was standing with me. "If I don't come back, people will come looking for me, and they will bring the police."

"That won't be necessary," she said. "We're not murderers. This all got out of hand. I'm only interested in providing the services people will pay for regularly. Some people need maids. Some people need cheap whores. It's all the same to me."

She sounded so matter-of-fact, and her voice added a touch of innocence to her words that was so out of place it made my skin crawl.

"What kind of black woman are you?"

"A successful one," she hissed at me. "A rich one. An independent one who doesn't have to take orders from any white man on this earth."

"You're selling people," I said, unwilling to grant her race-pride points for outsmarting the white man by betraying black folks.

"This country was built on selling people."

"Yes, *us!*"

"Then be glad for progress," Ezola said, standing up and offering me that twisted little smile again. "At least this time a sister gets to be involved."

67

I went straight from Paschal's to the *Sentinel* office to let Louis and B.J. know that everything was set and Ezola had gone for the deal. Louis listened to everything, then left us there while he went to meet Sergeant Lawson to finalize their plans for tomorrow. All I had to do was meet Ezola at her office at seven a.m., take her a notarized statement from Louis saying the series was off in case she had any last-minute cold feet, and then walk the girls outside.

B.J. turned to me after Louis was gone. "Why do I think it's not going to be this easy?"

"She's very pragmatic," I said. "What works better for her than this exchange? Nothing. All she loses are four girls, when what's at risk are all those other girls and all those millions of dollars you keep talking about. Not to mention her reputation. Why wouldn't she take the deal?"

"Because she's not used to being told what to do."

"Well, that makes two of us."

"Be careful, Cat. This isn't the movies.

People do get hurt." His concern was real, but his tone was wrong.

I looked at him. "Do you realize that if Celine Hudson is telling the truth, Etienne hasn't had to go through the circuit yet?"

"I know."

"And if we get to her in time, she won't have to, ever."

"I know that, too."

"Then you know I'm going to do this, right?"

"I just don't want anything to happen to you."

"Neither do I," I said. "So stop telling me to be careful and start making sure nothing does."

He was looking really serious, but this was serious business. He didn't have to tell me this was real life. I was the one living it.

"You weren't kidding, were you?"

"About what?"

"About being able to take care of yourself."

He still wasn't listening.

"Didn't I just ask for your help?"

He nodded and then gave me a slow smile. "Yeah, but first you made me beg."

I smiled back. "Just wanted to make sure you were paying attention."

"All right," he said. "You do your part, and I got your back."

68

Miriam was still staying at Miss Iona's, so I went by there when I left the *Sentinel* office. B.J. was going to meet me at the house later, to go over the plan for tomorrow one more time, but I wanted to tell Miriam. At first, I thought it would be better not to tell her anything until I actually had Etienne in the car with me, headed home. Then I started thinking about what she might have been through in the last five months. B.J.'s description of the lives these girls were forced to live was swirling around in my mind, and I wondered how damaged and drained Etienne might be. I wondered if she would still bear any resemblance to the smiling girl in Miriam's locket or if her captivity had robbed her of all that. The more I thought about it, the more I thought Miriam needed time to prepare herself for this first meeting. She would have to be the strong one for both of them until Etienne had time to heal.

Miss Iona was putting a roast in the oven when I knocked on her front door. Her steady beau, Mr. Charles, came to answer it, looking right at home.

"Well, aren't you a sight for sore eyes!" he said, leaning down to kiss my cheek. "Come on in!" He was neatly dressed in a sport coat and a nice pair of slacks. Still handsome at seventy-plus, Mr. Charles had always been a little vain. A dinner invitation from his sweetheart was a perfect excuse to dress up.

"You, too!" I said. "Something smells good!"

"Iona's in the kitchen working her magic. She's got Miriam working on the rice." Mr. Charles was originally from Charleston, and he ate rice with every meal. The first time Miriam had made him a pot of perfect rice, just the way her mama taught her, he wanted to adopt her. "Why don't you go out there and tell them there's a half-starved Negro gentleman out here who's looking for his dinner?"

"I'll tell them," I said, as he sat back down in front of the TV. Mr. Charles liked the Discovery Channel, and this was Shark Week.

Miss Iona and Miriam were buzzing around the kitchen like they were already aware of the hungry man in the next room.

"Hey, girl," Miss Iona said, peeking into the oven to check on the roast. "You're just in time for dinner."

Miriam smiled a greeting and crumbled some herbs into a pot of rice that was just beginning to boil. Haitians eat almost as much rice as South Carolinians, and she could cook it so that every perfect grain stood alone.

"I wish I could stay," I said. "But B.J.'s on his way to my house. I just needed to talk to Miriam for a minute."

"Go ahead," Miss Iona said, picking up the glass of wine she had been nursing while she prepared the meal. "I need to go out here and check on my sweetie anyway. Watching those sharks all day always makes him feel frisky."

And she rolled her eyes so Miriam would giggle, but Miriam wasn't even smiling. She was looking at me. "You have news about my sister?"

"Yes," I said. "We've talked to the people who are holding her."

The air seemed to leave her body, and she leaned heavily against the counter. "She's . . . all right?"

"I haven't seen her yet, but we've arranged to pick her up tomorrow."

She looked at me like she couldn't believe the words I was saying. "Tomorrow?"

The rice bubbled over on the stove, and I hurried over to turn down the flame and put the top on it. Miriam hadn't moved a muscle. I pulled out one of Miss Iona's kitchen chairs and guided her to it. "Sit down."

She did, and I sat across from her and took her hand.

"You are going to have to be strong, Miriam," I said gently. "Etienne has been through a terrible ordeal."

Miriam put her head in her hands like she couldn't bear to think about it.

"She's going to need a lot of support from all of us, but you know what she's going to need from you?"

Miriam sat up slowly and straightened her back, trying to pull herself together for her sister's sake. "What?"

"She's going to need all the love you've got."

Miriam's eyes filled up, but she didn't cry. I didn't expect her to.

"Okay?"

She nodded. "Whatever they have done, she is still Etienne. There is nothing they can do to change that. *Ever!*"

"Good," I said. "I'm going out early tomorrow, so let yourself in at the usual time. I'll be back there as soon as I can."

"Can't I come with you? She doesn't know you. She might be afraid."

She was right. *Terrified* would probably be closer to the truth. They all would be, but there was no other way.

"You can't come with me," I said. "I have to go alone."

Her eyes flashed. "With no one to protect you and my Etienne? I have to go."

"The police will be there already. As soon as I walk outside with Etienne, they'll move in."

"No shooting?"

"No shooting." I hoped I was telling the truth. "Don't worry."

Her fingers were tugging at the locket around her neck when she suddenly unfastened the clasp and took it off. "Here! Take this!" She pressed it to her lips and then handed it to me. "If you show her this, she'll know it came from me."

"I will," I said. "I promise."

"Catherine?"

"Yes?"

"You've done so much for us already, but may I ask you one more favor?"

"Of course."

"Will you pray with me?"

Her face was scared and hopeful and brave, and so young to be so far from her mother's arms. I hoped if my child ever had to ask some less-than-perfect woman to pray with her, that woman would have sense enough to say yes, and get on her knees. Which, of course, was what we did, right there in the middle of Miss Iona's pots and pans and perfect roast. We asked God to help us sing the Lord's song in a strange land, and then we asked for the strength to bring our Babylon sister home.

Amen.

69

There was only one message on my machine when I got home.

"Mommy." My daughter's voice was singing with happiness. She never called me *Mommy* anymore except in unguarded moments of absolute joy. "This is me. I got your message. Thank you, thank you, thank you! I can't wait to see you. I'm going to try to get an earlier flight if I can, but it's a holiday, so who knows? I've got exams all day, but I'll call you tomorrow. I love you so much. I can't stand it when we don't talk. Let's never do that again, okay?"

It wasn't necessary to remind her, even telepathically, that she was the one who had cut me off, not the other way around. But she had cause; I had admitted it. Now she was back! That was all that mattered.

70

When B.J. and I decided he would stay at the house again tonight, I knew it wasn't just for safety's sake. It was time. We were ready, and we both knew it. I had stopped for condoms on my way home from Miss Iona's, and since I didn't want to make a habit of making him beg, I asked him if he wanted to stay in my room this time. And he said yes. Just *yes*, like I'd asked him over to watch a movie on TV. Just *yes*, because everything that needed to be said had already been said. The message we needed to send now could only come through skin.

So we took off our clothes with the lights on so we could see who we were now and how we'd weathered the storms. His body, and his hands on mine, were still as familiar to me as the movement of my own hips. Even after so long apart, we came together like two halves of the same whole. We were like we were before, but better, truer, deeper. We made love like we'd been saving it up for all those years and this was the moment we'd been waiting for longer than that.

Wrapped up in his arms, I felt a part of my brain stop trying to think ahead, and I just relaxed into the moment.

"B.J.?" I whispered, my cheek against his chest.

"What, baby?" His hand was stroking the small of my back gently, enjoying the curve of my hip.

"Promise me something?"

He leaned back and looked into my face. "Anything."

"Let's live every minute of every day we've got. Okay?"

He smiled slowly. "Is that it?"

I nodded, loving the length of his body pressed against the length of mine.

"I promise," he said softly.

I kissed him then, and he kissed me back like he would never stop. Whatever was going to go down tomorrow would have to take care of itself. Tonight, I gave Burghardt Johnson all the love I thought he could stand; then I curled up in his arms and slept like a baby.

71

I woke up at five, and B.J. and I went over the plan one more time. I was to go to Ezola's office, where her secretary would meet me and make sure I had come alone. At that point, she would leave so the only people there to see the moment of transfer (on the cop shows, those are called potential witnesses) would be me and Ezola. She would hand over the four girls and I'd walk them out the front door. At that point, the Atlanta police would move in to arrest Ezola and I'd take Etienne home to meet her sister.

As I drove through West End so early in the morning, the streets were almost empty. Later on, they'd be clogged with people headed for the Falcons game or down to the newsstand to pick up the morning paper. But now everything was quiet, almost in a state of suspended animation, waiting for the day to begin.

It had already begun for me. I turned into the parking lot behind Mandeville Maids and looked around. It was empty. Ezola and Desiree were probably parked in the tiny underground lot that was just for VIPs. I wondered where the police officers were hiding with Louis and B.J. It would have made me nervous to know, so I hadn't asked. Now, I wished I had.

Desiree met me at the elevator with a curt nod and no other greeting of any kind. She headed down the hallway and I followed her, wondering which door stood between me and the four girls I had come to claim.

"Where's Sam?"

"Mr. Hall is on special assignment," she snapped, and pushed open the door to Ezola's office.

I stepped inside, looking around for Ezola herself, but Desiree stepped in behind me and kept walking. "What's going on?"

"There's been a change in plans," she said, opening a small door beside Ezola's desk.

"What are you talking about? She's supposed to meet me here at seven. She agreed." Had Ezola spotted our carefully concealed police backup? Had she decided to call off our deal?

"She still agrees," said Desiree. "Nothing has changed except the location of your meeting. Is there a problem?"

"Of course there's a problem," I said, trying quickly to consider my options. Was she bluffing? If she wasn't, as soon as we walked out of the building, the police would know something was wrong and swoop down on us. Then we'd never find Etienne. I couldn't risk that, but what could I do?

"This is not what I agreed to. What if I say no?"

"Then I'll have to call Miss Mandeville and tell her she can go ahead and transfer the girls to their new sponsors."

"Is that what you call them? Sponsors?"

"That's what she calls them," Desiree said, stepping through the open door into what I could now see was a tiny private elevator.

"That doesn't make it true," I said.

"Listen, Catherine." She sounded annoyed. "If you don't come with me, what's going to happen to your friends isn't pretty. Mr. Hall has been hyping his Miami connection way up on the fact that these girls are still virgins, and these guys are animals."

"What does that make you for being a part of it?"

"It makes me a Harvard MBA," she said. "Surprised? Don't be. Miss Mandeville liked to say that I was a success story to impress people with what she was doing."

"You were never a maid?"

"Do I look like a maid?" She sneered and held up a cell phone she was carrying. "Now, are you coming, or should I make that call?"

"Where are we going?"

She waggled her finger. "If I tell you, then you'll know as much as I know, and we can't have that."

"Even if I go with you, how can I be sure that she'll turn over the girls to me? If she reneged on one thing, she'll renege on another."

Desiree raised her perfectly plucked eyebrows. "You're the one who said you'd come alone and then brought the cavalry."

Damn! We were good, but they were better.

"We can't walk out together. There are people watching the building."

She raised her eyebrows even higher. "No shit."

Harvard was out the window now. We were playing by street rules, where smarter and stronger always came out on top. *So be it,* I thought. "If they see me without the girls, they'll know something's wrong."

"They're expecting to see me leave right after you come in, right?"

"Right."

"Then that's what they'll see."

"How?"

"This elevator goes down to secured underground parking. You'll get in the trunk of my car — don't worry; it's clean. We'll get you settled in and make our exit without a hitch. They'll still be waiting for you, and we'll be on our way."

This was getting scarier by the minute, but we were in it now, and there was nothing to be done but *go with the flow*. "If you think I'm going to get into the trunk of your car and go God knows where, you must think I'm as stupid as you are crazy."

She looked at me. "It's your choice, but I think you should know one thing."

"What's that?"

"Before they give your girls to these guys, they're going to tape their hands and their mouths with duct tape so they can't fight back and nobody can hear them screaming."

I stepped into the elevator beside her, and she punched the button for the garage. I wanted to punch her. "Did they teach you this at Harvard?"

"No," she said, cool as a cucumber. "I picked this up right here in Atlanta."

72

The trip took about twenty minutes. Of course, she had confiscated my cell phone, and since I couldn't see anything, I had no idea where we were going. Desiree had music playing loudly, so I couldn't even pick up any sounds from outside. Her car had one of those switches that opened the trunk from the inside, but what good did that do me? I wanted to go wherever Ezola had told her to take me. If I knew anything, I knew where she would be was where I'd find Etienne. I only hoped that someone had been suspicious when they saw Desiree leaving and followed her, but why would they? Her departure was part of the plan, and the truth was, I was probably on my own.

When the car finally came to a stop, Desiree blew the horn to announce our arrival and popped the trunk from up front. I didn't wait for her to give me permission; I scrambled outside and looked around. We were in front of a large house that seemed to be located in the middle of a whole lot of great big Georgia pines. The road we took was the only way in or out that I could see. The overgrown yard and shuttered windows made the house look unoccupied, but it wasn't. The first person I saw was the guy with the ponytail coming across the grass in our direction. Somebody was definitely at home.

"Anybody follow you?" he said to Desiree, keeping an eye on me.

"No way." She shook her head, and then spoke to me like we were girlfriends. "Mr. Wilson thinks I'm not ready for the big leagues."

He ignored her, took hold of my arm, and started walking me toward the house.

"Tell her I'll be back with her sponsors by noon."

"You better be," he growled over his shoulder. "We ain't got all day."

Desiree climbed back into her car and drove away without another word. If the sponsors were coming here, that could mean only one thing: the sale of the girls was still on. The man Desiree called Mr. Wilson opened the front door, and once we were inside, he locked the dead bolt and released my arm. The house was nicely furnished, and I could hear the low drone of a TV nearby.

"I want to see Ezola," I said, trying to sound braver than I felt.

"She wants to see you, too," he said, pointing toward the living room. "Go in there and sit down. I'll tell her you got here."

He said it as though this were a social call. I walked into the living room and looked around for exits, wondering if I should run for it while I still had the chance. The television in the corner was tuned to the Playboy Channel, and two blond white women with obvious implants were making fake love on a bed covered in black satin sheets. I sat down. *No.* I couldn't leave Etienne here. If these girls were in this house, we'd all go free together, or we'd all go down together.

When I was a kid, my mother told me a story about a serial killer who captured eight Filipino nursing students and herded them into a bedroom in one of their apartments. He had a gun, and he told them that if they tried anything, he would kill them all. They were so terrified, they were completely immobilized. So, over the next few hours, he took them one by one into another room, tormented them, and then murdered them. Only one escaped by hiding under the bed.

What I wanted to know as she told me,

even as a kid, was what were the others doing when they were left in that room together between the murders? He didn't tie them up or drug them or knock them out. He depended on their fear to keep them rooted to that spot until he had killed them all, one by one.

There are crazy people and mean men everywhere, my mother said, folding the paper with the photograph of all those dead girls and putting it aside. *But there's almost always more of us than there are of them, so remember these two things.* My mother held up one finger and then another. *Don't let them separate you from your sisters, and always fight back.*

Her words came back to me now as I looked around this ordinary room, searching for clues or escape hatches. I could imagine Etienne and the others cowering somewhere close by, too scared to grab one another's hands, dash off into these pine trees, and run like hell. All I had to do was find them in this great big house and teach them the lesson my mother taught me: *Stay together and fight back.* I hadn't bounced around in the trunk of a car for twenty minutes to come out here and surrender to an evil woman and a man with a ponytail.

Ezola walked into the room, followed by Mr. Wilson, and looked at me. I looked right back.

"Did you really think I was that stupid?" she said.

Wilson sat down near the TV, his eyes glued to the screen.

I stood up. "I think *this* is stupid. We had a deal."

"It's too late to make deals," she snapped. "And we both know it. Once you call the police in, all deals are off."

"What are you talking about?" I reached in my purse and pulled out an envelope. "I've got a letter from the editor of the *Sentinel* right here."

She shook her head, looking disappointed. "Sit down and stop waving that thing around so we can have this conversation and be on our way."

That sounded promising. I sat back down as far away from Mr. Wilson as I could.

"It's too bad we couldn't work this out," she said. "You were a great help to us. The perfect early-warning system, but that damn reporter just kept digging around, didn't he? He just wouldn't stop digging around."

Ezola had hired me to let her know who

was looking at Mandeville Maids, and I had willingly supplied her with all the information she needed. It had all been a big setup.

"So you never had a problem with Sam, did you?"

"My only problem was with you," she said. "But now it's over; you know it and I know it."

"It'll be over as soon as you give me what I came for."

"And why would I do that? So you can waltz out of here like some kind of hero and they can come take me to jail? For what? After all I've done and all I've built, for nothing? Now I'm going down because of four little bitches who aren't worth my time or yours?"

She was getting worked up, and that was the last thing I wanted. "Then let me have them. The police don't even know I'm here. They're waiting for me to come out of your office."

"How long do you figure they're going to wait?"

"Long enough for you to get as far away from here as you need to."

"Don't be ridiculous!" Ezola raised her little voice, and Mr. Wilson glanced up, but seeing no problem went back to the Playboy girls, who were now taking a candlelit bubble bath together.

"You're still underestimating me," she said, "but you know what? I'm going to use that to my advantage, just like I always do. And once it all goes down the way it's all going to go down, you'll have plenty of time to think about old Ezola Mandeville and how she was a lot smarter than anybody gave her credit for."

"I never thought you weren't smart."

She leaned forward and looked at me like she had caught me in a lie. "Then why are we sitting here?"

"Because we made a deal."

"You keep talking about that damn deal!" she said, suddenly angry again. "Okay, let me tell you what the new deal is. The new deal is this. I don't care whether you run those stories or not. I'm leaving Atlanta as soon as Desiree gets back with my friends from Miami. They're prepared to pay enough to take over the network Sam and I have put together so that we can disappear for a while. Sam's on his way to the Bahamas right now to get things in order for our little hiatus. Once the heat dies down, I'll start over, and believe me, this time I'm not going to waste my time on a bunch of damn maids. There's always more people who want to *do* dirt than there are who want to clean it up."

"What's all that got to do with me?" Every possibility was a nightmare, but I had to know.

"Didn't I tell you? At first my friends were a little hesitant, what with all the bad press, so I threw these girls in as a bonus. My sponsors like the idea of six virgins at one time. They think it's good luck."

What did she mean, *six* virgins? "I thought there were four girls."

"There were four," she said, nodding thoughtfully, "but you have to add the two we picked up this morning at your house."

"My house?"

She sat back, enjoying my surprise. "I told you you were still underestimating me. We picked them both up this morning, right after you left for my office. Of course, we were watching your house and when they showed up, one right after another, I couldn't believe my good fortune."

I felt like she'd kicked me in the stomach. Had Miss Iona and Miriam come over to wait for me there? They wouldn't do that. Not today. Besides, Miss Iona was nobody's girl. "What girls?"

She ignored me. "They're two of the prettiest ones we've got; wouldn't you say so, Mr. Wilson?"

His eyes never left the TV. "They're not as young as the others."

Ezola chuckled at that, fingering her pearls and looking at him with the affection of an indulgent aunt for a mischievous nephew. "He really likes the younger girls. Once they hit sixteen, Wilson thinks they're over-the-hill."

I swallowed hard so I wouldn't faint or throw up. This was no time to fall out.

She turned back to me. "But in the case of these two, he's prepared to make an exception."

"You're not making any sense," I said. "Who was at my house?"

"That little bitch's sister, the one who's been working for you, but Mr. Wilson said that when he got there, he found the bonus prize."

She turned toward Wilson again. "What did she say her name was?"

"Phoebe," he said, his eyes glued to the girls as they toweled off each other's towering silicon titties. "Her name's Phoebe."

I stood up and reached Ezola across the room in two steps. Not as distracted as he appeared to be, Wilson stood up, too, and grabbed my arm before I could grab her neck.

"Where's my daughter?" I said, shaking

so hard I thought I'd shake loose of his grip, but I didn't. "If you do anything to hurt her . . ."

Ezola stood up in my face as close as she could without touching me. "You're not in a position to do much of anything, are you?"

She was right. Wilson's hand on my arm was large and cruel. I couldn't even move. *Think, think, think!*

"I'd throw you in, too," she said, "but you'd be more trouble than you're worth — to me, or to them."

B.J.'s words came back to me. *She doesn't like to be told what to do.* The girls were about business. Her interest in me was personal.

"Let me see my daughter," I whispered.

Ezola sat back down, but Wilson still had hold of my arm. "Of course you can see her, Catherine. It's only fair. Just think, she came home early just to surprise you, and it turned out we surprised her instead. You two will probably have a good laugh about it later."

Her face was a tight mask, and her smile wasn't a smile at all. "You know this isn't personal, no matter what you might think."

She was still reading my mind.

"There's just too much money to be

made for you to mess it up trying to save the world."

"I want to see my daughter."

She glanced at her watch. "You can see her right now if you want. The rest of them, too. Desiree will be back with their sponsors in a minute, and once she gets here, they won't have much time to talk."

"Why?"

"Because Wilson always tapes their mouths first."

73

They were all in one big bedroom up a flight of stairs and down a long hallway. There were two young guys in huge, low-slung jeans and black hooded sweatshirts stationed outside the door. I recognized them as the arsonists from the other night. They were the first guards I'd seen, other than Wilson. They were leaning casually against the wall, talking to each other, but when they saw us coming down the hall, they tried to sort of come to attention.

"Open the damn door," Wilson growled as we approached it, and they practically fell all over themselves to do it.

I stepped into the room quickly.

"Mom!" Phoebe cried out, and ran into my arms.

"Are you okay?" I said, hugging her, but not as long as I wanted to. I leaned back to look into her frightened eyes, searching her face for signs that someone had harmed her in any way.

"I'm okay," she whispered.

Over her shoulder, Miriam and a young

woman I immediately knew was Etienne were sitting on the bed in the windowless room holding hands. One woman was lying down on the bed with her hands over her face, and two other women were sitting on the floor, their frightened eyes full of hope that I had come to save them. I could tell they had all been crying.

"Is everybody okay?" I made my voice louder than it needed to be. I had to suck the victim energy out of this room, and all I had to use was the sound of my own fearlessness.

They all nodded, and I looked at Wilson and the two young guards standing in the doorway, my arm still around Phoebe's shoulders. There were three of them and seven of us, even if we were scared. I wondered if they had guns.

"Can I speak with them alone for a minute?" I said, still talking loudly.

The girls were watching me closely. Even the one on the bed had taken her hands away from her face and opened her eyes.

Wilson frowned at me, and the two wannabe Wilsons did, too. "Say what you have to say right here."

I released Phoebe gently, pushed her back toward the others, and lowered my voice as if I wanted him to hear me, but not the women. His boys leaned forward, too, like two little evil clones of their ponytailed boss.

"They're all virgins," I said. "I want to show them some things that will make it easier for them."

Wilson's face was a mask of meanness. "Ain't nobody tryin' to make it easy for them."

The two guards snickered and punched each other.

"And better for their sponsors," I said as suggestively as I could.

"They ain't supposed to know how to do nothin'," he snarled. "They just supposed to be virgins."

"But . . ." *But what?*

"Shut up," he said, turning back to the guards. "I'm going back downstairs. Tape them up like I showed you and then come get me."

The shorter boy looked startled by the request, but said nothing.

"You got the piece?" Wilson said to the taller of the two guards, who had a baby face in spite of all his gold teeth.

The kid fumbled quickly through his oversize pockets and came up empty. "I musta left it in the car," he said sheepishly.

Wilson looked disgusted. "Then go get it!"

The kid hitched up his pants and shuffled off down the hall as quickly as he could without them falling off his slim hips and settling around his ankles.

Wilson turned back to the first guard, who was still standing there looking uncomfortable: "You got the tape or what?"

The kid looked like he'd rather have misplaced the gun. These guys were as bad at being guards as they were at setting fires. *We can take them!* I thought. *If I can just get these girls not to be too terrified to move, we can take them!*

"Leroy said he was gonna get it," he said, pointing accusatorily down the hall after his long-gone comrade.

"You get it," Wilson growled. "Or I'm gonna blow your stupid brains out."

The kid started down the hall at a trot, holding his britches with one hand. "I'm gonna get the tape, man. I know where he put it at, so I'll be right back."

Wilson turned around and looked at our tiny, cowering band and then back to me. "Fuck it," he said. "I'm gonna get the damn tape and do you bitches myself."

Then he slammed the door and locked it behind him. Phoebe ran back to me, but this time so did Miriam, dragging Etienne, who was even lovelier in person than she was in her picture. I strained to hear Mr. Wilson's footsteps to be sure he had really left us locked in, but unguarded. He had! He expected us to wait here for him to come back and tape us up like a bunch of hogs on their way to the slaughter. Well, he had the wrong bunch of girls. We might go down, but not without a fight!

"What are we going to do, Mom?" Phoebe said, her voice shaking with fear. "Who are they? Are they serious about —"

I cut her questions off. "They're very serious, but so are we," I said in a voice I'd never heard before. I wasn't just Mom anymore. I was the voice of our resistance!

"What can we do?" Miriam's voice was almost a whimper.

"You must all listen to me carefully and do exactly as I say."

Phoebe, Miriam, and Etienne stood together, watching me, wondering, I know, what I had in mind. I was wondering, too!

"Go on, Mom," Phoebe said softly. "We're listening."

The two women on the floor nodded. The girl who had been lying on the bed sat up and held her knees close to her chest.

"Do you speak English?" I said, aware of how little time we had.

The girls sitting on the floor nodded yes.

The one on the bed just looked at me.

"Miriam, you translate for her," I said.

She nodded and went to sit beside the girl on the bed, translating for her softly as I talked as fast as I could without confusing them.

"There are only two guards, plus Ezola and the guy with the ponytail. There are twice that many of us."

"But they have a gun," Miriam whispered, like I might have overlooked it.

"It doesn't matter," I said, hoping that it didn't. My mind was racing ahead, trying to *think, think, think.* "If we stick together and you do exactly as I say, we'll be all right. Do you believe me?" I looked around at their frightened faces. "Do you believe me?"

Phoebe spoke up first, and her voice didn't tremble. "I believe you, Mom."

"I do, too," Miriam said, still sounding scared, but a little stronger.

The first step in staying alive is always to believe you can, and I had never believed anything so strongly in my life. We had to stay alive. I hadn't had a chance to tell them what I knew, and they hadn't had a chance to tell me what they knew, and that exchange is what our lives are really about. Sometimes, it's all we've got.

"All right," I said, "here's what we're going to do. . . ."

That was when we heard the sirens. My heart leaped into my throat. Had the police followed us? Had our reinforcements finally arrived? The girls froze, and I did, too. Too scared to hope. Too scared not to.

Then we heard the sound of cars screeching into the yard at high speeds, and then the sound of someone beating on the downstairs front door the way only cops do, and people shouting, glass breaking, more shouting, and somebody screamed. We didn't know who it was, but we knew it wasn't one of us. We were all present and accounted for, listening, praying, determined to be strong, but longing to be rescued just in case we weren't strong enough.

Phoebe was holding my hand, and Miriam was holding the other one, and I realized we weren't huddling in a scared little clot anymore. We were standing in a circle, and we stayed in that circle even when we heard voices coming up the stairs, until I heard B.J. calling my name and I knew they had found us, deep in the middle of all those Georgia pines. Only then did I start hollering.

"B.J.! In here! We're in here!"

Thank God! Thank God! Thank God!

"In here!"

"Stand back!" he shouted, and somebody hit the door hard enough to break that pitiful little lock, and there was B.J., right up front, and behind him, three of the biggest police officers *ever*, and Louis right behind them. Then we all started hollering at the same time and hugging one another and hollering some more, and the police officers asked us if we were okay and we said we were, and B.J. hugged me again, and all I could do was hug him back and try to realize it was over. It was finally over.

"How did you find us way out here?" I said.

"I told you I had your back." And he hugged me again. Hard.

"But how —"

"Don't worry about it now," he said. "I'll tell you everything later. I promise."

That was good enough for me. I gave him another quick hug and looked around for Phoebe. Across the room, Louis was trying to get his arms around her and Miriam at the same time, and the girls who had been sitting on the floor were hanging on Etienne, and the one who had been curled up on the bed was hanging on all three of them and crying and smiling, and so was I. Then Phoebe extricated herself from Louis and hurtled across the room back to me, and she was still crying a little bit, and I was, too, so we just stood there holding on to each other like we'd never let go, but then over her shoulder, I saw B.J. watching us with such longing, and I knew he was waiting to see if this was the time for his introduction, and even in the midst of all the confusion, I knew it was.

This was not the way I wanted it to be for them. This was nothing like the perfect moment I had imagined. But if there's any truth to the saying, "All's well that ends well," it was perfect enough indeed. So I turned my daughter around to face the smiling stranger, and took her hand in that mad swirl of people and policemen and answered prayers.

"Phoebe," I said as if we were alone in the room. "I'd like to introduce you to your father."

She squeezed my hand so hard I swear she almost broke it, but I didn't care. *"Daddy?"* she whispered.

He didn't say a word. He just opened his arms and she walked right into them like she belonged there, which, of course, she did.

74

If this were a fairy tale, I could tell you that on the same morning I went to the headquarters looking for the girls, in the middle of her breakfast at Thelma's, Celine Hudson suddenly remembered hearing her escorts talking about a club near Miss Mandeville's house, and when she called to tell B.J., Sergeant Lawson of the Atlanta Police Department knew exactly where it was. Once they had a starting point, it was only a matter of time before they discovered Ezola's evil hideaway and burst in at the very last second, just like the heroes do in the movies, right before everybody lives happily ever after.

If this were a fairy tale, I could tell you that Ezola and Sam and Desiree and the ponytailed Mr. Wilson and his two sorry commandos all went off to jail for a long, long time. I could tell you that the prostitution ring was broken up and the girls found homes with families who loved them, and Precious Hargrove took over as interim president of Mandeville Maids and hired me as her vice president of operations, so nobody lost a job during the investigation, including Celine Hudson, who was getting her GED and trying to lose a few pounds.

If this were a fairy tale, I could tell you that Miss Iona finally retired from the *Sentinel*, and she and Mr. Charles took a cruise around the world and then another one. I could tell you that Louis and B.J. made the *Sentinel* the fastest-growing black newspaper in the country, with fifty thousand paid subscribers and a staff of four full-time reporters. I could tell you that Aretha had her baby and Kwame cut the cord, and Hank Lumumba announced his candidacy for city council from West End, and Blue and Regina Hamilton did a fundraiser, and Phoebe and her daddy were thick as thieves.

If this were a fairy tale, I'd probably have to confess that two days before Christmas, Amelia and I put on our long white gowns, and Phoebe stood up with us while Amelia married Louis at the same ceremony where I married B.J., and we promised to be true until death do us part. But this isn't a fairy tale, so I have to tell you the truth: Amelia and I both wore red.

ABOUT THE AUTHOR

PEARL CLEAGE is the author of *What Looks Like Crazy on an Ordinary Day . . .* , which was an Oprah's Book Club selection, and *Some Things I Never Thought I'd Do*, as well as two works of nonfiction: *Mad at Miles: A Black Woman's Guide to Truth* and *Deals with the Devil and Other Reasons to Riot*. She is also an accomplished dramatist. Her plays include *Flyin' West* and *Blues for an Alabama Sky*. Cleage lives in Atlanta with her husband.